] *The Swing at the Gates of Eternity*

The Swing at the Gates of Eternity

] AN ELIZABETH CROMWELL MYSTERY [

Charles Ryavec

EXPONENTIAL PRESS, SANTA BARBARA, 2026

Once again my heartfelt appreciation to the enormous efforts of my editor, Eric Larson, who took the raw materials of the initial drafts of this story and made them coherent.

C.R.

][

Exponential Press
Santa Barbara, CA

ISBN 978-0-9980221-6-1 (hardcover)
ISBN 978-0-9980221-7-8 (paperback)
ISBN 978-0-9980221-8-5 (e-book)

Book design: Studio E Books, Santa Barbara

*A little town stuck far away in some obscure hills
attached to the rest of the world by a dirt road that
swerves dangerously through ugly trees and a fog so
dense no one else thinks about making the drive though
occasionally strangers will come by mistake and take
a brief look around then realize how unimportant its
buildings and residents and beliefs seem whereupon
they'll turn back not moved enough to tell anyone
they'll ever know the rest of their lives that it crossed
their circuitous minds once.*

—Dennis Cooper

] *The Swing at the Gates of Eternity*

] *Chapter 1*

S HE WAS LOWERED to rest under a marble stone inlaid with a piece of obsidian etched in gold letters. JANUAR, a word of private meaning in her native language, wasn't the month she entered the world. The word referred to something else unknown. Her facts were like that.

A photograph of some of her people went into the good earth with her.

I read from Dorothy Parker: "Epitaph for a Darling Lady."

On the way back to San Francisco, I stopped at an inn with sufficient elevation to offer a continuous view of Atascadero Creek. A glance exhausted the pastoral view of my own death.

"I don't need this," I said. It was all I needed. Do this thing right. No shortcuts. The coming twenty-four hours were spoken for. I headed off to the Red Hen Tavern and uncorked.

THE SONG was without meaning, except it was sad, with intervals in the lyrics where the singer cried, and that was it for how many moments of expecting a clarification of what the singer was sad about, who knows? I didn't count, but a sad song, no more no less, while I waited on the edge of uncertainty with no idea where I was or why I was crying. Then steps from somewhere and a hand on my shoulder and the realization of who I was. The bartender was repeating "Elizabeth" and patting my shoulder. That must have been when I quit for the night, with a glass of tired ice I couldn't get out of my hand. I needed help.

I fell on the sofa at home and pulled a blanket over my head and passed into the rest of the night and on through the morning and then some, and a phone rang—in a dream? The fourth and fifth rings ended the dream. I hoisted my purse onto my stomach and got the phone to my head and said, "This is she."

The voice on the line was calling itself a doctor. I couldn't catch all the syllables in the name. Might have met him elbow to elbow on a bar last night. He worked for William. William Emmon. Yes. Oh, yes. I'd just recently shoveled dirt into his wife's grave.

Doc needed a favor.

Reason to listen. I put the phone on the other ear. "What?"

"I don't know what the problem is yet," he said. "Not all of it."

I held the phone up to my face: 2:08. The afternoon. I must have slept. Becoming aware that the grandfather clock on the mantle was my clock on my mantle, I built a reality around a voice, as if Doc pulled a chair to eye level and summarized the current state of affairs: William was home from the hospital within the past hour. Would I sort out a difficulty? Could I come over right away?

"I'm dressed," I said. He called a car. It was on its way.

The William Emmon house was on the steep end of Grant just up from Jack Early Park and down and around the corner from the Kearney Open Space. Across the street from Emmon was the fabulously wealthy side of Grant. Two connecting estates filled a walled-in presence for a long block. The view from the street was a fortress with majesty and exclusivity, until the estate and the location of a murder became one and the same in the papers, and we got our look inside. What we all imagined: majestic and exclusive.

I let myself out on the Emmon side of the street in the skinny driveway of a skinny garage with a skinny door. It wasn't poor over here either. Wealth was packed wall to wall in skinny homes on five levels.

Way off out on the Bay was a ferry sliding along, seeming to pass right over the head of a woman not fifty feet away in the next driveway. Torn from a leather clothing ad, she was in black pants and black boots. A summery blue blouse left her neck and shoulders bare above the cleavage—a lot of skin attractively out there for a summer date—a lousy predicament in the freezing wind that was tearing up Grant.

I see her problem. She's locked herself out, no coat, sifting through ways to dig herself out of a hole and not getting any-where. Now there's me arriving, and I'm going in where it's warm. I waved her over. Join me. The way she didn't acknowledge the invitation was freaky. She kept staring at me, eyes glazed over, out of it, like a stoned face sending the kind of vacant looks that harbor thoughts that don't get you anywhere. All her mistakes at once made sense.

At the door to the Emmon place, I was six feet above the street, and it was colder and windier. I banged the knocker.

A stout blonde in Swedish braids opened the door, looked at me, and made a space for me to squeeze past her. I put a foot back and turned, pointing away from the door.

"The woman there," I said, "she must be freezing."

"She moved out," the braided woman said.

I took a position on the sill so the door couldn't be shut. "She's hardly dressed."

"You're letting the cold in."

I motioned a come-on-in with another sweeping wave. Again she defied the invitation. No surprise if she couldn't process infor-mation. She had a phone. The crazy thing, she had my number. My phone buzzed.

"*Je veux, pour composer chastement mes églogues.*" I digest-ed the French. What was going on in her head drew a blank. I stepped inside.

"What's the problem," I asked.

"There isn't," she said.

The door shut behind me like it was meant to stay shut. The braided woman took her leave of my presence. See who answers the door the next time I come calling.

Bushes in pots decorated an elevator. A diminutive woman in white gloves pushed a button and the door closed. When the door opened I stepped out. A man and woman in blue and white medical outfits expected me. The doctor I'd spoken to over the phone reintroduced himself, introduced his assistant, and gestured to chairs positioned for a *tête-à-tête*. I should hear something serious before I heard anything else.

Large oak pieces stood against opposite walls to give a small room the appearance it wasn't empty. Above these was a line drawing of the inner hall of the Palace of the Legion of Honor facing a monochrome of the length and breadth of the Bay copied from a famous photograph taken from a flying boat while the Golden Gate was under construction. A hexagonal stained-glass window was behind the two of them. It put their images into basic colors reflected in a tinted glass floor.

"You called me," I said.

"Mr. Emmon collapsed on the kitchen floor last night," the man said. "A roll of paper towels fell on the stove. The emergency room physician thought his fall was due to smoke inhalation, but his speech is slurred. They wanted to keep him over. Mr. Emmon refused. He insisted we call you, but I'd prefer you call back day after tomorrow, at the earliest. We'll know more. I'd be in a better position for a decision."

"I was with William yesterday," I said, "putting his wife in the ground. He left the burial grounds with one of Ingrid's sons. Nobody said goodbye to me for him. Could he want to catch up?"

"He didn't say."

"What if I just said hello and goodbye?" I said.

"Okay, but if he asks for a cigarette, or requires the facilities—if he asks for anything—please call me immediately. I'll be here."

The woman pulled double-doors toward herself and stepped to one side. I went in past her.

A pair of three-cushion sofas sat end to end in the shape of an L, which fit the tidy dimensions of the room, but backwards, the mirror image of a welcoming design. The set-up had closed off a cluttered dump, not worth a description except that for a dead certainty the maid had been told to stay out for this year.

A rectangular glass table served both sofas. A clearing had been created in a corner of the table for a dozen red roses and a card balanced vertically on edge against a vase. The display was within a hard forward lean of where a man was planted on the far cushion next to a dog crate. The crate was empty. The card was unopened. He hadn't leaned to bother with it. He was wrapped in a blanket as thick as a rug. The flaps of a cap covered his ears. His feet were in booties. William was set up to survive my visit. A nod was "Hello."

He was worse for the day since I'd last seen him, but he was the William I'd always known, x-ray eyes running up and down my frame inside my coat, inside the foundation garments.

"You will leave us alone," he said to the woman at the door. The doors closed. It was a while till the silence ended with a click.

"My apologies, Elizabeth. I'm guaranteed another hour on this earth, if I don't put effort into it. Are you able to hear me?"

"You're fine, William. I don't want to take up the last hour of your life."

"Drive me to the desert."

His hand made a tiny loop counterclockwise to his lips, meaning that on the other side of an interior wall closest to me was nourishment.

"Anything, please help yourself," he said. "The refrigerator, cupboards, please, wrap something up, take it with us."

"If you'll join me, I'll accept water with fizz in it."

His eyes widened an instant, a memory rekindling an historical antagonism. "We took you in, a stray blonde on a street corner. You haven't changed, Elizabeth."

He had waited twenty-five years to throw that back at me. Where else would I be? I was seventeen and looking for a night school to finish the eighth grade and pick up a junior high school diploma.

I dropped onto the sofa and crossed my legs. "How long are you staying on this hunger strike?"

He raised his arm. A finger pointed at the back wall. "Behind the photograph of the old man is a safe."

"You don't owe me anything," I said.

A hand poked at the wall facing him. "Over there, the signature on the painting. That's the combination."

"William…"

"The money's not for you."

I've been asked from time to time to hustle over to a friend's place. They're sick as a dog, lower than a snail's belly, on the edge of climbing over the rail of a bridge. Pick up liquor, medicine, hard stuff, any something to get them through. From time to time it was reasonable to look at the question: What if they die, and I'm at the wheel? This request from William was familiar.

I was aimlessly shuffling a foot under the table where the dust had settled itself undisturbed. When I was starting out, William and Ingrid bought a business with a nice address and gave it to me. I was in business, a dominatrix. After I was earning real money, I couldn't find them. They would sniff it out when I was putting the word around that I was looking them up with the whole debt to be delivered on one check, wiping the slate. They were always gone fishing.

I got up and did the signature, ROLF, three turns to the right, left to eighteen, then right, left right, spinning the dial. The safe opened, and there it was, what the safe was designed to keep safe: money. Four stacks of paper plugged the opening. My first thought was that I was looking at upwards of quite a few millions in American currency, and what was I supposed to do with it if it wasn't for me? I pulled out a packet of hundreds held together in the middle by a paper wrapper. On the wrapper was "100" handwritten in red ink. The packet was more like something I'd call a brick; the hundreds were uncirculated, and while I could fan them like a deck of cards, flat in my hand they seemed stuck to each other as if glued. Ten thousand dollars didn't take up much volume. Not a real brick's worth, anyway.

I held the brick out and asked, "What do you want me to do with it?"

He held out two hands. I pulled him to his feet. It took a minute. Then he was balanced, and then, a step and a step, and, strength summoned, he dropped the blanket off his shoulders. He indicated a medical bag on the sofa.

"You want me to put the money in the safe into the bag?" I said.

He nodded.

"Are we exercising poor judgment, William? Shouldn't we leave this to the lawyers?"

"I'd like to sit down," he said, "until you finish."

I put him at the end of the sofa where I'd been sitting, and put the medical bag next to him. That left a cushion free where I could dump the contents of the safe, see where we were at. Fourteen envelopes indicated a thousand dollars each, presumably ten hundreds. Bunches of hundreds were collected in paper clips. Wads of smaller denominations were paper-clipped or rolled in rubber bands.

The hundreds came to seven hundred seventy-six thousand and two hundreds. The rest of it was hard to estimate, at least a few thousand, but an upper limit I couldn't say, less than ten thousand.

I put the hundreds in the bag. Left the rest on the sofa. It's what he wanted.

"My lawyer took the car keys." His eyes rummaged around the room. "In the kitchen, four green containers. The one with the sugar: dump the sugar. Keep the key."

I cleaned up the key and tucked it in a pocket and wait-ed while William had the nurse come in and shuffle through pharmacy sacks and bottles on the sofa. She dropped pill bottles into one sack, all but one. She held that one out.

"Give him one of these under his tongue if there's pain in his chest. He'll let you know." I put that bottle in a shirt pocket. "Can you give an injection?"

I nodded.

"She held a vial of liquid at eye level. "A shot of this, if he stops breathing. Pound his chest. You never know."

"If you want anything in the house, take it now," William said to the nurse. "Back a truck up and take it. Elizabeth will confirm with my lawyer." He took a short breath. "I would appreciate some help to my car."

William's car was in the garage on a turntable that rotated one hundred and eighty degrees so the car could exit hood out. I pulled the front fender to the edge of the street and shut off the motor. The doctor buckled William in. The nurse handed me a bag of bottles, repeating earlier instructions. That stuff went into a storage bucket between the seats. The medical bag full of money rested at William's feet. Nobody shook hands. Nobody wished me well. Probably some legal liability in it.

I turned on the engine, released the brake, and lifted my hip from the seat. My hip buzzed. A reminder. Pick up something for dinner. I shut the engine off to look at the situation I was in.

"Where are we going, William?"

"Five south until Bakersfield. I know the exit when I see it."

I got off 580 and circled around to a Chevron station and topped off the tank. As I went into the store, my eye caught the last ray of light in a damaged front fender. The reflection gave back a deep green shade, one of those richly layered paint jobs that can be mistaken for black or just a dark something or other when out of the sun. The chrome around the right headlight was held in place by red plastic tape. The wheel rim had been spared, and the crumple hadn't reached the hood, not significantly, not so the hood would fall off in a high-speed turn. On a two-door coupe, a bump with a shopping cart will look like a hell of a smash-up.

I loaded up on a weekend's snacks. In the car, I tore a sack open with my teeth and talked with my mouth full, enunciating well enough.

"I met a young woman on the street as I was coming to see you," I said. "A weirdo with a taste for cold. One of yours?"

"Aubrey, Aubrey Babcock," he said. "What else did you think of her?"

"She was not carrying, thank God."

"Ingrid's star translator. Plays with Latin phrases. Like a priest in heat. Snaps at you in German and smiles. Expects you to click your heels."

"Used French on me, a sort of non sequitur while freezing to death." I exchanged an empty for another bottle, held the wheel with a knee, opened the bottle and held it in front of him.

"Ingrid's memoirs," he said. "She wrote in German. When she got sick, she hired Aubrey to translate them to English."

No hold-ups, a big if, and it's a straight ride to Bakersfield. I maintained a steady speed at the speed limit. No idea what it would take to lose a fender.

After a while William said, "When Ingrid didn't wake up… Thursday. What is that? Thursday…Friday…Saturday…Sunday—three days, four days, what the hell, days and days. This morning I left a cigarette on the paper towels and passed out. At the hospital I sobbed—I came home and gave Aubrey a half-hour. Pack up and clear out. Ingrid was dead. Aubrey had her money."

I let the road go by a while. "She had some reason to talk to me."

"You're all I've got, Elizabeth." He caught his face in his hands and made a sound like a laugh. "A hell of a way to go."

I gave that a few minutes. When the memory died, I asked, "How did you two meet? Honestly, I couldn't see you and Ingrid meeting."

"I was a Florida boy," he said. "I was a steward on a chartered yacht. We met a boat near the Bahamas. Took on six young women, Europeans, a boat out of Genoa, none of them more then twenty. Unusual. Most of the time the boats we met came from the islands, mixed blood and dark, all kinds, all points of origin. In Miami a customs agent wasn't where he was supposed to be, and the cargo came in duty free. I dropped five of them off at the address I was given, all except Ingrid. A man was waiting for me. He gave me some money and the keys to a car, and said goodbye to Ingrid in German. He said to me in English that I was known as a reliable man. I was never ever to imagine that the woman I was taking to California wanted me to touch her or speak to her unless spoken to. That was the job. A free airline ticket back to Miami came with it. Leave the car at the airport drop in L.A. Everything else was none of my business. That's how we met."

"You were with her for fifty years."

"Sixty-two," he said. "Where along the way did I fall for her? I thought she fell for me when we dropped the car off in L.A. I was ready to catch my flight to Miami. She asked me to find a hotel for us. All I could think was she'd spoken. I obeyed."

"Romance?" I said.

"She wanted to show appreciation. I made an executive decision."

"The appreciation lasted sixty-two years," I said. "You must be good."

"You can cut the snark, Elizabeth. You could have had it with me…Elizabeth. I offered to show you how good. You might just drop what you don't know anything about. You didn't know Ingrid, honey. She tortured people, and I don't mean like you do it. I never made the mistake thinking she loved me. The thing she felt for me was always a minute of appreciation that was left over from a job she got me stuck in.

"The first night at the motel she made a call. A man had been supposed to meet her that day in L.A. when we arrived. He didn't show. We took a train the next day to a station in the desert. First time I saw Mojave. A woman met our train and took us to Inyokern. When we got to Inyokern she and Ingrid spoke

English with each other like old friends with a lot of catching up to do. I didn't say two words in two days. I was warned not to go wandering off in the desert, which never occurred to me. I got my three squares and a pillow to lay my head on. I expected at any moment the woman would run me over to the bus station at Mojave. That would get me back to L.A. and Miami. But the strange thing was they took me around with them in the backseat, like I was their pet, and they felt some responsibility."

"Around where?"

"Some old mining camps across the Nevada line. The woman was older than me, not by much, four years. I was twenty-two, Ingrid was several months upwards of eighteen. The two of them were the adults. The main gate of a naval weapons testing range was less than a mile from where we stayed. Above a security checkpoint, you could see way off in the distance a hill with a B in white letters. That was for 'Burroughs,' the base school. The woman was a language teacher at the school, French and Spanish, a U.C. Berkeley graduate. She spoke German with Ingrid on the occasions when there was something to hide from me. When they thought I was catching on, they whispered or went off together to speak out of my hearing. I felt like a puppy leashed to a fence."

Why he didn't get on a bus and leave wasn't a question I ever needed answered. He was leashed to Ingrid, and she knew it before she asked him to get them a motel room. They were destiny's companions from that moment she decided this was her guy.

"I wish I had a cigarette," he said. The cough hardly had the effort in it to remove air from his throat. It had lost all life along with the dying face that had darkened and begun to shrink. There was a bottle of water in my sack within reach. I offered. I didn't hear anything. If he had a cigarette, I wasn't mule-headed enough to not let him out. He didn't.

"What is it, William?"

"It's hard…to talk."

We turned off Highway 5 just below Bakersfield, and, except

for Tehachapi, passed a dozen names I never heard of. In the starlight was the desert. Another hour and we passed the turnoff to Inyokern. William said to count off six and a half miles, then put the brights on and look to the left for a dirt road and a gate.

I saw what I thought was a road cutting perpendicularly off into the dark. I slowed and let William decide. This was it. I took the dirt road easy for a minute till we arrived at six boards, four in a rectangle and two more crisscrossing the diagonals. The gate was closed.

"The hinges are over there on the right," he said.

A rubber inner tube held two posts together. I got that off and gripped a post with two hands and walked the gate open. The gate swung clear of the road without dragging.

My coat caught on something. I tugged without freeing myself, then saw the problem was a strand of barbed wire. In the lights ahead was more road. That would serve as an introduction to an announcement. I got in the car and said, "There's nothing up there, William."

"In two miles you'll see some buildings."

I was the driver. The end of the road was anywhere I said it was. Big talk. I kept going.

For a mile we were on a gradual upward slope. Then the slope suddenly went up a notch, still not to where I'd call it steep, but that's where his interest suddenly rose, which must have been a remembered feel for this particular sense of change. We came to a place where he said, "Stop." Other than a clearing ahead, there was nothing visible until I turned the lights off. Then a rocky landscape appeared all around in a familiar slice of moon. Patches of darkness shaped themselves at a common angle. It was here he wanted out.

He said nothing, a man waiting for a foot to follow a thought.

"Look up, Elizabeth. You can see the Milky Way. Right over your head. There's a cot in the trunk, a sleeping bag and a pillow."

I helped him to the front of the car, and got him steady against the good fender. He waved a hand at the desert stars sprinkling a few wooden frames that jutted over a promontory above us. These were familiar stars. He was at rest. This was some sort of headquarters where important decisions had entered his life, for all I knew.

I set his cot up next to the car and got him on his back, his head on the pillow, and zipped him into the sleeping bag. The instructions were to be back by ten that morning with a bottle. "Not coffee," he said.

He gave me two names: a woman in Mojave, another in the Granville Estates up around the Sacramento River somewhere.

"The money," he said. "Divide it in half."

I didn't bother to close the gate on the way out. Heading back to the Inyokern cutoff, I made a reservation at a Holiday Inn in Ridgecrest.

] *Chapter 2*

THE HOLIDAY INN was off a road that was off a road, a clean-looking boxy building that stood not quite alone. An auto parts outlet looked walkable. At night that couldn't be estimated.

I wrote down the names William had given me on motel envelopes. I located the two single hundreds in the bag and put them in my coat pocket. Expenses. I turned the heat up, showered and flopped on my back, stuck, in the moment, with the thought that William was alive. What might be reasonably expected of a responsible adult? The legal blowback from this mess worried me. I could get him into professional care and go home, having robbed the guy of the right to his own walk into the sunset. That didn't worry me.

What would happen came to me now as a declaration that what I had done was the right thing to do. Then that ping-ponged and loop-de-looped in the place in the head that knows when I've stepped in it, and the night was just beginning. This night wasn't going to let go.

I needed a counselor. I called Susan Ferenci. I left a message at half past one that she was my lawyer. Much appreciated if she might call as soon as possible.

It was not three minutes later her call arrived. "Hi, Elizabeth. So what's the matter?"

"I just left an old man alone in the desert on a cot. He wants to die there. He wasn't dead when I left him. I think I should go back and talk him out of it. That's what's the matter."

"Is this assisted suicide?"

"He was in San Francisco yesterday under medical care. He asked me to drive him here. The doctor taking care of him must have protested, but it was the doctor who called me to say that William wanted to see me. He must have known what William wanted. When we got to where he wanted to be for the night, I set him up on a cot. He asked. A night under the stars would do him good."

"He was checking out?" she said. "Would you say you assisted?"

"We didn't have an agreement. I owed him."

"A last wish?" she said.

"I was with him a few days ago when he buried his wife. I owed her."

"Where are you?" she said.

"The Holiday Inn in Ridgecrest."

"Do you inherit?"

"He gave me two names and several pounds of hundred dollar bills to drop off with them. I kept two hundreds. I suppose I can give them back."

"It's late. Let me skip the stupid questions for now. You skip the explanations. Call nine-one-one. Tell them a life is at stake. Time is of the essence. The person you speak with will keep you on the line while they bring the police into it. They'll talk it over. The police will come to the Holiday Inn. They'll want to know where they can find William. They'll need you, go with them. They'll take you in a squad car in the backseat. They'll ask questions, friendly questions, to pass the time. You can give them your name and address, basic contact information. They can look up the rest. Don't answer any other questions. They'll ask about your business, the English Department. They'll want to understand, and so forth. Respectfully refer them to me and give them my number. Don't refer to your rights. Don't get caught up in their behavior, a friendly inquisitive 'what did you want to kill this guy for?' I'll fill them in on the Constitution. Call me as soon as you can…and remember: do not answer questions! You know all this. If I say it, however, I can bill you. Go to it."

IT was ten in the morning, like a morning a year from now. Eight hours had passed, in which interval I hadn't slept, had no liquor, no candy, no change of clothes. It was good enough that William was in Ridgecrest Regional Hospital with vital signs. I had told the night nurse that nothing was too good for William Emmon. I could bring cash over; she could take what she wanted. There was more when that ran out. I got schooled. That's not the way a hospital did business.

Eleven in the morning. I was in my motel room in towels with William's doctor in San Francisco. He got me to William's lawyer, the guy paying him, Brendan Hopkins, of Abarbanel and Hopkins. The next-to-last step was closed when I put Hopkins and the hospital together. There was William's car, and there was a nonstop flight, Bakersfield to San Francisco, the next day, Tuesday. Otherwise, today I could go through LA. I passed it up.

There were two grocery sacks on the desk, three hundred and eighty-eight thousand in each. I ran a thought over an adjustment involving a dozen hundreds, a fee distributed equally between sacks. Was I entitled? I didn't want that argument.

I stuffed the sacks in the bag, and put the NO HOUSEKEEPING sign on the door handle. I washed my hands. I went into town, my bag in hand at all times, and picked up fresh undies. I went back to the motel and changed, and tossed yesterday's pair in the shopping bag and dropped that in the trash. On the way out of the motel lobby I wiped my sunglasses casually, getting a look at a deserted parking lot. I put the bag on the passenger seat. I set the navigator for the Monica Parker residence. I had some money for her.

I'd recommend a desert visit to just about anyone, once in a lifetime. I'd go in November, and do your driving in the daytime. Keep the window open some. The smell is different, but it's not the smell. It's what you see, pretty much exactly as it was seen a hundred centuries before anyone saw it, a thirsty landscape with a hard life. I'm not into rock formations or earth movements, and know next to nothing about them, but I've no quarrel about this sky as a cover to die under.

I turned off Highway 14 at Billings St. in the unincorporated community of Mojave. Four blocks down I made a left on Tierra Grande and parked across the street from 2026. I opened the gate over a stone walkway, shut it behind me, and pushed the bell of a single-story wood-frame house with a scrub grass lawn on two sides. I heard the bell. When nobody appeared, I did it again, and went out to the street. There had been a man on a porch on Tierra Grande watching me as I passed. I walked the block to his fence and waved and stood there. Have a word with him.

In a neighborhood bereft of wonders, whatever he had to compute about me waving a hand at him from the other side of his fence, he wasn't going to bring it up with me. A woman with a big head of gray hair pushed the screen open and came to the edge of the porch.

"What do you want?" she asked.

"I'm looking for Monica Parker. I rang the bell. Nobody home."

"Check at the Brown Bear. It's the café next to the Valero station on Silver Trail. She owns it."

There were photographs all over the place at the Brown Bear. They hung from just below the ceiling to waist level, images of movie stars from the silent era, mining locations, and life a hundred years past; Death Valley in the summer, and the bleached bones of oxen where they quit and dropped. It was lunchtime at the Brown Bear. A stool at the counter was free. I watched two people in the kitchen doing a dozen tasks in one continuous motion. Plates appeared on a stainless steel shelf over green slips of paper, in turn snatched away by a couple of thirty-ish ladies feeding the crowd in the booths, perhaps its fifth generation of customers.

The man to my left at the counter leaned his head to the woman to my right and suggested we all introduce ourselves. I crossed my arms and stuck two hands out and said hello, and I was Elizabeth Cromwell from San Francisco.

"They're not hiring," the woman said. "You can leave your name."

"Just here to have a quick word with the owner. She around?"

The woman turned her face to a hall running off the end of the counter. "The hall ends at her door," she said.

A voice behind me: "She's always busy. Best, knock. She'll wave you off. Go in anyway and stand with your hands folded. She'll put the phone in her lap and let you say what you have to say. If it's short."

"You can wait till quitting time," another voice said and laughed.

The upper half of the door was four glass panes. Beyond these was a window letting in sunshine on the head of a woman with a phone at her ear. At the far side of a pile of stuff that accumulates on a desk in the restaurant business were a boot and a bandaged foot.

I knocked, but I wasn't waved away, so there was a missing step and I knocked again. Again no wave. I turned the knob gently and went in on little cat's feet and waited in a formal posture for my wave in here, after which I could go out and come in again, and that's when I was noticed.

The occupant of the boot and bandage looked at my chest and said, "What's that?"

I pulled a shopping sack out of the medical bag. This is for Monica Parker."

"What's in it?"

"A lot of money."

"You must be out of jokes. Let's see what might interest me. Toss it over."

I slipped a leg at a time around the open door of a dull green safe. I reached the sack to the edge of the desk. She rotated her chair sideways to the desk and got a grip on the sack and pulled it to her side of the desk. The other hand pulled the sack open. She tilted the opening to get her face up close. She hauled out a packet of hundreds and studied one side, turned it over and studied the other side, and thought a long time. She put the phone to her face and told it to call her back.

She held each end of the packet in two fingers. "This'll get ya a fine lunch. Or is this for your entire natural life?"

She pulled out another packet, checked both sides—a habit with hundreds, I guessed—and dropped both packets in the sack and cuddled the sack on her lap. "A refund from Safeway?"

"A William Emmon asked me to give you the money. He didn't say why. I didn't ask. He's in the hospital in Ridgecrest."

She picked up the phone and said, "A double-double, and a coffee volcano." She looked at me. "Hungry?"

As a matter of fact, why not? I ordered what the woman at the counter was eating. "I'll have a tuna fish sandwich with chips, and a vanilla shake."

There's always a personal touch or two decorating the boss's office, what you might expect, but not quite, like the boss getting off a shot at a charging lion. That was one photo. A photo on the desk had her buried up to the neck in sand. Over many years, for every two items that came into this office, maybe one went out, and a huge volume of accumulation shrunk the working space to a channel that took three turns getting to the desk. Shelving stacks had overflowed. Life was lived leaning backwards in a chair. She didn't enter the office the way I did. The window behind her chair was the window in a door.

She pointed at a collection of office materials on a chair. "You can set that stuff on the floor and take your lunch sitting down."

She put the sack of money on the desk and pushed it away. "Not bad for tuna and a shake. You run money drops for people?"

"My first," I said.

She nodded at the medical bag. "What's in the bag?"

"Another sack," I said.

"When do I get the other sack?" she said.

"For someone else. I'm returning to San Francisco tomorrow."

"That's interesting." She took a second. "Why didn't this Emmon give me the money before getting sick?"

"I drove here to find him a place to die," I said. "That was a day ago. He should have been dead by now."

She was encouraging. "Then you could have kept both sacks."

"I could have."

The office door opened. A woman with a tray on one hand over her head squeezed her skinny self through little openings. She swung the tray in a handsome arc to to a foot above the table. A double-double must have been a burger oozing its innards dressed up in a skirt of fries. A black bowl held a voluminous cone of dark ice cream with white sauce flowing from the summit. The eruption. I slid my chair up to some boxes in front of the desk. I got what I ordered.

The server said she had to leave early today. Monica asked if this was for just today. It was. The door closed. "Don't wait for me."

I took a bite. After the joy wore off some, Monica eased in the suggestion she was entitled to some personal questions. A "Fine" made it out of the side of my mouth.

"This man Emmon pays you to bring him to the desert to die, and then he doesn't come through on his end, and you honor yours. It doesn't exactly add up, not exactly. I'm thinking why not give him his money, and you take off. How old is he?"

"Eighty. Or so."

She left her burger to ripen some. She scraped a spoon alongside the volcano and licked it clean. She used the spoon like a bandleader would keep a tune going with a baton. "Never been an Emmon in Kern County."

"I only know one," I said. "A Florida boy."

"You didn't tell me your name."

I gave it to her and tossed out a hunch, "You never heard of a Cromwell around here, either."

She pushed a hand around a table next to the desk till she uncovered a laptop. She booted it up and said, "William Emmon," at the same pace she could have typed it with one finger.

"Emmon's not online. A guy with money to burn in Mojave, you'd think a crazy CEO of something going out of business."

She googled my name.

"Now you, am I getting this right: you are known as a dominatrix?"

"Right on," I said.

"The English Department. That your business?"

"Twenty-four years."

"Neat snapshot," she said. "That's one handsome whip you have there. Emmon got it with that?"

"He was never a client. At one time I knew his wife. We spent a while in the desert camping, somewhere around here. It still looks like it looked then. The desert was her spiritual journey. I didn't catch it."

"I wouldn't camp out there without a gun. Never did, anyway." She watched me get to my limit on the shake. I gave out a heavy breath. This far and no more.

She rotated her computer to one side. Get the screen out of her sight. She licked her spoon clean, inspected the surface, and put it on a napkin. She rotated her chair to where she could look at me full in the face. We were about to take each other seriously.

"I don't have friends, Ms. Cromwell. I've been thinking why I've been thinking about that. Thought I'd come to terms there with that side of life by now, but we all get a kick in the keester once in a while. They say expect it when you least expect it. Right off when I saw your web page I was thinking this truly gorgeous hunk of woman eats alone, sleeps alone, no pool, no pets, no outdoor activities. Just like yours truly. Also tells me you're an honest woman, puts in her nine to fives, rain or shine, and I'm thinking that's more than just an impression. It would be nice to have you drop in on the old girl once in a while. Like to know more about this English Department. I take it you're a punctuation enforcement agent. There's the straight and narrow with the *p*'s and *q*'s, and all the other directions get your pupils a bit of correction. An honorable profession, if there ever was one.

"What I'm saying is, take your sack. If Mr. Emmon pulls through, tell him sorry. Tell him I never heard of him. I never heard of anyone giving anyone who never heard of them this kind of money. Not in Mojave. There's something felonious in this money. Somewhere. I stole a pineapple when I was twelve. Hope this money doesn't open that can of worms. Hope you're not part of this money. If you're not, and I'm sure as sure you're not, come back any time. Lunch was on the house."

Tucked in between the Brown Bear and the Valero station was Lloyd's Wheels and Brakes The office was empty, but a car was up on a rack in a service bay. The guy working had his back to me. I called, "Lloyd?" to him. He turned after a long quarter of a minute, and looked at me. I'd come to the right place. He said, "Yes." He looked at me and meant it.

"I have a car next door." I pointed. "It's that one with the bad fender. I'm thinking of driving it to San Francisco. I'd appreciate if you had a look at it. Should I get it repaired?"

He didn't have to do any more than look. "I'd have to order parts. I won't find anything local for this baby. Lotus Evora, twenty twenty-one. It'll cost you."

"The owner's in the hospital. They'll take him back to San Francisco. I thought I might drive the car back. It would have to be driven back, or sell it here."

He went over to the car and took a knee and reached an arm under the fender and worked his hand around. He stood up and brushed his hands. "You can drive it. I can get you some better tape on it. Make it look prettier. Match the green. Who patched this? They were in a hurry."

"Not me."

"Say thirty dollars?"

"It's a deal," I said. "Just curious: Monica Parker, she owns the Brown Bear. She's lived here a long time?"

"Her father owned it. It's older than him. The Parkers have been here a long time. Why?"

"I just wondered. When should I stop back?"

"Give me a minute." He came back with a roll of dark green plastic tape and got busy getting the tape replaced.

"You here about Monica's father?"

I shook my head. "Would I be?"

"He was murdered. Forty years ago, almost. A detective drops in now and then. Some women detectives these days. They ask if I remember anybody remembering anything." He stood back. "My best work. What do you think?"

I unhooked my wallet.

"I was just kidding," he said. "It's tape."

I had a hundred in my pocket. I pushed it at him, a favor to a fellow blond.

"When you need that fender fixed," he said, "we can talk about that hundred."

Leaving Mojave I checked messages. There was one from Hopkins, William's lawyer. William died at 1:37 P.M. I went back to the Holiday Inn and told them I'd be checking out in the morning.

] *Chapter 3*

IN THE MORNING I left a message with Abarbanel and Hopkins: I'd be in San Francisco at or before two; I'd leave William's car in his garage; I'd toss the keys in as the garage door came down. There was another thing. William had asked me to deliver three hundred and eighty-eight thousand dollars in cash to a Joanna Dempsey. There was a Dempsey family in the Granville Estates. That was the place he meant, but there was no Joanna listed. If I didn't make contact with Joanna, there'd be twice that much, in cash, to return to the Emmon estate for reasons I would explain. Another thing: I'm thinking of keeping a couple hundred for personal expenses. Then again, we'll see.

Some feelings left over from a sleep not quite shaken off in the morning held me at the edge of the parking lot, wasting a minute thinking I'd likely have to return to Ridgecrest with a lawyer. Minor matters disposed of, that would tie up the life of William Emmon for the record.

I took a left onto Highway 14 southbound just as the sun was coming up over a ridge in the east. It was impossible to think that anyone ever got from there to here. They just did, and the Holiday Inn was the proof. On all sides was a subsistence environment for growth that most of the year looked dead, a tapestry of rounded gray weeds that endured all the way to those mountains,

and kept going to more mountains and on and on—the vast lands
the trains of wagons crossed, for the simple routines of wrack-
ing labor, tearing minerals from the ground, lifting them to the
surface, hauling them out of here, exchanging them on a dollar
basis for a roof and two or three squares. In a couple hours I'd
be north of Bakersfield on I-5. The morning was getting brighter.

I stopped at one of those gas stations where a road crossed
I-5. I bagged a coffee and a roll, paid at the counter, including
forty dollars of gas, and noticed helicopters circling on a screen
mounted high on a corner shelf at the wall. I was seeing the Bay
Bridge.

The cashier put coins on three dollars and held his hand flat
for inspection.

"What's going on?" I asked.

"They hit eight-eighty, two places, and twenty-four. The dick-
head we got for a governor closed all the bridges. If you're going
to San Francisco, you better get over to one-oh-one as soon as
you can."

"They hit eight-eighty? What does that mean?"

"They took over the freeways."

"Why?"

"Collect tolls. That's what they say on the news. This guy got
out of his car on twenty-four. Killed two of 'em. They showed
the bodies before, but not now. You know, the kids will see dead
bodies. Can't have that."

"Do they say when they'll have the bridges open?"

"They drove school buses onto the freeway. Blocked the
on-ramps. The freeways are elevated along there. The cops can't
get to them. A lot of guns up there, and innocent women and children. They don't want innocent people getting shot." He made
change for the lady behind me. "The cops will wait 'em out."

He shook his head. "Radicals, don't want to work a steady
job."

"I can't use the Hayward Bridge?"

"Closed. An abundance of caution."

The major arteries on the West Bay were solid red on the traffic app, cars not moving, or barely. A bit better on the west side, but again solid red through the turn in San Jose and, with the exception of a few sections here and there, most of 101. 280 was yellow, green above Palo Alto, but you had to get to it. I made a reservation at the Carleton in Monterey. I'd be there in three hours. I was in the green to Salinas and all the way to the coast.

It was the off-off-season. A room with a balcony looking out to an unremarkable shimmer on Monterey Bay wasn't too bad. I found a shop a few doors down where I could buy a cheap change of clothes. I ordered hot food, Italian, room service.

A text message arrived from Abarbanel and Hopkins via the secretary, Ms. Haskett: the Dempseys of Granville estates were not in touch with their daughter Joanna. It had been some years since they heard from her. The mother said Joanna once shared a place with some girls in Albany, but that was a while ago and they could have moved. She couldn't say where she was now. Joanna once was associated with a woman by the name of Jasmine.

A second text: A link to an online news article from last Thursday's edition of the *NewsEagle,* an independent paper in Berkeley. The brunette in the photo was dressed in three-tone olive-drab camouflage, worn-looking, like real war surplus available in a thrift shop on Mission. Missing in the counterinsurgency outfit was the over-the-shoulder grenade belt. The article was bylined Haley Nalls. There was a link at the bottom to a speech by the redhead, who was identified by a single name, Jasmine.

LOCAL WOMAN ENCHANTS CROWD

Jasmine spoke on Monday without ambiguity: "I owe you honest bullshit," she announced. "U.C. thinks they have you by the cunt. What do you say? May I hear you? I don't hear you! Make them hear you! The lily-libs whisper you aren't acting in your best interests. You're not rational. You don't read Robert's Rules of Order, Revised.

We were a trickle yesterday. We're a fast-running river today. We're a power in history! United! Nothing will stop us!"

The answer arrived loud and clear in the chant of a crowd estimated in excess of two hundred: "Power now! Power forever!"

I propped my phone on a thingamajig that the Carleton provides for when you want to set it up no hands, a miniature television. I called Haskett. When I got a hello I said, "Okay, you found Jasmine."

"Jasmine *is* Joanna Dempsey," she said. "According to Ms. Nalls, the writer. Just a second, I have an address in Albany Hills."

"What are they unhappy about?"

"Didn't ask, but I did find out Jasmine's group will be constructing the articles of a new American constitution in Albany this coming week." A laugh followed.

"Thank you for the information, Ms. Haskett."

"You're very welcome, and while I have you, we understand you're carrying a considerable amount of cash on your person."

"Keep it to yourselves, if you would, please. I'll be by."

] *Chapter 4*

A N OVERNIGHT letter was on my desk. It had arrived two
days ago from a Mr. Benedict, an investigator with Advanced
Inquiries, Inc., Stamford, Connecticut. He had enclosed a brochure. They were the most active agency in Connecticut in the
business of locating missing children. He'd met with a Detective
Cole of SFPD, who had spelled out the peculiarities of Aubrey
Babcock's situation. She was last known in a living/employment
arrangement in San Francisco.

Mr. Benedict left a message: a meeting at my convenience.
He was familiar with police procedures when notified of missing
kids with histories of emotional trouble. His advice to Detective Cole would guide as much of the department's stretched
resources as could reasonably be allocated. The fact was they
wouldn't find Aubrey unless she came to them via some kind of
crime—either as a detainee, or in some relation to a complaint
or a felony, or as a body.

On his return east, Mr. Benedict had made the drive to
Westport to deliver his report to Mrs. Babcock, Aubrey's mother, in person. He hoped to get authorization for a second trip to
California. He had learned that on the night of her disappearance Aubrey had made a call to me, the last call that could be
traced to her number. So authorized, Mr. Benedict called me. He

suggested that a visit to the English Department was worth his while. He came across as that rare bird who could pick through the superficialities that inhabit young lives, and tap the tragedies. Aubrey worried him. We agreed to meet.

Today was the start of the third week since Aubrey Babcock had last called her mother.

My postal address is on Stafford Avenue. A high steel-mesh gate is set back off the sidewalk in the narrow gap between a schlock shop known as The Electric Voice House and Lee's Export/Import Emporium. On the gate is a lock with five rotors, each with the numerals one through five. Visitors to the English Department enter their code. If entered correctly the lock opens. The visitor enters and steps onto a cast-iron circular staircase that drops two full turns to a narrow passageway that leads to another fifteen-foot drop to an alley running parallel to Stafford. Before reaching the second drop, they pass the entrance to the English Department.

The door was open. I stepped aside. Benedict was mid-fifties, none of it disguised or denied—paunchy, conservatively trimmed white hair, thinning but with enough left to fool around with, a curve in the spine that stuck his bifocals forward over his chest. An excess of fine dining in a floppy face. A crested coat of arms centered a maroon tie.

He looked satisfied that he'd done his share in life. A nod at me carried a curiosity around the quiet furnishings of my waiting room.

We didn't start out chummy. Head lowered, he passed two sides of the room and turned to look back at a closed door on the first wall. His eyes went to the top of his glasses, focusing on a cluster of whips at a distance, various sizes sorted by length, draped over pegs. Well, I wasn't in the pottery business.

In the office I took the swivel chair at the desk. A solid oak chair at the side of the desk would put the desk between him and me. He angled it to face the bronze sculpture on the open side of the room. A riding mistress with a hunt whip, gripped two-handed behind her back, authentic down to a raised eye-brow, held his glance.

"An arresting piece," he said. "Armand Klein?"

"A gift from him," I said.

"Thank you for seeing me, Ms. Cromwell. I appreciate your time. Mind if I look around a minute? I've never met a woman in a business so well barricaded."

He started in on a photo of Theda Bara, a thumb gripped behind his back, and advanced along a dozen photos on the wall, noir advertisements of the nervously tinged dispositions of Hollywood legends. Step by step he kept on saying nothing until he stopped at Louise Brooks. He pinched the bridge of his glasses in thumb and forefinger, and raised the frame off his nose. To do what? It's what he did.

"The English Department," he said. "You play English teachers?"

"Women in authority," I said. "All sorts; say, physical ed instructors."

"No favored literary predicament in that case?"

"More likely, push-ups. In most cases I'm informed they want me to order them to do things they can't do. A basic punishment fantasy."

"How did I get to be me, they wonder?"

"If we're meeting regularly, we'll get around to discussing the oddities of masochism, such as whether they can whip me."

"And?"

"I laugh and pat their cheeks," I said. "A reminder: If they want their house painted, call a house painter. Tell you what, Mr. Benedict, you're looking for Aubrey Babcock. How can I help?"

"You study people," he said.

"It's a competitive business," I said. "An ear for what people want, it helps."

"You told me about the time you saw Aubrey. All of a minute. She had just been kicked out of where she'd been living. She was waiting for you. I recall, 'impervious to cold,' 'off her rocker,' 'possibly dressed to meet a date, but couldn't imagine the man she'd meet.'"

"Afterthoughts, a few days after. I recalled what was odd about her. You asked if I thought she would harm herself."

Lightly, he rubbed the flesh where the line of his jaw was a hard substance once upon a time. He was checking his shave with the tips of three fingers and thinking.

"If you don't mind an observation, you're exceptionally attractive."

"And exceptionally unavailable," I said, exceptionally patiently.

He smiled a frown. "I put people on their guard, Ms. Cromwell. I haven't stopped trying to fix myself. What I'm asking is, would Aubrey be attracted to you? Not sexually, necessarily, but an attraction. I ask because you said she had a disturbing fixation in her face."

I put a foot on the desk reflexively, and took it off, restoring half the lost poise, and crossed my ankles, dignified but comfortable.

"Aubrey was coming on to me, but not that way," I said. "The gale coming up Grant was sooo cold. A good chunk of her tits above the nipples was bare. Date or no date, her situation didn't make sense. If she were locked out of her house, she would be doing something else."

"A quick impulse to offer a hand was there and gone?" he said.

"I waved her over. She didn't respond as I expected. As I said, it was freezing."

"A normal person would take your offer, go inside with you. No way you had of knowing. The mind Aubrey uses is stripped of your experience of warmth. It's not warm inside. How did she look?"

"Unpredictable," I said. "A look that could be dangerous. I've seen it enough to respect the risks."

"You were concerned, as far as it was possible to be," he suggested.

"Not to any degree I cared to notice for long," I said.

"The concern remained?"

"A bewildered sympathy," I said. "You're getting at what?"

"You were the last person to see her on Grant. As far as I know."

His hand lingered in contact below an eye. That left a constant looking from the corner of an eye.

"She say anything?" he said.

"You know French?"

"When I was thirty-nine, my doctor said I wouldn't make forty. I should walk once in a while. I've been doing the Cote d'Azur. I've picked up dialect."

"Je veux, pour composer chastement mes églogues." I waited.

"Coucher auprès du ciel, comme les astrologues," he said. "Should I go on?"

"That's what she said to me."

He was resting against the doorjamb. He pushed off into his Hamlet routine, a thumb clutched at his back, head down. He got to the door in the reception room in under two minutes. His shoes were the silent type. I didn't hear a step as a step, a steady prowling. He returned and passed me. He let go of his thumb and tapped a knuckle on the door to my dining room, as if to say, "What's in there?" He turned and ran the thumb over an eyebrow. It didn't take the puzzle out of his vision. He wiped his eye all the way to the other door. Off again on the second go-round. He was back in his chosen two minutes.

In my presence, finally, a question: "What did you answer?"

"I told you, it was freezing. About then my knocking at Mr. Emmon's door paid off. The door opened. I went in. The door shut."

He took off wandering again. Another minute went by. A wall tap here and there. He was moving. The question came from the other room. "And the door stayed shut?"

"Probably," I said. "I got in an elevator."

"Baudelaire wrote that poem under a twelve-syllable-per-line scheme that is distinctive to French poetry," he said. "I'm sure you know it, alexandrine—the major stress on the sixth syllable. Under this scheme, Baudelaire was pressed to craft each line to respect the twelve-syllable condition, which may, in turn, explain the inclusion of words like *'chastement'* and *'églogues.'* They make each line verbose, and attain his self-imposed syllable count. A translation seeks to respect the alexandrine form of the verse while performing a literal translation. You can see this by counting the syllables. However…that's not what she wanted from you."

"She threw a phrase at me. How did I know what she wanted? I didn't care what she wanted."

He almost patted me on the head. "You will know soon." He put his right index finger in the air. He wasn't pointing at the ceiling.

"*Chastement* is pleasant to the French ear, given the silent 't' at the end. To you it's a French word of three syllables. Chastely is a clunky adverb in English, hardly seen outside the OED. The same general comment for *églogues* and its English equivalent. Both French words fit quite nicely. I think *églogues* was mainly used to rhyme with *astrologues* in the next line, which gives the poem a pleasant tune and feel, summoning the high bells and their calm hymns blown upon the wind in the next lines. The word itself is uncommon in current-day usage, given its specialized meaning in a pastoral poem, where 'pastoral' is, for Baudelaire, a withdrawal from a cosmopolitan setting to a rural place where one fantasizes an idyllic life."

"Okay."

"Apropos, *je veux* doesn't mean 'I would,' but rather, 'I want.' Yet the dream-like setting argues for 'I would' in English."

"I would have said, 'I want to compose my eclogues chastely.' I screwed up one word."

"This isn't an exam, but your translation is fatally flawed if you hoped to discover what she wanted with you."

"Give me a break. She was a nut. I'm beginning to wonder about you. Could I interest you in sitting down?"

"Gadzooks! Sitting. I'll die. Gave up tobacco, liquor, French fries. What I survive on now would substitute for sawdust. I eat a lot of it, though. You own this place. Do you insist?"

"How did you take tests? Did teachers let you walk around, knocking on the walls in Morse code?"

"You picked that up. Good for you."

He leaned an arm on the wall. A muscle might have accidentally gone off on its own. A smile flickered. A hand ready for the accident wiped it off.

"Aubrey's request was not for a thoughtful translation with Baudelaire's original twelve-syllable scheme. She wanted to jerk a reaction out of you. A considered opinion? I'd say that if you'd come through, she would have given you a fact that she could trust you to comprehend."

"Am I worth talking to?" I huffed.

"In so many words, that was her intention. You were going in, while she was going...where? She had two seconds. Were you in her league? Can you dash off a *New York Times* Sunday crossword between Grand Central Station and Columbia? Mom says Aubrey did. Got off the subway train and threw the paper away. Another triviality." His eyes flickered, communing somewhere within himself. His hand shook a dramatic back and forth, an instructional gesture: note well.

"For some reason, her mother knew your name. I discovered that later, and it puzzled me. Rule of thumb: Always meet the mother twice. We met at her home in the early afternoon, tea time, formalities and worries. When I left, I went to a park and waited ten minutes and called to say I'd lost a key ring. I'm a habitual recidivist there. It was between the cushions. She handed it over at the door.

"I remembered the Latin award on the wall. Very old school stuff. And the French award. And the Italian and German awards. The apple of her mother's eye. Before I knew it we were back inside, another round of tea. It took no effort on my part to admire the world of Aubrey, a girl who would have skipped two grades, but a shy girl, a bit on the small side.

"Best all-around decision? Keep her at age level. The school and the mother worked out a schedule with private tutors. And then she fell for *Rebecca*. She was twelve."

He put his hands in his pockets. One pocket had heavy coins, a couple quarters. I could hear them exchanging places.

"There followed an unhealthy declaration: She and Rebecca should live together, or die together. Rebecca should not marry. That put her in a clinic for gender evaluation. She came out a schizophrenic—my word, but the niceties they use these days have obliterated the diagnoses for voices in the head. Drugs and doctors beat the disease. What her mother said.

"She was also brains and hard work; a lot of brains and a lot of hard work—unbeatable. An incredible ear for the poet's tongue, *summa cum laude*, Yale. Graduate studies and the highest life of scholarship opened, but she went off to a book agent in New York, sifting the day's catch for some devotion to the daily grind of the unemployed. For two thousand a month she lived in a hole in the ground. In Aubrey's case, a sign of independence, the sign the experts actually were hoping to see. As they were beginning to despair, she turned her back on a career in the classics—and for what? A hand-to-mouth post at the lowest level of a literary agency. Literature? I misspoke, paperbacks, the reading materi-al of prisoners on life sentences, of Dallas housewives between airports. If that wasn't enough, she left the purity of a Yankee hearth and home, and found a translation job in San Francisco."

"You said you drink tea. I heard you say it."

"You want to shut me up," he said. "Between sips, or other-wise?"

I went in the kitchen and hauled out the fine service, heated water, and held the tea tin at eye level. He nodded.

"Two bags?"

"One, if I may. Please."

I poured. He sat on a chair. He took three teaspoons of sugar, a tad of nonfat milk as he licked his lips. I crossed my legs and looked at him across the rim of a cup.

"The sad tales of San Francisco," I said. "They have no bottom."

"That's another thing. How did the mother know your name? And why remember it? I wanted to get to the bottom of that connection."

"How's it going?"

"Brick wall so far." He settled back. "The mother assured me they were a close-knit team. Aubrey and her mom had a moment for each other every day. There was a call one morning. Aubrey was excited. She'd left her job. She was packing. There was a job in California. She didn't have it yet, but the job was bound to happen. A woman was dying, a German woman named Ingrid. She was writing her life story. For some reason that Aubrey didn't mention, the woman needed a Latin scholar. Aubrey's next call was from JFK. She was getting on a flight to your fair city. After that, the calls stopped coming every day."

He twisted his cup, thumb and finger, in short arcs, passing time, linking nothing to nothing.

"Ms. Cromwell, I invite you to share the moments when I close a case. In a few days from now, the toughest part of this job, I tell a parent they have no idea who their daughter is, and I have no idea where she is."

"You suspect foul play? I mean, beyond faulty mothering?"

"A disgruntled sex fiend? Two ships passing in the night? Intellectual upper crust Connecticut girls do it differently."

"Ingrid was dying," I said. "Aubrey must have known."

"The mother said the afterwards was all in their arrangement. Aubrey would keep her key to the house. When the translation was finished, Aubrey would take it through to publication."

"And then William decided to die," I said.

"That he did."

"And was unkind enough to kick her out," I said.

Benedict hadn't touched his cup for a minute.

I thought about the fridge. "Day-old coffeecake?" He shut his eyes. Oh, the memories.

"What do you live on?" I asked calmly.

"Flax seed meal, seeds, peanut shells You got any sunflower seeds? No? How about rice, any kind of beans? Most anything green, except M&M's."

"Why do you look for kids?"

"They're not hard to find. You figure out which friend is lying. Tail them. Adults have a right to run away. I find a woman for a husband, then what happens when I tell him where she is? It's out of my hands."

"Dirty hands?"

"Not if the contract's adequate." He veered off. "Ingrid. Ingrid what? And where? Dead? Like the Third Man was dead."

He was right. I knew more than he did. I could feel a tiny spot low on the shoulder blade, a small itch at the moment. He scratched his face and scratched at it. It wasn't making him look any smarter. He was smart regardless, even dumbed down.

I brought out half a cake, two plates, a knife, two forks, napkins.

"Last chance, Mr. Benedict. I'm peeling off a cellophane wrap, placing the knife where two pieces might be separated, and I'm asking you, 'Say when.'"

"He seen his opportunities and he took 'em," he said.

I poured another cup.

"I hope there's a next time, Ms. Cromwell. I'm filling a fork and pulling the fork against gravity, slowly, to my lips. I see two pennies on my eyes. I'm in the heaven where I can have my cake and eat it too."

"I forgot the whipped cream," I said.

"Speaking of whips," he said, "how does one compliment a dominatrix to her face?"

"Say something nice?"

"The word on the street: One never encounters a lazy pun at the English Department."

"How about a run-on sentence? I'm familiar with the sense of something needed from me, that extra in the design of a caning, if I may drag the subject of talent into my profession, that just comes from an instinct, a soothing hand, a kiss on a cheek, an expression of lust, or passion, or concern in a threat, delivered in a whisper, a warm breath in a whisper, encouragement, some sort of emphasis filling in for the thing they never had. It's the substance of a repeat business."

He formed a thought and held it, or just pursed his lips. "I didn't mean to interrupt," he said. "You mentioned whipped cream."

He cleaned his plate and lost his mind thanking me for day-old cake. "If you need a gumshoe with time on his hands, you have my private number. Was there mention of a tour?"

That put me in a think. He thought he was hearing a no. He was thanking me, pushing onto his feet, but I patted the air with some fingers fluttering, like take it easy, relax.

"I can give you a tour," I said, "but I'm retired, if I can make it stick."

"Not asking for services, merely an immersion in the grandeur."

The other door in the waiting room was a reproduction from photographs I'd taken in a Portuguese monastery. It's where the "tour" of the English Department kicks off. They all go through this door. I selected local reclaimed wood, worked into a medieval design, imitating the style that appeared in Europe when they needed powerful doors. It swung on iron hinges.

"The other side is serious business," I said.

We entered stacks along a narrow aisle between a wall of book shelves and a free-standing shelf.

"Seven stacks is shelf space for thirteen thousand items," I said. "I had the ceiling removed. The stacks now rise spectacularly to the ceiling above, anchored on guy wire. A small room has assumed the stature of a big room."

Coming out of the stacks, I stepped onto a low platform. I sat in a pumpkin-colored wingback chair. On either side were card catalogs. Benedict fiddled with the quarters in his pocket.

"I'm an eighth grade drop-out, Mr. Benedict. I'm greedy; a nice word for an uneducated book addict. Flagellants began storing their porn with me, and then it was Thackeray, Melville, Tennyson, as they retired to smaller digs. Left me their treasures. When they offered, I never said no."

Spreading my hands in abundance, I said, "All this was free. Time went on, more porn and more classics. I have a librarian who does the selecting. I've cornered self-published sado-masochism, scribbled on anything: three-hole lined paper or parchment, from novels to office memoranda."

"Where'd you train? Expertise, I mean."

"I consulted with a colleague until I could cross my own bridges. Took to role-play within limits. Queen Elizabeth is a steady request. Among men and women, a couple elections back, they asked for a paddling, a hard one from Hillary. Had a hunch she'd win. Instinct isn't everything."

I rose and led Benedict on. We passed the big ladder on wheels that maneuvered between the stacks. At the end of the far wall was a circular staircase that took us a flight up and onto a U-shaped balcony. More walls of books surrounded the mountain of storage in the cavern.

"You might have noticed," I said, "we're on the Dewey Decimal System. Every item gets a card. Porn is collected uncategorized. Fitzgerald and Hemingway are together, a peculiarity of my librarian. During the pandemic we got our treasures into a computerized catalogue. That's an ongoing project. Books keep coming."

At the curve of the U were three medieval doors with semicircular arched tops.

"Door number one," I said. I brushed the handle with my fingertips. His choice. I pushed it open, stepping back. Rough-hewn boards and a narrow bunk, an imitation of a monastic cell: chastity, obedience, discipline. Conspicuously absent was a crucifix. No emaciated figure on a cross.

"You have a keeper there," he said.

He was alluding to a life-size oil painting of a bare-breasted prioress shaking out the lashes in a multi-tailed knotted whip.

"Gifted in lieu of my fee," I said. "He overheard himself discussed in a parent/teacher conference: he'd never amount to anything. A millionaire these days. No better spot to immortalize his success."

Door number two had a plaque: B-200. "Have a look?" He opened the door. The canes in the umbrella stand in the corner made it clear what the next half-hour would be all about. If door number one was a dose of pain to make us feel better about something or other, here—face to face before the desk at the far wall, where the headmistress, Lady Smythe-Jones, receives the shiftless, the absent-minded, the dim, the shirker, the insubordinate, the cheat—door number two was correction, improvement, instruction, the laying down of the straight and narrow.

"Almost done." I followed Benedict through door number three. He wandered around the foot of a canopied four-poster bed, satin bedcover, velvet drapes. He was holding his thumb again, as if there was something to figure out. It kept him from touching, as if he didn't want to muss up a classic prop. He examined a mirror in back of a vanity table. Then he was checking the drawers. What was inside?

"No whips for this room?"

"Oh," I said. "I bring them up and then bring them back downstairs when we're finished. Nobody's complained."

"I see a wedding bed. Proposals of marriage?"

"You get points," I said. "Tease and denial. The fantasy is I'll break down and fall in love. I won't be able to resist them. Anyone else, yes. Not them."

"Do they get bored?"

"When we get bored, the heart grows fond. They put their head in my lap and we listen to a violin concerto. They have me, and they don't have me. The best of all possible worlds."

We went downstairs. Benedict took in the stacks with wide-angled appreciation.

"How many?"

"Including upstairs, fifteen thousand four hundred," I said. "We're a lending library, selectively. My librarian knows where to put his hand on a title."

At the door he asked, "What'll you do now?"

"Without a junior high school diploma? It'll get harder and harder to look in the mirror. Two notches on my forties. The big five-oh up ahead."

He turned, and said. "I've been worrying: *Chastement mes églogues*. The image created is vivid, given the French feel of the last word. You can't translate it literally into English. You need the adjective here. There is no decent adverb. It's a struggle for the noun. You'd have to go with: *I would when I compose my solemn verse*."

"Apropos?"

"Aubrey. In case you two meet. Impress her."

His mind tripped past obstacles easily. I was surprised he hadn't found Aubrey. I shut the door.

] *Chapter 5*

THE SLOPE OF my section of San Francisco is steep, so while my mailing address is on Stafford, I walk straight out of the basement three flights below street level into the alley between Stafford and Milpas, the next street over. A seven-sided bronze plate in the basement is decorated with the days of the week in Chinese characters. It was laid a century ago and might be worth some money, and someday I'll have it looked at. It covers a drop to a sub-basement that extends under the alley to metal rungs bolted to a wall. The ladder still works. Above it is a trapdoor that opens into a stairwell, which ends at a back door to the ladies' room on the third floor of a restaurant across the alley on Milpas. I could enter unseen. I could sneak in and sneak out for a free lunch. The bootleggers who once had access to the trick are dead. If they were available, they'd be closer to a hundred than ninety, so not too available—likely past communicating with.

This all has to do with Bob Corning, then and now. He had requested a meeting for services way back when he became the youngest Lit chairman at U.C. Berkeley. (He's still the record holder.) Nobody got his English Department mixed up with my English Department. The risk of being spotted doing business with mine gave him pause. This at a time when I had a rule: I met clients on my premises only, for my own safety. On the other hand, I was star-struck by literary royalty. I didn't want to miss him.

With Bob it always seemed an unseen hand was guiding a discussion. Bob put on a certain kind of Ritz, a repertoire of fussy speech that sent mildly pretentious half-formed challenges to a listener for a bit of help. "Let's do this thing together: I have an obsession with covering my tracks, and please get me over the hill on this." There I was, on the spot, and as dumb as it was, there it was: the underground passageway, a suggestion. The challenge of secrecy was now a puzzle in Bob's thoughts. The rest of the phone call was the fun of getting the stuck parts unstuck.

The trouble, laid bare, was that he had to go back through the restaurant the way he came in and face questioning, which meant passing off a wholly ridiculous story about where he'd been for two hours. The restaurant staff would have no basis on which to call him a liar for just one disappearing act. They'd have to claim where he had been. So it would work once—awkwardly, perhaps—but not once a month. But he *had* to do this thing once. Bob's joy was the nonsense routine. Just see how it worked, people confronted with crazy and never getting to grips with how the *crazy* was done.

I would have loved a seat in the peanut gallery, but had I been there, I would have ruined the act laughing. No matter, the gold separated from the dross. Bob recovered the dross at a pizza place in Berkeley just off campus. There we wrote a play about a politician who accomplished a variation of the restaurant peekaboo with a lady of the night.

Bob's problem of secrecy disappeared, but not in the way I ever could have imagined. We met for seven years in that pizza joint, usually in the same chairs at the same table, mining material randomly from the essential life histories of the servers. I never caned him. We enacted our scenes in writing.

Currently I'm not accepting new clients, easing into retirement, taking contact from established clients as time permits, hopefully the usually convenient ten-to-twelve slot. That's when the call came in. I didn't recognize the number. She said she was Mrs. Bob Corning. Odd, for the reason that I hadn't heard from Bob in at least ten years, just to pick a big number. It could have been more. I had heard he moved to Santa Cruz, and then left California.

Mrs. Corning apologized for the intrusion. Bob needed a favor. She was asking on his behalf. He couldn't ask for himself.

"Bob's in a nursing home in Austin," she said.

"He can't call?" I said.

"He can't talk. He growls. You might understand him; I can't. For that matter, he can't dial. He had a bicycle spill coming down a hill. He survived that one, and then took a second spill. A year previous there had been a bicycle crash in traffic. He was making less sense, not day by day, but each week his speech got worse: less communication, more noise. Now it's baby babbling and this horrible growling in his throat."

"What's the favor?"

"Bob left some boxes with a friend. I went to his friend's house. Nobody was home; his phone number was not in service."

"There's no one else?" I said.

"Bob has many friends, Ms. Cromwell. Friends are not an option. I wouldn't have called you otherwise."

"I was a friend," I said.

The voice grew tired. "Nothing would be gained by asking for clarification. I find this subject impossible. Could we simply meet? I'd like to give you a photograph."

"I'm free at noon," I said. "Say half-past. It would have to be close by." I gave her a street corner. She was in Walnut Creek. This time of day, give her an hour.

I left the English Department at noon, walked to Union St., grabbed a coffee, and did some window shopping and meandering until I got to the commemorative statue of volunteer firemen on Columbus Avenue. I sat on a low stone wall next to the statue and thought about men worth memorializing in bronze. The fireman with the bugle had a handlebar mustache tipped up at the ends. For the risks he was taking, he was on in years, fifty anyway, maybe sixty. His right arm was raised in the posture of an oration, but his mouth was firmly shut. The other man had a woman in his arms, a life just saved, unconscious.

The afternoon was cool. The two old women who passed wore winter coats. A young guy in denim happened to be passing the section of curb where a car going in the opposite direction pulled in. A woman got out and had to give him a look to get him out of the way—the kid spat on her. A City tussle of the passing moment.

Strategically placed to be immediately recognizable as the woman Ms. Corning was looking for, I stood, dumped my coffee along the edge of some grass, and dropped the cup in a wire receptacle. Meeting time.

She was in dark business attire, heels, and a maroon pea coat. She had the bearing of a woman of status and responsibilities, a fair degree of sex appeal at the end of middle age. She was meeting a woman who had taken up years of her husband's interest. She kept her hands in her pockets.

Face to face, she took a hand out of a pocket. I took a piece of paper handed me and noted a name on one side, Travis Rhymes, and an address in Woodminster. The other side was blank. The name and address didn't mean anything to me.

She took a photograph from her pocket, an indoor shot of a man facing the camera, his hands tied over his head, a woman on her knees sucking him and another woman behind him with a whip and a smile, waiting for the photographer to say, "Say cheese."

"This would be Champ," she said. "It's the buddy name Bob used for Travis. It was in one of Bob's appointment books."

To one side of the scene was a man in a chair, watching. It was Bob. Bob wouldn't want to be seen floating around the Internet like this.

"There are other photos?" I said.

"In the boxes," she said.

Okay, I got it, what's in the boxes should stay in the boxes.

I rubbed the side of my nose in appreciation of why I would be the one to look into the boxes. Coming along when I did, when books were no longer the keepsakes that had once gone to the next generation, clients drove up to the back door in the alley and unloaded the kinky-arty kind of stuff along with the collected works of Zane Grey, Freud, the metaphysical poets, and classic after classic.

I was thinking about the steps that would be involved under the simplest possible circumstances. "I'll drop by this address," I said. "There are a lot of if's, but let's say I return with the boxes to my place. How long are you in the area?"

"I leave tomorrow."

"It's a long shot," I said.

"If you would," she said, "please shred the lot."

She paused.

"There's this one other thing," she said. "Clearing Bob's study I had to decide what to do with his old appointment books. I came across the name of this kid in a Catholic school, Colin Ryan, an artist–poet. He kept coming up page after page, book after book. He sold poetry and stories out of his garage in Oakland. It seemed some school administrator called one of Bob's colleagues to let him know they had an up-and-coming Shakespeare on their hands. Would the department have some time for him? Bob bought up Ryan's garage, everything he did. It will all be in the boxes."

"Shred it, you're saying?"

"No, Ms. Cromwell, I'm saying in some circles this Colin Ryan is a writer. I'm saying, he's all yours." She looked down, ran a hand across the back of her neck, looked up and said, "I actually paid for a book of Ryan's poems: *Needs Emphasis*. You read it?"

"Bob put me on to him," I said. "I don't recall any poem in particular."

"'I, the Lash.' Cute. In your business, I would have thought you'd commit it to memory."

"I would have put it to use instead," I said. A poor counter. I was opening up.

"How is that? This English Department you operate. How would you put a poem to use? I really am curious."

"You mean after they're undressed, you want to get the low-down, stroke by stroke?"

The smile on her lips shot me a double-edged *touché*. The English Department was a snob title. She raised her eyebrows by way of getting to an insight into this need of mine to torment other women's husbands; or was I happily unmarried; or was I interested to know if she could forgive me?

"Mrs. Corning, you don't want to bother with where I fit into society. I'm a sex worker. That's how the City describes my work. I'm vulnerable, but there's high ground I can defend. If we're honest, we'll both walk away hurt. I'm not about to stoop and let you take a stab at a vital organ. The men who see me and decide they're getting a fair deal with the English Department are smarter than I am and know English better than I do, and know they know more."

"I'm sorry, Ms. Cromwell. Think of this experience as an indication of how far I've fallen. Bob put you on the high ground. Just what excited my husband's critical judgment exactly? I want to understand that."

"The plays he was writing? A sounding board was what I was most of the time."

"Give me a break, Ms. Cromwell. I'm not that far gone. I know when I'm getting a low-grade con job. My husband listened to you. I mean…listened! He recorded your every hiccup, encomiums I would have gotten on my knees for. To put the matter as honestly as I can, I…just…don't…get it."

Her eyes disappeared in a very slow blink. She wanted a confession that sounded authentic enough to supply a bit of comfort in reason, but phony enough to pass me off with *I don't mind if you don't matter.*

I left the subject. She was holding an envelope meant for me. It bulged.

"Mrs. Corning, Colin Ryan dedicated five novels to a girl he was in love with. He called her Sally Monroe. She killed herself.

It's what spurred the novels. They're famous, the Sally Monroe cycle. If you give me whatever of his is in those boxes, you're passing up what might someday be more than a fortune."

"Could we settle what I owe you?" she said.

I went on with what needed to be said.

"Ryan's style was haunting…original…went straight into me." I had a think: "*Emotional, Comma, Aura, Grasp, Arbitrary.* That's the cycle. They may not be in order. I'd recommend the first and last paragraphs of *Arbitrary.* When a writer rises to the level of Ryan's kind of fame, and he's still a miserable soul, that's getting at something inside your husband that he didn't show."

"You're a shrink?"

A shrug. It was all I could offer.

She held out the envelope. I took it. "If I can't retrieve the boxes, I'll let you know."

A woman passed pushing a baby carriage. I had shifted a few steps out of her path, the right of way a privilege of motherhood. In a moment, without taking her eyes from the woman Mrs. Corining said, "What did I miss?" She spoke to my face. "He trusted you."

"Not with a child."

Her body jerked. "He offered?"

"I wouldn't have accepted." Easy to say at the moment.

"Bob unartfully managed his absences in our family life," she said. "Not very original. It only required my acquiescence to ridiculous lies. I knew his erotic interests, as much as I cared to know them. Do with the boxes as you see fit. I trust your judgment."

She called a car. "We lived in one house for thirty-eight years. I'm trying to say we held it together for thirty-eight years. Never had the slightest hint from him how to get things going for us."

I walked back to the office. "Wild midnights" was what Bob called the occasions with his crowd, his art pushing the assertion that a whipping could be an act of love.

] *Chapter 6*

CIELITO LANE in Woodminster is a squashed semicircle attached at two points to a loop. The connection looks like a dog's body with two crooked legs, the way Egyptians left us their take on dogs. It's what the geometry provided in the hills up here below Skyline Blvd. My driver stopped and said, "This is it." I didn't see a house. I took his word for it and got out. There were three levels of growth, short, medium, and timber, the latter being large evergreens that in some decorative commingling overhead became this day's sky as I stepped off the street onto the driveway. A square stone column with a hollow space for a cement mailbox and metal door provided a number, 3833, consisting of embedded red stones in turquoise.

A paved incline ran a distance parallel to the street. Then it cut back a hundred and eighty degrees to an incline parallel to Cielito the other way, and then a ninety-degree turn up and onto a brick drive that had a semicircular run around the front of a two-story box.

The architectural style stuck a veranda along the front of the house, and continued its ample width around both sides. Debris had accumulated on the porch steps. Not an inch of ground was raked. Leaves, tangled in small branches, clustered between bushes, still zones that stayed put in knotted shapes in pretty much any gust. The whole place had a rundown appeal, like the opening scene in an art film getting you ready for the old man in the rocking chair long after an end-of-times stock market crash. Nobody had been here since the seasons changed.

I cupped my hands at a front window for a look inside. The rooms on either side of the entry foyer were empty, with vertically growing vines in three colors in the wall paper, a pattern not immediately periodic, and not cheap. If I bought the house I'd think of keeping it. Along the side I passed a main living area and a dining room, and then around back, a breakfast nook and kitchen that caught sun in the morning. An alcove in a corner was fitted with a washer and dryer. The middle of a counter was cut out to accommodate a refrigerator. Plenty of counter space left for a microwave.

The house next door on the north was another massive thing of the same era, but ornate. Four octagonal window frames projected from its south side in a two-tone of bright apple green and avocado. A wire fence about four feet high was strung between wooden posts, dividing the properties. It ran through grass and trees to the far side of a thicket, the north side manicured, and this side's growth splendidly left to its own.

Heavy double doors beside the back steps covered stairs to a lower level. Basement windows were half above ground, the lower half set in window wells. Bob Corning's boxes could have been stored down there or left on the second floor, but there were no outdoor steps so I couldn't see the upstairs. A massive wooden ladder was propped against an oak. Its feet were overgrown in weeds.

A wall of fitted stone of varying sizes set the boundary on the south side of the house. The house had not been centrally placed between neighbors. On this side of the house I estimated five short paces from house to wall; the north side was three times that far to the fence.

Another oddness in design, the wall didn't go all the way to the back of the property, but stopped where the back veranda ended. A section of wire fence filled in the rest of the distance from the wall to the rear property line. I was liking what I could do with the house. Plenty of room for my library. Enough left over for a lady of leisure.

In the middle of the wall was a gated doorway. Again odd, and again easily fixable. The gate was propped open. The ground at the gate was hollowed out, a well-traveled path between yards. I went to the gate. On the other side, a man in skimpy shorts, bare above and below, sandals and no socks, was wrestling a wheelbarrow onto its side, dumping a load of mud. He worked a shovel into the mud, shaping the mass into a tight mound. On the other side of the mound was a castle. Two of the turrets came up to his chest.

The details of the mud castle did justice to coffeetable images of the real things along the Rhine. Crenelated walls surrounded an interior of four turrets. Exterior stairways connected all four from the shortest to the largest. The man pulled a knife from a holster on his belt and began chipping at the edge of an upper window in a string of windows in a central turret. A square satisfactorily cut out, he dabbed into the interior. He applied wet mud to the sides of a window opening in the turret, and smoothed it with a trowel and fingers. The workmanship caught my admiration.

"Beautiful work," I said.

He hiked his shorts up and bent over the turret. Nice structure in the man. He dropped a flat spoon-like tool with a long wire handle into the open top of the turret. This he operated with another tool: a thin knife that apparently scooped dirt into the spoon. Out came a little shovel-full of dirt. That's the way to hollow out a turret.

I was standing behind him and to his side. "I was looking for your neighbor, Travis Rhymes?" I said.

He straightened up and turned his head. Two steps turned his body to face me. Pale blue eyes and a swimmer's appeal, more sinew, less bulk.

"You know Blake?" he said.

"I was angry with my friend?" I said. "That one?"

"You auditioning?"

"How'd I do?" I said.

"You must know what you're getting into."

"Just a reminder. I'm looking for the owner of the house next door."

"I remember. Looking for the neighbor. You have an appointment?"

"Just dropped by to say hello," I said.

"I moved here in early June," he said. "Haven't seen anyone…although, wait, about a year ago Blake was looking for him."

"Him?" I said. "The owner of the house here?"

"Yes. The house there." He pointed. "You were just looking at it. Blake heard he stopped in at an establishment near the Duboce Triangle for sex. Blake took a position there just to meet him."

"Why didn't Blake come here to meet him?"

"She heard that his wife lived here."

I could just as well meet the wife, I thought. Then again, Bob would have left his boxes with him, not her. Better meet him.

"Thanks," I said. "Just to make sure I understand: This Blake can get me to Rhymes?"

"My guess? She doesn't know where he is. What I said was, the owner of the house here, Travis Rhymes, was visiting the place where Blake worked. That's where she met him. He became one of her regulars. Since then, things have changed."

"They split up?" I said.

"That's my guess. As I said, the owner of the establishment near the Duboce Triangle would know how you would reach him. I don't know the establishment's name, but it's where Blake ran into him."

"Don't let me keep you," I said.

A straw coolie hat lay on the ground. It went on the turret, last thing before a step back and look-see. He changed the tilt of his head as he changed positions. A frown and pursed lips decided he had aced the turret. The slant was okay.

Without looking at me, he said, "I watched you come up. You don't have to leave by the drive. If you go over to the front corner of the yard, you'll find a landing and brick steps and a handrail."

"Thanks," I said. "Beautiful work." I said it plain, like I meant it. I did.

"In case the owner drops by," he said, "who should I say is looking for him?"

"He hasn't been around for a long time," I said.

"I just wanted your name."

"You've been helpful. I may have an idea that may get me to the owner. Blake worked at a location in the Duboce Triangle, and the owner visited that place. He has known tastes. I know that much. I might know that place. Thanks."

As I was backing away I gave him Elizabeth. "It won't mean anything to him."

"It does to me. "I'm Stan. In case."

Things began to jell all around.

From just one spot as I crossed the drive, the house shimmered in light. Slanting across the front windows were mirror images: perfectly reproduced reflections of trees. They and I moved oppositely, keeping a watch on each other. At the corner was the landing I was told I'd find. A few worn bricks were inscribed with 1922, laid by a company by the name of Apex. As they say, the house bore witness to time, so you might say its time was up—a tear-down that wouldn't survive first contact with new owners.

It was the style I liked, though, tucked away in isolation. I fought through brush grown heavy across the steps. Near the bottom was a worn outcropping of stone. An oak bench was grimed and nestled into a nest of branches, but still on its feet. It faced straight out to the Pacific, set here before the Bridge. Next time I would get some snaps of the house. I got on a knee and took a picture of a bunch of green and blue beyond.

] *Chapter 7*

MONTORGUEIL STREET in the Duboce Triangle is a row of tall, narrow two-address buildings dating from when each structure was an upstairs and downstairs, separate dwellings that over time had gone into single ownership. My colleague Jade had picked up the combined 1121 and 1123 as a business and residence. They had gone on the market together, a total reclamation at the end of a fifty-year life. The upstairs became her living quarters, and the ground floor put to use for customized services, similar, in the conventional aspects of comparison, to the English Department. Unlike me, she operated at street level.

A raised porch was secluded in three shades of bougainvillea that swallowed clients in the soft enclosure of anonymity. On the side of the house was an exterior stairway. I entered the residential area from the upstairs kitchen. I washed my face and hands and passed through sunlight to curtained darkness in a room overlooking the street. Off that room was an unoccupied bedroom suite. Jade was up and around. I went downstairs.

Robin, Jade's security man, was seated in front of a monitor. He watched over the proceedings of this fetish brothel, the House of Jade, established in 1994. Jade's original business predated this location by some ten years.

Robin's powers of persuasion derived from an absolute understanding that you're sure as sure you didn't want to know what would happen if he became upset. I'm a good six feet in heels. I feel small around him when he's sitting.

"Hi, Robin," I said. "Touching base."

Robin rolled his chair away from the desk and swiped two fingers across his brow. The sweat of a close call. He was sometimes required to intervene in a session, if things got out of control.

The goings-on in the room on the other side of the wall were on the screen. I leaned back against the door frame. A man in a prayer position was shining a boot on a woman's foot with his tongue. The woman was giving him instructions as if nothing the man ever did the rest of his life would be quite so important as what he was doing this instant. One of his hands was working hard on his cock.

"Mistress Melissa," Robin said. "A trainee. Her timing's off. She's six minutes over. Jade's Rule: An hour is fifty-nine minutes and sixty seconds. I'm giving him another minute. But it doesn't look like he'll last that long. "

"Say something nice," I said.

"The session will end without gun play."

"Jade's in back?" I said.

"Working on a pitcher of lemonade in the garden. Grab a glass in the kitchen. Take the chair on the back porch."

I sagged.

"You look peaked," he said, probing for some him-and-me chumminess.

I scraped a lip on my teeth, like this peaked stuff could come off.

"You must be tired of hearing me say, 'ravishingly beautiful.'"

"Will you love me when I can't play that card anymore? Speaking of which, losing the thread, you ever consider running your own shop?"

We all knew he'd only separate from Jade on a gurney, out the door feet first.

"What if the English Department beckons?" I said.

"Where's this coming from? You okay?"

I went to the door. I held on to the doorknob. "I just came from a house on a hill. Maybe the house and the hill that I will own someday. Come hell and high water, I want it." I pointed to the monitor. "He's done."

Out in back, Jade was in a rocker presiding over a flower garden, a hardback in her lap taking up tender loving care. I bent over and kissed her forehead.

I had been in attendance at her seventieth birthday party, one of a gang of seven of her own disposition, plus her sister, a well-married lady from the North Shore of Lake Michigan. And there was a woman friend of some significance from Carson City, an American flag above her heart, as if she would be undressed without it. All of us were a little louder than usual. The afternoon was a brilliant success. The question came up during the presents ceremony what Jade wanted but wasn't getting, something for her eightieth birthday. Well, she wanted us back next year. And happiness and health.

Well, she would be eighty next year, and at the moment she looked me over with a frown, a combination of crafty and concerned.

"How's the reading?" I asked. I sat and stretched my legs.

She raised an eye. "Very old biography," she said. "Briefly, Claire Clairmont was Lord Byron's mistress and the mother of his daughter, Allegra, and, less certainly, Shelly's lover. I'm trying to catch up to you in my golden years."

"I'm trying to get some balance in my life. Look at Little Miss Retired."

She closed her book on a napkin. "You're just a kid. What are you?"

"In my forties," I said. "Looking through catalogs for the perfect hammock."

"I mean," she said, "what's going on in that head of yours?"

It was eleven o'clock on a cool morning. We were out of the

sun, but with the wind in the leaves, the backyard was sprinkled in shimmering spots of light. No threat of fog till afternoon, but this late in the season the sky just might go gradually through pale shadows all the way to lamplight.

I poured myself a glass of lemonade. Skipped the ice bucket.

"Ingrid died," I said. "You know?"

She didn't. Her eyes narrowed, her lips closed, a face of limited sadness for what has to happen. After a second, "How's William?"

"Dead too. Not many days after. I pitched in with him for a decent casket for Ingrid. The place of interment was an old vineyard on the north side of her property."

"I was there years ago," Jade said. "A dirt road ends at a creek where a bridge washed out."

"How's Randi?" I asked. Randi was one of the dozen or so women on Jade's payroll.

"Hurt her wrist. That was in May. A case-hardened cripple now. Keeps it wrapped in an iron lung, blessed by a faith healer. Can't swing a twig. She says she'll be back when she's her old self."

"Sorry to hear," I said. "And Joan of Arc?" A nickname in common use, but never in her hearing.

"Turned thirty-six, went into the furniture business, making a living from bondage furniture and leather tackle. Works out of her sister's house."

She swiped her finger in her lemonade, inspected the tip, flicked her wrist, "Be gone." And licked her finger. And tossed a look at me. "What's the occasion?"

"Travis Rhymes," I said.

"Champ? In here a couple months ago."

"How would I find him?"

"If he weren't hiding?"

"Is he?"

"You tell me. What happened when you called him?"

"I didn't. The number Bob Corning had is disconnected."

"Bob? Champ wouldn't be hiding from Bob."

"Travis Rhymes has a house in Woodminster. I want to know what he would let it go for." I held up a palm outwards, the universal sign of honesty. "That's all I want to know from him."

"Champ has a couple places in Beverly Hills. Would they do?"

"My information is he met and fell for a sweet young thing name of Blake, and, as it happens in a coincidence, the meeting was on these very premises."

She stuck a forefinger at me. "You want Blake. And ask her where you can find Champ." She moved her finger around in calculations. "What's so great about this house?"

"My library will fit, with a room or two left over for quiet contemplation."

"What happens to the English Department?"

"Haven't got there yet. First things first. My books need a home."

Jade flipped her book up, took out the napkin and moved a ribbon to the page she was saving, and closed the cover. "We've had good times, Elizabeth. Not enough, though." She spread the napkin and put the book on it. "Ham on rye sound about right?"

She got a phone from her coat pocket and called in an order. "Twenty minutes," she said. She called Robin to let him know to expect a delivery from Samson's Sandwiches. In the meanwhile, she'd appreciate it if he would open that unopened box from the Biscuit Factory. She put the phone to her chest. "Cabernet Franc?"

She studied her phone and called Robin again. "Could you see if you can reach a Mr. Travis D. Rhymes? There's one in Woodminster, also a listing in Santa Monica. Any which way you can get him, or someone who can get him, let me know, please."

Fifteen minutes passed. Jade's phone buzzed. She put it on speaker. Robin said, "There's a Ms. Whitman on the line. She works for Crystallized Entertainment. You might want to talk to her."

A woman's voice said, "Hello."

Jade said, "This is Jade speaking. Am I speaking with Ms. Whitman?"

"What business do you have with Travis Rhymes?"

"First of all, would you say he's missing?"

Jade looked at her phone. "That's funny. She hung up."

Robin arrived with a tray and a bottle of wine. I moved my chair to a table under the gazebo and set it opposite Jade. Robin removed the lemonade pitcher and put it on a curved stone seat at the side of the gazebo. He set the serving tray on the table, two curved rows of rectangular biscuits, arranged in an arc. Two wineglasses clinked upside down between his fingers. He turned his hand over and removed the glasses. The cork was already out of the bottle. He poured a finger for Jade to do the routine. "Excellent," she said. "Lightly chilled." She nodded. Napkins and eating plates were set and glasses, appropriately filled, clinked to our health.

"Robin, if you would, do we have a photo of Blake handy?"

"I'll check."

She set me straight. "You're exercising an adolescent rebellion, Elizabeth. Don't get me wrong. Age appropriate. Do not forget, forty-two, a very dangerous age."

"I like the house," I said.

"I shall support you in whatever decision you come to," she said.

"It's a big house. As I said, my library will fit. My books, they're all I have."

"When you're no longer one of us, will you still see me?"

"I want to do something else with my life," I said. "I might hire a yachtsman and sail."

Lunch arrived. Robin cleared the table and set out the sandwiches. "Mustard or mayo?" Robin read my head wiggle: "Thin on both." Robin backed off two steps, turned and went inside.

Neither of us ate much. Jade might have been thinking that if I was so hell-bent on retiring, I could save her some phone calls looking for people I had no business looking for at forty-two. Get an agent, let them find Rhymes. While they're at it, they will run across homes in the hills that are on the market, ready for occupancy. But of course this is America. It's a free country, and Elizabeth Cromwell will do this her own damn way. And what's to complain about? I took her nose out of some stupid book. Byron? Get a life.

I wrapped the uneaten half of my sandwich in a napkin. The corner of the eaten half was two chunks of toast, complete in itself with an artistic existence. I left it as it lay. I gave a potato chip a rest. Deep down Jade liked something about me. A unique privilege, she let me kiss her forehead once in a while.

She pointed her finger, as if to say, just a second, one more thing. "Come back!" A strict foot stamped the bricks. A command.

I put a hand on her shoulder. "I'll give you a call about the retirement thing, one way or the other."

I looked back from the porch steps. She watched my line of sight. It bounced off a terracotta pot deep into a domain so far away she couldn't possibly not have to worry about me. I waved myself off and poked my head in on Robin.

Robin was not all sunshine. He reached a hand out to tap a finger on a book, one of two dozen stacked in his work area. The book was held upright and open in a plastic frame. I had a look. He was studying inkblots.

"They say you can't cheat," he said. "So why am I looking at someone else's answers?"

"What is it, Robin?"

"I appreciate you dropping by. It's her best medicine."

"She seems sharp."

"Each day she slips a little more."

A folder was squared off at a corner of the desk. He opened the cover and unclipped a photo of a brunette. He slid the brunette to where I could see who he was talking about. "Here's your Blake."

"A last name?" I said. "Or a first name?"

"Just Blake. That's all she gave us. Two things to know. She stiffed a client. The guy flew in that morning from L.A. to meet her. She didn't let him know she wouldn't make their appointment—on purpose. She got some other girl to take her place."

"What was her side of it?"

"I left her a message to discuss that with me. No callback. That was her side of it."

"Jade took her back, though?" I said.

"Jade didn't like losing her. She had animal magnetism—a greyhound. I'm a tortoise. You know, repeat business is basic human decency."

"Big mistake," I said.

"Saw it coming," he said. "She walked out the door with Travis Rhymes. Never heard from her."

"She didn't give notice?"

"She fired us. Fucked Jade over. Jade gave her a break. Of course, latching Rhymes was pay dirt." He looked at an inkblot. "Watch your back with her."

] *Chapter 8*

I WENT HOME and got a feel for what I'd have to consider if I wanted to get a toe in real estate in Woodminster. Travis Rhymes's address wasn't in the listings. Sort of irrelevant in that case getting a real estate agent? Then again, if the house suddenly appeared for sale, I'd want an agent working for me; but then again, why ask around? Why share my knowledge of a vacant house with realtors? What they don't know might preserve an advantage. With plenty of money, and pressing interests, selling a house could have slipped Rhymes's mind. Not too likely, but he must have had some reason for letting the house sit vacant. He could be ready for an offer and a deal that gets done in a hurry. All I had to do was find him.

I climbed under the covers that night with a laptop and pulled up a satellite image of 3383 Cielito. It all looked the way I remembered at ground level. I slept on it, and greeted the new day slowly, not quite ready to get up. There just seemed to be some misunderstanding in the night that demanded a reckoning. I took the printouts of the Woodminster area in two hands and thumped the bottom edges, squaring them up. There on the top sheet were those skinny dimensions of the Rhymes lot. I checked. It was the single oddity among a dozen bunched properties. It was too narrow. I sat there undoing my earlier disregard of the

dimensions. Why did I think the wall was constructed on a neighbor's property line? Had Rhymes, or a previous owner, sold off
that half, and the buyer built a skinny house? It seemed doubtful
that a neighborhood of the Woodminster sort would sanction
lot-splitting, nor would it be legal.

Less unlikely, say pretty for sure, it wasn't a split lot and
nothing had been sold off. The little stucco house was on the
big house's property, and the wall had been set up to provide a
private space for a guest, or for a renter. Okay, if Rhymes owned
the little house, the question is—if I was thinking right—who's
been paying the electric bill in the guesthouse for half a year?
Had I asked Stan the wrong questions?

It rained overnight. The forecast said clear in the East Bay
until late afternoon, but in the hills of Woodminster dark clouds
in a blue sky were bundles of swirling showers, intermittently
annoying getting up to the house. The steps arrived at the corner
of the lot, coming into the Roman patio. Already a few clouds
were dark over the higher elevations past the freeway. A bibli-
cal ray of light from the heavens had landed on Mount Diablo.
Traffic was a soft hum, not yet the constant roar you get during
a rain. Several seasons' worth of pine needles had entangled and
formed a carpet, bunched higher on the windward sides against
circular columns. Their carpet spread out beyond in a curved
pattern. Where it reached a raised section of the driveway, it left
a clear swept boundary to the cover of the veranda. It was the
preferred route the winds took up here, and I followed it to the
veranda of the main house.

A folding table had blown over in the vicinity of a chaise
longue. I pulled the table upright and shook off of it what would
shake off. The dirt would have to be scrubbed and the wood
lacquered again for any recovery of the grain.

A lounge pad had once been sparkling white satin. I turned
it over and sat on a barely dry surface and crossed my legs, like I
would if I owned the place. Just beyond the end of my feet to the
southeast were the inland regions this side of the Golden Gate.

I knocked on the door of the darkened main house for the heck of a no answer. From the veranda I could see that the upper windows of the guesthouse were dark. Nothing lost, nothing gained in the visit. I started to call a car. I turned my head getting the phone under my hair and caught a glimpse of a shape that blinked in the thicket that bounded the back fence. Stan broke into a clear narrow lane. He balanced a brown paper grocery sack on top of the back fence. He held the sack and held the fence, and suddenly let go of the sack, hopped over the fence two-handed into the backyard, and grabbed the sack. Aware that he was not alone, he pointed a hand in my direction and swung his arm to the wall and jabbed a finger at what could mean the open gateway to the guesthouse.

"Meet you at the house," he said.

The front door was open. He was waiting. "I thought you'd be back," he said. "If you're inclined, come on in."

I went into a room with a sofa and two chairs, two small tables, a large table with a television, two identical lamps, and a couple high-altitude photos of Bay landmarks. A bed was visible in the next room. A kitchen and dining area were all of a piece with the living room. It was modern, built, say, within the past fifteen years, a low ceiling, track lighting, with the amenities limited to what it was, a compressed space with plenty of class and comforts for a bachelor pad on a hill.

His stuff was all over the places you might think of sitting, other than on the floor.

He unloaded vegetables from a grocery sack onto a counter, and interlocked his fingers and gave me another option.

"I was intending a salad. There's plenty for two. You want to pitch in on that job, the counter is yours. I don't do alcohol. Sorry. Tap water isn't bad up here. Anything stronger, there's coffee and black tea. That over there is the electric kettle. You don't see equipment you need to make a salad, check those drawers. Some open dressings are in the fridge."

"You give more information on lunch preparation than on your neighbor," I said.

"I know salads. Don't know neighbors." He opened the refrigerator and held a package for consideration. "Some tofu? I know tofu."

"You expected me, you said."

"I've been expecting somebody to show up and give me ten minutes to get my ass out of here. Almost half a year I've had the place to myself."

"Any ideas about me?" I said.

"Yesterday you showed up in the busiest hour of the morning. So you have no regular employment, unless you're a realtor, but then a woman with your looks, realtor or not, distrusts an isolated locale." He rubbed his chin. "I needed a theory to cover a fearless beauty. I knew the owner's mistress. You might hope to be another one."

I laughed. "Not even close."

"You never met him?" he asked.

"Not even once," I said. "And anyway, why would a mistress come to an empty house?"

"Didn't know it was empty? Found out her guy walked out on her. Meets a dope playing in mud. Next day she has a second thought. Decides to come back, catch the dope with his feet up, and ask him to pass a message to the guy who walked out on her?"

"Not bad," I said. "And the dope invites the mistress in for lunch. Work out an arrangement?"

He snapped his fingers. "Struck out?"

"Oh, please," I said. "Don't even think things like that."

"What's the answer?"

"Off chance I meet the owner," I said. "See what kind of offer he'd entertain for his house."

"Will you keep me?" he said.

"First item on the lease," I said, "you'd work without a shirt."

I must have looked honest and uninformed. "You want to buy this place?"

Moved by some impulse towards my salvation, he motioned me to follow him. We went outside, turned to the left front corner of the porch. He spoke in a strong clipped voice, as if he knew the way the wind blew around here. His nod fell on a red brick wall about two feet tall that went from the house to a wire fence in the back.

"I built that," he said.

His finger pointed at the mountains. "Back there. All that ground's been shifting. Eons of shifting. The wall here? When I got here, it was down there." He pointed at an area beyond the line of the porch. "To build this house, they cut a notch out of the hillside. That cleared a level surface. To stop all that ground above from moving, they stacked bricks against the raised section, you know, like extra careful, but only a single layer, like not too smart. Cosmetics. The bricks were jumbled when I got here. They planted a row of trees in a line. Well, see for yourself."

The trees had invented their own line.

"Your future lot is on the move." His hand swept over an expanse of even ground in front of the porch. "I hauled back fifteen cubic yards of earth." He pointed at the mountains again. "I moved it all back up there. One load at a time. There's a carbon footprint for you."

Fifteen didn't sound like many yards. But if it weren't, would he have mentioned it? "That's a lot of earth," I said.

I'd been working him over with little flicks of admiration. Salads and physical labor had kept him sporting a body. He was ten years my junior…thereabouts. One of nature's gifts.

"One castle to go," he said, referencing a pile of mud.

We started inside. He stopped to say, "There was a structure here before. A foundation is still in the crawl space. Some initials in the stone. I'm assuming they identify the builder, a guy named DWH."

We went inside. I ran an eye over a head of lettuce, red and green peppers, two green onions, radish, celery, and a bag of sunflower seeds. I could handle salad makings. A cutting board was next to the sink. A knife was in the drainer. He took his lumberjack shirt off. A hooded sweatshirt from Marburg was underneath. He pushed the sleeves up and washed his hands. I took the opposite side of the kitchen island. He got busy setting the table.

"Call you Elizabeth?" he said.

"I'll always smile."

"Incidentally, Stan is the accented syllable of Konstantin. Stick to Stan, or I think I'm talking to my mother."

I found a bowl worthy of ingredients for six, and fluffed away. I cut open the bag of seeds, distributed half, and circled a rubber band on the package.

He sliced a slab of tofu in fifths and stuck them in an air fryer. He pushed the button on the tea kettle. "I'm having a French roast, supermarket grade. You?"

"Sure."

"You size men up fast," he said.

I blinked a blink at him.

"I'm safe," he said.

Oh, that. "You've lived here since when?" I asked.

"June first," he said. "The letter from the math department arrived beginning of May. I had till the end of June to clear my office. This hacienda came available and I took it."

"Where did this opportunity come from?" I said.

"Blake. We met up here at the Space Center. I was on my back scribbling on orange paper, crumpling pages as they got full, arcing them unerringly into a trashcan. I got up and started looking through the can. Had I thrown away a vital step? I retrieved my scribblings and got on my back again, unfolded them, studied each, crumpled them, now certain the chain of steps was useless. Threw them back where they belonged. A black leather boot appeared next to my head. A voice told me to hold her ankle and tell her what I was doing. That's how we met."

I looked like I always look when men want me to know something important about their adventures. I got a radish between my teeth, and gave it a slow going over. An inquisitive stare synthesized an instruction: "Go on."

"She cleared away misunderstandings. She was a sex worker. If I was inclined, call the Snarky Owl, ask for a bartender named Sue—her moniker. From then on it would be five hundred dollars cash, and I could call her Blake."

He watched me think. "Whatever you want to know about her," he said, "I don't know. And who's been paying the utilities you might ask? The light switch keeps doing its thing."

We dressed our own salads. He made the appreciation sound on the first bite. He smiled and pointed his fork at me.

"The day I was fired I was due to meet Blake. I told her I loved her, but now that I was unemployed I had to watch my pennies. An hour later she called me. This place was available. It was free."

"Blake was living here then?" I said.

"The domain of the mistress."

"Five hundred is a lot of pennies," I said. "You were fortunate. She liked you. Not always the case."

"At the time I could afford true love."

He stood and looked confused for an instant. "I had a photo of her. I'd have to look." He sat down. "I moved my stuff here and waited for her. It didn't occur to me I could live here alone, and nobody would show up and give a damn."

"So far," I said, "five months and free?"

"What it is," he said. "The last call I got from her was the offer: I could move in here. She was frightened."

He went to a shelf next to the refrigerator and picked up a small paper bag. He put the bag at my left hand. He nodded at the bag: "I found this here."

I unwrapped a rubber band and looked inside. There was a fingernail file and a light gray paperback, pretty good shape for a first edition, 1961, Frantz Fanon, *Les damnés de la terre*, in all-lowercase along a tall, thin green rectangular cover, the identifier for the publisher, François Maspero, Paris. A preface by Jean-Paul Sartre. Quality recommendation.

"The nail file might have been a bookmark," he said. "It fell out when I took the book out of the sack."

He spread out browned slices of tofu on a serving dish. There were five.

"I could cut one in half," he said.

I nodded: "My compliments. Delicious."

Robin's opinion of Blake was lodged in my brain in opposition to her act of generosity toward Stan.

"You think Blake might be up to something?" I said.

He sat at the edge of his chair, stuck out his legs, and leaned back. He took a spoon in thumb and forefinger, and tapped a rhythm on a knee. "This free ride in Woodminster? If she's up to something, she's taking her time."

"Travis Rhymes owns this property," I said.

"You know more than I do."

"I'll come back to that," I said. "You had your meetings with Blake here?"

"We began our dates at the Snarky Owl," he said. "Ended our dates over sundaes at the Snarky Owl."

"You assumed she lived at this Snarky Owl place?"

"She said she'd lived there off and on. Where she lived, I didn't care. When she called to say I could stay here, she said she had moved out."

"She doesn't own it. What in the world was she thinking?"

"I'm not completely sure she was living here, but I'm not blaming myself for believing her. I didn't knock at the main house. Blake had been living in the guesthouse. Circumstances changed. I could have the guesthouse. I'm still waiting for clarification. Why not?"

"I'm struggling with how I'll ever get this property under my name."

A silence endured quite a lot of small hand motions. It occurred to me that if I told him about myself it would make me look like an authority on something or other. Okay, Blake was a sex worker. This gave me an opening for a fact-based opinion without risking too much anxiety.

"I'm a sex worker," I said. "It runs me into the subject of loneliness. We could dwell on one end of that connection."

"What's the other end?"

"Loneliness," I said. "Both ends. What I'm saying is you were special to her, obviously. She selected a guy stretched out on a lawn. Way out of line with the generally agreed-on protocol for introductions. A sex worker solving the loneliness thing day by day, she was susceptible to taking on a trial lover."

"She charged," he said.

"She protected herself. Emotionally risky, and she knew the risks. She told you she was another man's mistress. Same reason. Protect herself."

"She steered me to this house when I needed it."

"It all might be the way it looks?" I said.

I cleared my plate. "You were walking up here from below the freeway. Where were you before you went over the fence?"

"A pedestrian underpass. It's not far to the shopping center on the other side of the freeway."

We washed up the dishes and lingered outside, exchanging possibilities.

"I'm not hard to find…till I'm kicked out. Something to know: I'll walk a mile for pistachio."

I gave him my personal number. "I always answer."

I went to the edge of the promontory, checked my footing, slowly backing to my right, tracking the edge along the outer curve of a steeply terraced drop. From where I looked back a third story was suddenly visible on the main house. The builder had stuck a windowed box at the top of a gently pitched section of roof. I put my mind inside for a guess at what the view in all directions would look like. There was nothing to not like. It was as if this day of the year and this time of day was when you bring yourself up here to pitch this house on the heath.

An argument I was in love with the joint was getting easy to prop up. I was already thinking of it as half mine. House-hunting can sound scathingly silly.

At the office I checked online for faces on the faculty page of the U.C. Berkeley math department. Stan wasn't there. Naturally,

I wanted last year. That might be in the most current yearbook. They might have a copy in the math office, or I could go to the university library. I found the guy I wanted online: Konstantin Arnold. Specialized in algebraic geometry, Harvard undergraduate, Princeton doctor of philosophy, two years at MIT, two years at Berkeley, currently specialized in mud castle construction in Woodminster. Several talks he had given were available online. I spent a few minutes watching him at a chalkboard explaining why Reshevsky Cohomology Groups for Projective Toric Varieties was a thing to study. My guy was sporting a T-shirt.

We'll meet again?

] *Chapter 9*

THE RIDE UP Albany Hill was steep but short, not much of a minute; whatever, my ears popped when we stopped at 435 Altair Drive, the last address of a dozen places on the leeward side facing away from the Bay.

The house was halfway up a tree-lined climb to a park at the mound of the hill. Built outwards from the street, a wide driveway of a car's depth filled in a parking area fronting a double garage, which gave the place the appearance of a duplex, but there was only the one address with a couple air conditioners on the second floor.

Something significant in the grand scheme of things in this section of Altair Drive, however, was visible. A printed sign on an easel announced: THE NEW CONSTITUTION. That's what had dragged me up here—or better to say it had come to the attention of Brendan Hopkins that Joanna Dempsey, aka Jasmine, would be at this address, at this time, with the new framers of a new Constitution of the United States. The amount that William Emmon wanted delivered to Ms. Dempsey wasn't cash any longer. I was carrying a bank check for three hundred eighty-eight thousand dollars.

At the far corner of the garage was a sign on a stick mounted on a Christmas tree stand. An index finger pointed to the right. Underneath was: THIS WAY. The finger pointed to steps that ran down and around the side of the house. A man on the top step was employing an arm managing gestures that kept up with remarks he was directing at a woman holding both her elbows. She might have been the back end of a queue that wasn't moving, or maybe the constitutional convention was over, or hadn't started yet, or it was full and they'd run out of room. Whatever was going on inside, or was scheduled and should have gone on, a woman in a chair against the garage had the time-on-her-hands look of an older type out for a celestial event, say an eclipse of the moon, but it was too early to look up, or she had looked up, and she'd get back to it. Or she owned the hill.

I asked my driver to hang on a second. I was about to step into the open air when a moped pulled onto a cement pad just off the driveway. The rider dismounted and took her helmet off. She was a long-legged attraction not much into her twenties, with two-tone maroon hair. The look wasn't making its way readily through my delicate sensibilities. Did it or did it not harmonize with what she was wearing? The outfit below the waist was stretchy black stuff, tight the whole 360 in the crotch. I was looking at her for a fashion verdict. The woman in the chair was looking at her for her reasons. The man at the top of the steps was looking at her the hardest.

She got busy with a hand in a backpack, extracted a thin wallet, unhooked a clasp and let a press pass drop open facing me: HALEY NALLS, NEWSEAGLE.

"Heard of you," I said. "Saw your article on Jasmine: the event at Berkeley."

"If you don't mind my asking, you are?"

"Elizabeth."

She said my name out loud as she wrote. She waited. Nothing more from me. "First names, then. I'm Haley. I prefer to meet people who are late for meetings. As you can tell, obviously. That's why I'm late. Why are you late?"

"Not late enough," I said. "I'd hoped the meeting would have broken up by now."

"You want to meet Jasmine? Mind my inquiring?"

"A private mission," I said.

"Fair enough." That out of the way, she clicked a pen and stuck the point at me. "Hope we meet again. "

An ambulance had passed me going down the street as I was arriving. Three men and a woman were a few car lengths up the street, milling around as if in discussion of what the ambulance had been about. Nalls looked in the direction of the discussion, like not enough to listen in to. She headed to the gray-headed lady in the chair by the garage. I got out and followed.

Nalls skipped the introduction and asked, "What was the ambulance for?"

"A man fell asleep in his car," the woman said. "The car was locked. The paramedic used a piece of metal and a wire. He was in like Mickey." She added a comment of journalistic significance: "They found banana peels. The man had eaten four bananas while the engine was running."

Nalls wrote that down. "In his sleep?"

"Good question. They couldn't wake him to ask."

The woman in the chair lit up. The pinched end of the object of interest was getting itself massaged in a thumb and forefinger. Her upper arm was planted on an elbow. The wrist was waving the smoke through a fortuitous current of air, passing the sweet aroma to all assembled.

Nalls re-situated herself to the side of a column of smoke, all business, pen ready. "I'm a reporter with the *NewsEagle*," she said. "Would you mind answering a few questions?"

The woman's wrist flicked the joint up an inch and back. "Depends."

"You know anything about this new constitution?"

"What you could put in a thimble."

"By any chance are you Jasmine's press secretary?"

"Nope."

"You know her?"

"Enough."

"Okay, the new constitution," Nalls said. "So there's an amendment process in the constitution we already have. Jasmine have a position on that?"

"Get your head out of the sand."

I could see Nalls's pen thinking, "Can I quote you on that?"

No answer. Nalls had a stab at clarification. "What sand would you be talking about? Seventeen eighty-nine, and all that?"

"Pick any sand you want. Pull your head out."

"Fair enough. I'll pick seventeen eighty-nine and the amendment process. Jasmine has abandoned the current foundation of the United States. That's what you're saying?"

"I'm not saying anything."

Nalls tried from another angle. Let's all reason together. "Okay. The eighteenth-century document was for putting a country together. Amendments were for holding it together. We're coming apart now. The parts will require an agreed-upon operating manual. Is it fair to say that Jasmine is offering the United States a new operating manual?"

"Your words."

"May I have your words? What parts are we talking about?"

"The nations."

"These nations have names?"

The woman who'd been holding her elbows stepped into the interview. She introduced herself as, "Virginia Willis-Ashford, assistant director of development with Perfect Media Vectors."

The authoritative tone pulled our interest to the announcement.

"I believe I can answer that. We're embarking on a documentary on 'Nukon,' N-U-K-O-N. Of course there's the who, what, where, when, and why. We expect the details will change. We expect the organization's aims to evolve. We hope to be with Jasmine the whole journey. The fundamental point to keep in mind is that new eras require new directives. The Constitution of seventeen-eighty-seven was a roadmap for the formation of a union of thirteen separate entities. The new constitution will be a bridge spanning anywhere from nine to fifteen distinct political parties within four to seven distinct nations. These numbers are guesstimates. The idea is not to become specific as to how the country fragments as the country fragments, but how the fragments function organically with developments."

Nalls stopped scribbling. "What do you mean by 'the whole journey'?"

"We want to be at Appomattox Courthouse when Lee rides in on Traveler."

"What if the four to seven nations fragment, but agree to carry a grudge against television?" Nalls inquired. Willis-Ashford paused in silence. I couldn't get the question into focus either, if that was Willis-Ashford's problem.

"I mean," Nalls thought a second, "each nation would censor the media of the other nations, don't you think? I mean, isn't that the reason for splitting up? They don't like each other."

Willis-Ashford did a wide sweep around the essence of the question.

"Of course, we've done a prudent stepping back, calculating odds against live streaming. The Tower of Babel is what the new constitution is all about. Hate can be an expression of love. Shared values preserved in written documents will be up for debate. Just in case."

"Just in case?"

"There will be conflict, an expected ingredient of our documentary. The weekly episodes of the documentary will run concurrently with adversarial gatherings, but they'll be peaceful—everyone sitting in their own den, the exchange of multiple viewpoints. We call the strategy 'content modulation.'"

"'The Tower of Babel.'" Nalls squinted as she crossed a *t* in a squiggle. "That show went strong for a few seasons. Then the project became unworkable. Wasn't that God's idea? All those languages?"

Willis-Ashford was on it: *"Come, let us go down, and there confuse their language, that they may not understand one another's speech."* She then provided the modern answer: "You people always forget: the descendants of Shem. Life goes on. There are other seasons, other series. Media will unite the tribes of the Lord."

I rolled one eye. I kept my face in one piece.

Nalls looked over Willis-Ashford's head, apparently out of pointless questions. Her pen thumped a page for what else might go in the notebook, and then she turned around to study the guy at the corner staring at her. "Who's tall, dark, and handsome over there?"

"He won't be your story," Willis-Ashford said. "He can't get you to Jasmine. He's my gopher."

Haley looked at the woman in the chair. "I'd like to talk to Jasmine when she's free."

"There's a door inside the garage," she said. "On the other side of the door is a closet. On the other side of the closet is a bedroom. On the other side of the bedroom is the meeting."

"I can watch from the bedroom on the other side of the closet?"

"I might let you in. Or you can go down the stairs there to the left. They go to the first floor, one floor down. You can hear everything from the garden."

"When does the meeting end?" Nalls asked.

"Could go on all night—that's why I mentioned the bedroom. Crack the door, stretch out on the bed and listen in."

I broke off from the show and stepped onto the walk at the corner of the garage and stood still, looking east from the heights, a bird's-eye view of the community below. Many lights come together.

Stairs went down to the base of a lower level of the house. A walk went along the house. It ended at three steps that descended to a small stone patio that followed some architectural philosophy governing the integration of land and structure. From one end of the patio you went straight into a kitchen, open to a view of both sides of the house. The kitchen was lit but deserted. Above the kitchen was an upstairs patio and a large enclosed room separated from each other by glass doors. I was next to stairs that led up to the patio.

I went partway up to where I saw heads and shoulders in a line along a window. A woman standing above them was providing the voice I heard.

Inside was a common purpose that ventured out in the night with nothing less than a new American design. They turned their backs on this basic American story, sick to death, the new young in a greater childhood. Shouldn't a despair that would lead you to desert a two-hundred-year-old document come out of a four-story cold-water walkup off an alley?

The stairs to the balcony were blocked by the back of a folding chair with a note taped to it: NO ENTRY. I folded the chair, propped it against the rail, and slipped past sideways to a gate on the patio. A woman saw me. Then a half-dozen looked. Two of them looked at each other and stood. The tall one with the reddish hair came outside. The other one remained at the sliding door.

"You read the sign," she said. "Go back the way you came."

I jiggled the envelope I was holding. "This is a bank check for Joanna Dempsey."

"To repeat, go back the way you came."

"Fine," I said. "Happy to do that. And the check will go with me, to be returned to the account it came from. The effort I'm making now to get the check to Joanna Dempsey will be considered sufficient to close the matter. The three hundred eighty-eight thousand will go to the State of California."

As I went back down the stairs, in my mind's eye I held up phantom hands, palms out, silently saying, "My hands are clean."

I turned at the bottom of the stairs. A voice above said, "Just a minute."

The voice was not exactly desperate, but it was sharp. It didn't want to be ignored. I took a breath, stopped and looked at the sky. The redhead whom the *NewsEagle* called Jasmine put a foot on the lowest step, about my height in combat boots.

"I'm Joanna Dempsey," she said.

"Here," I handed her a photograph from the desk of Brendan Hopkins.

"That's me," she said.

"Here," I said. I handed her the envelope. "Life is good."

She turned the envelope to get the corner ripped open. I had taken a step backwards, duty discharged.

"Could you wait a second?" she said.

Why not? I gave her a second.

She studied a legal-size piece of paper. "Who is William Emmon?"

Not the easiest of questions to answer.

"He gave me a bag of hundreds," I said. "The check is your half."

She wasn't content. "Why?" she asked. "I never heard of a William Emmon. Is this a donation to the cause?"

"Not that he said."

"He's dead, I'm assuming?" she said.

"He gave me the money," I said. "The next day he died. I called your family. They said I could find you 'with Jasmine.' You might do them a favor, let them know you're using the name. The name helped. I gave the cash to Emmon's lawyer; he gave me the check. He found you."

"What do I have to do?"

I pulled my hands apart, a benediction. "Enjoy." In less than a minute her face had drained of self-confidence. Her face couldn't move. I felt odd, leaving a job performed as prescribed, but that somehow felt unfinished. Sorry for someone coming into money, like a check from the insurance company, and that's all she wrote: you cash it and the deceased has done the last thing they could do.

"Is your father dead?" I asked.

Her eyes swelled slightly, and reddened. If she didn't speak, she wouldn't break.

"I'm sorry," I said.

"He swam out too far," she said. "Why do you ask?"

"A coincidence, perhaps. The other half of the money went to a woman whose father was murdered."

"It wasn't a murder," she said.

] *Chapter 10*

I WENT TO the street to call a car. Two guys on the sidewalk were invoking last thoughts: "I don't think there's a right or wrong way. He was cashing in, ate his last banana, and didn't stick the landing."

Behind me I heard, "Elizabeth."

It was Haley Nalls. "You want a lift?"

She folded her notepad and hooked a pen in a holder, released the pad above an open backpack and looked in after to see if it got there.

"I've got an extra helmet," she said.

"I've got a question for you," I said. "Jasmine's father drowned. What happened?"

"You lost me. How does someone drown?"

"You're following Jasmine's career?" I said.

"You have something?"

"I just gave her a check for more than a third of a million dollars. A man asked me to give her the money in cash. She never heard of him."

"Anonymous campaign contribution? I am interested. You have a name? Just a sec."

She pulled the pad and pen back out of the backpack, and stood with the pen poised.

"William Emmon," I said.

The pen scribbled on the pad. "Address? Phone number? You wouldn't have the bank and account number? Beautiful, if you could nail that down."

I waved a hand at her pad. "If you stop asking me questions, I can get to what I want to tell you."

She pulled the pad to her chest. "But you won't forget Emmon?"

"Emmon gave me a stack of cash. I gave the cash to his lawyer, who had a cashier's check made out to Joanna Dempsey, for three hundred and eighty-eight thousand dollars. According to Emmon's lawyer, that's Jasmine's legal name. But she never heard of Emmon."

Nalls tapped a fingernail on her crown.

"This past week I offered the same amount, in actual cash, to a Monica Parker at a diner in Mojave, also a gift from William Emmon. She never heard the name either, and she wouldn't take the money. Her father was murdered. Joanna's father drowned."

The pad and the pen went back in the backpack. Nalls looped her arms through its straps.

"There's a story here all right," she said. "Listen, I'd like to do an interview. I can't pay you. I'm a volunteer. If they print my story I get mileage and access to office doughnuts while my editor scribbles on my free lunch coupon. What about now? What are you doing?"

"I was here to see Jasmine. I saw Jasmine."

"Let's walk up the hill," she said.

The keys in her hand went into a pocket. "I'm puzzled," she said. "This new constitution is a promotion for a television documentary: America fragmenting. I could never have come up with this scam."

"The exposé will be quite the satisfaction."

"When I heard about this constitution," she said, "I couldn't imagine what Jasmine was thinking."

"Use it. A good line," I said.

We settled into a steady gait, like a couple soldiers, left, right, eyes set where the next step falls higher in a slow rhythm against gravity. Sooner than later the forehead would tip into a sweat.

"A man at the meeting recognized you," she said. "Mistress Elizabeth Cromwell. I looked you up. Illustrious owner of the English Department. I know what English is, and Department, but together, what is that?"

"What *was* that. I'm seeing a few long-term clients till they're done with me. But basically I'm retired—a job in itself in search of a real job."

"What's the meaning of the English Department, I mean?"

"A way of drawing a sharp line, what I do versus what I don't."

"What don't you do?"

"What I'm told to do," I said. "Anyway, Mr. Dempsey drowned. Do you know anything about that?"

"Some fishermen saw a body floating face down. His clothes were in a boat a ways off. His ID was in his wallet. Cash, credit cards, car keys, all there. They decided he went in for a swim."

"That was it?" I said.

"The coroner's findings? Dempsey was in the water no more than an hour. Might be a suicide. That what you mean?"

"Monica Parker's father was murdered," I said. "No question there."

"What are you thinking?" she said. "William Emmon killed two men? Paid off the children?"

"I knew him," I said. "He didn't kill anyone."

"But you're asking," she said.

The paved road went left at the top of the hill. A narrow pebbled path went right, off to a fenced-in promontory on the other side of the hill, where we stepped onto a small gravel patch that looked over some decorative fruit trees and then out onto the patchwork of Albany. In the not-too-distant distance was Tilden Regional Park, and further to one side, the Berkeley Hills. A nostalgia for the forgotten prairies where I grew up was out there in the dark spaces between the rows of light. In the City I don't think of the past. Not that way. I took a step back and turned away from this unexpected experience. A moment was enough.

"You were looking for Jasmine," she said. "Journalism is a shady business. Never know what I'll hear if people think they know more than me."

I caught her eye, a quick question, "You know a lot about Jasmine?"

"A political career on the move. I'm sticking with her. I sit on the edge of the bed in the morning and ask myself what comes next. I'm always stuck on what to do. You know, that twinge at the end of an essay."

"You're missing something?" I said.

"And hope it's not the punch line." She looked in the direction of the wail of an ambulance. "I'm worried."

"Jasmine?" I said.

"She talks like somebody with a grip on the uses of power. I don't buy it. A huge power, so huge she won't accomplish a thing that gets her near it. It'll be there when she commits suicide—a girl falling out of the sky."

She fiddled with her phone and pulled up *Musée des Beaux Artes*, and held the phone up to show an image: Icarus, terrified, falling through the sky upside down. "The old masters were never wrong."

"They had the gender wrong," I said.

"Them was the olden days. The world barely notices either way."

We descended the hill in silence. She hooked herself into her backpack, mounted her moped and put-putted it into the street facing downhill. She smiled with a downward nod that was easy to interpret—an invitation to put my arms tight around her middle.

"One drink," she said.

The Cat's Cave didn't have an address. The girls in the know knew. We had a drink, or two, and some songs, new in our times, and between songs, while a lot of drinking was going on, I was introduced to Tops and Aurora. The four of us had to sing a song and drain our glasses before it ended, and when they were empty, I knew I was fond of Stan.

When I got my key in the door of the English Department, I was, yeah, the times they were changing all the time.

] *Chapter 11*

THREE ALLEYS made a triangle in the industrial boonies
of Emeryville. You came out where you came in, at a row of
color-coded trash barrels at the edge of a curb at the back end
of a company that shipped goods in trucks with a lot of wheels.
A couple of these monsters were parked end-to-end, splitting
the road. Across the street were four addresses strung together
under a sawtooth roof, up-down-up, at the peak of which was the
profile of an owl in a red tuxedo and spats. He was puffing on a
cigarette holder. Back when the cigarette fell out they must have
developed affection for the old bird.

A dirty two-story brick wall gave a worn, down-at-heels charm
to cracked cement steps that led to a basement entry. The Snarky
Owl had earned its authenticity. It had survived, like a kid's toy
recovered from a grandparent's attic.

The slow burn of lost love was coming from an open door.
Pairs of legs were twisting to the bittersweet lyrics of "The Tennessee Waltz."

In my hearing a couple was moaning in rhythmic rises and
falls. The very feminine figure in the pair had chosen a green
satin tunic, tiger-striped leggings, and ripe banana-yellow heels.
She knew the tricks to throwing things on, as if by the merest

of accidents she came out the most recollected girl of a new evening. She also knew the tricks to manipulating knobs under clothes. The couple's radiant faces were inching to the top of the steps. They had the on-and-off attention of the corner of my eye, aware they were on stage.

The Snarky Owl was at one corner of a gated entrance to a back parking lot, brightly lit. There were a couple of smokers in close proximity, concentrating their efforts on nothing much, just making the night air feel good enough to get out and light up. A lady in faded jeans was taking stock of the contents of a cup. What she was thinking was not putting her at her ease. Slowly she tipped the cup against the bark of a tree. When it was emptied, she took some time screwing the cup into the spaces of a chain-link fence. She took some more time aligning the band of a wristwatch.

Stan was sockless in sandals, jeans, an open jacket over an orange T-shirt with an equal sign between a P and an NP, but the equal sign had been canceled sort of with a slanted line through it. I was a bit dressier, pickleball shoes, ankle socks. True to a fate steering us, we met just short of body contact on the first bars of Patsy Cline's "Crazy."

"Which hand?" he said.

In each was the same whitish-gray paperback with a pale green rectangle along the front edge identifying François Maspero, Paris. I took the one offered and opened the cover, a first edition, 1961, of Frantz Fanon, *Les damnés de la terre, préface de Jean-Paul Sartre*.

"The one you're holding," he said, "is from Blake's grandmother's basement in Lodi." A Post-it note was stuck to the cover. In blue ink: $1,550.00.

"That much?" I said.

"The current ask on the L.A. market for a copy in fine condition."

He opened his copy to a middle page and riffled a few pages with his thumb. "I mean, that's when everybody is making rational decisions, in possession of complete knowledge. These came to us free."

I rewarded him with the "good going" look. He was frowning.

"A book prefaced by Jean-Paul Sartre isn't a thing you overlook to take with you."

"So there's some doubt Blake stayed in the guesthouse?" I said.

"You did have that hunch," he said.

"An expensive oversight," I said.

"Oversights are not Blake. If she left it, she didn't want it. Didn't know its value maybe. For that matter, Blake and French don't go together."

"Takes you for a bumpy trip," I said. "Blake's grandmother's basement? You'll need to explain that."

He pointed at some bushes at the back of the parking lot. "It takes imagination from here."

Except for a few bare patches, the fence on the far side of the parking lot was covered in bougainvillea and bushes of plain green, the year-round display of color in the warming era. Stan parted a patch of foliage. He stepped into an illuminated opening. The path underfoot was worn down. A large arc had been cut in the wire fence. It left a door-like flap that curled open to shoulder height. On the other side of the flap was a culvert in the shape of a deep V, a good ten feet down to the bottom, perhaps more, like a dozen or fifteen feet, but the slope on this side was interrupted in the middle by at a wide gravel ledge.

"Watch how I do this," he said.

A ladder lay against the cement slope. Two prongs reached a foot over the ledge at the top of the slope. Stan bent at the waist, took a sure hold on both edges, tested his grip, and inched a foot down to a rung, then both feet on the rung, and headed down step by step.

At the bottom, he held his hands up backwards and wiggled his fingers, as if fanning his face. Next to him was a royal blue tent, illuminated by the lights of the parking lot on the other side of the culvert.

"Your second home?" I asked. I had to hear him deny it.

"Just visualize the steps," he said, "you know, little by little, and you're here."

I could visualize any number of things. I could jump. The idea didn't scare me, because, of course, I wouldn't. At some indefinable moment I felt the courage to give this a long second thought. The terror? He'd see my big ass. I could ask him to cover his eyes. Or was that the deal? When he asked me to meet him here, who in a million years could have guessed this angle? Points for originality.

"Get your hands right," he said. He clenched his left fist. Then the right fist clenched. "That's it. Now the right foot." From the second foot on he kept up a "good," slow and steady.

When I took my first look down, a hand flattened against my upper thigh, a great deal more support down there at low altitude than was necessary. Then two hands on two upper thighs. The entire kit and caboodle was safeguarded in the compressed effect of a U-shaped seat on a swing. Steady as she goes, eyes wide, victory. I was good.

The way my bottom slipped between his hands to a fine firm hold at my waist had me thinking the bridge we were crossing had been crossed somewhere on the ladder. He opened a flap of a blue plastic tarpaulin to a chamber. Inside, a plunge in temperature. Chastity would hold its own in here. A woman treads cautiously, if only for the reputation of all women.

Metal pipes at right angles formed a rigid cube of about four paces by three paces, and enough height to stand without stooping. A Tiffany lamp hung from a screw in a board running between pipes. A wire came from under a corner and ran up a vertical pole to the top of the structure, and back down to a second lamp on a table with space to spare for a couple of piles of whatever needed a place for handy reference. Beside it stood a metal box with wires that might heat up a corner of the tent by five degrees. A bookshelf stood at the head of a cot. Wooden palettes kept our feet above a blue plastic foundation. A torn pair of running shoes and a pile of socks and shorts stuffed a second bookshelf underneath a chest. The arm of a sweatshirt was knotted to a hanger. Stan pushed a blanket aside and sat on the cot. I got the desk chair.

I unbuttoned the top button of my coat. Make myself at home.

"You're probably wondering?" he said.

"What should I wonder?" I said. "Blake and you down here?"

He was motionless, as good as a fib.

"The cot?" I said.

Enough said.

"Blake knew a boy in high school," he said, "a year ahead of her. He won a Westinghouse award in math. They're rare. I looked up awards given in California about twenty years ago. A math award was given to a senior at Lodi High School in two thousand six. I went to the library. Blake was in the yearbook as Sandra Truesdell, and the next year."

"You went to Lodi?"

"I stopped by the address she was living at back then. The lady who answered the door was too unlike her to be her mother. Stepmother? An older sister, rough-hewn? Neither, as it turned out, she was a Heather Nelson, a cousin once removed. Anyway, she wanted to know when Sandra was getting her father's junk out of the basement."

"The Fanon," I said. "From the basement?"

He leaned forward, elbows on knees, and pushed himself up. He pulled a folded piece of paper from a back pocket, and held it to me. "Which of these doesn't belong in Joseph Truesdell's reading list?" he said.

A list of books my eye hit quickly: *Symptoms and Remedies, Scaff's Bible Dictionary (Student Edition), Holy Bible (Revised Standard Version), Practical Guide to Prescriptions (1967), Children's Guide to Knowledge, Treasury of American Humor, Creative Divorce, The Wellness Encyclopedia, Baby and Child Care, Les damnés de la terre.*

"Did I mention Mr. Truesdell was murdered?" he said.

"Unsolved?" I said.

"I checked the *News–Sentinel* in Lodi for what I could get on the status of the Joe Truesdell murder. A young guy at the desk hadn't heard about it. He thought I had the name wrong. We got that fixed. Thirty-four years unsolved and thirty years forgotten. The kid in the office had been confused, thinking of a second murder twelve years later: a Lodi man killed his brother-in-law. A different case in every respect. No murders in Lodi since."

"Two murders in thirty-four years," I said. "Not the murder capital of California."

"Heather Nelson was still mystified: nobody would think of hurting Joe Truesdell. The world's most considerate human. He tipped the night clerk handsomely for an out-of-town room. A redhead went in with him—class way beyond anything ever seen on highway twelve. Which raises *the* question. Where did Joe find the redhead? And what did he pay her with? His bank account was hardly dinged. A fifty-dollar withdrawal. Enough for a room and a bottle. That was the other puzzle.

"I'm not doing solutions," I said, "just throwing something out. Who inherited?"

"Heather said that Mrs. Truesdell and Sandra moved in with Joe's parents. The proceeds from the house were put in trust for the girl's education. The mother moved out; lives with some guy in a log cabin these days. Heather said I wouldn't find the daughter anywhere near her mother.

"When did Sandra become Blake?" I said.

"She went to Stanislaus State, Stockton campus, half a year. The grandfather died. There was no falling out between her and her grandmother. There never was a falling in. She moved out, took a new life as Blake, and found a home at the Snarky Owl.

"Left alone, the grandmother promised her sister's daughter—that's Heather Nelson—full access to the Truesdell house until her—the grandmother's—death, provided Heather took care of her till then, assuming, reasonably, that the grandmother's death would come first, and assuming that afterwards it wouldn't matter."

"What wouldn't matter?" I said.

"The afterwards. Heather was expected to provide for her own future when the grandmother died. In that event Heather would move out. But Heather's health deteriorated to where she couldn't take care of the grandmother. That state of affairs arrived a lot sooner than expected. Sandra wasn't interested. She left the grandmother to Heather. Heather had the grandmother moved to a nursing home. The state of things currently."

"You asked Heather about the Fanon book?" I said.

"We spent most of our time on 'life isn't fair,' the Lodi chapter of the story. Heather's in bad shape physically, but not a geriatric in the head by any stretch, sharp actually, aware she's on the ropes: a whole new blood system has taken over all kinds of colors. Legs might have to come off."

"There was a second Lodi murder, you said."

"Henry Wilmot. His murder is endlessly interesting. People never stop talking about the alibi. Papers run an annual follow-up. A guy named G.W. Logan got convicted and sent up, eventually confessed a few years ago, came out on parole after twenty-three years served. But the case will never be closed in the public's mind."

"Wilmot? Logan?" I said. "Don't recall the names."

"Garrett Wilkes Logan?" he said.

"No help," I said.

"Henry Wilmot?" he said. "Logan's brother-in-law? No?"

He put his fingers together in a prayer position. "Heather said Logan swore so often that he would kill his brother-in-law that if Wilmot showed up dead on Mars everyone would know Logan had done it. You wouldn't have to know how. In fact, the forensics were open and shut. The only thing was that Logan had an alibi. He had been somewhere else. The only other thing was that Logan didn't know where he had been. He had arranged an abduction scenario with a redheaded Hispanic escort. She had transported him in the trunk of a car. He had fresh whip marks to prove he'd been engaged in something other than killing Wilmot. At trial Logan's defense team produced expert testimony that it would have been impossible for Logan to produce the effects himself."

"There were two people in on the frame-up," I said, "if Logan was telling the truth. A pretty far-fetched alibi if he wasn't."

"That's the discussion: Logan was in that scene. Known in fetish groups all over Sacramento. Those favoring conviction thought he was too clever by half. They believe Logan decided he'd stake his freedom on far-fetched. But Blake was convinced Logan was innocent. Heather said that's what started Blake's visits with Logan in prison."

"Was Henry Wilmot buddies with Joe Truesdell?" I said.

"No association there in anyone's memory."

"How was Truesdell killed?" I said.

"Cyanide."

"And Wilmot?"

"Five bullets to the heart."

"Redheads play rough," I said.

"Very high-end redheads. That's how Blake tied her father's death to Wilmot's."

"Was there a copy of Fanon found at Wilmot's place?" I said.

He brushed his hand past my thigh. "Didn't think of it."

"When you called this afternoon," I said, "you said you had something important to tell me. I'm here. Blake is not why I'm here. If you can't get her out of your life, it would be a kindness to me to please let me know."

"Well, it's about those locks," he said. "There's a lock on the back door to the kitchen of Travis Rhymes's house—the main house next to the guesthouse where I've been staying. As you enter the kitchen, along the wall in the room to the right are boxes with a name, Robert Corning. May I be blunt?"

"I can handle blunt."

"There was a wife who came around one day, looking for

some boxes that might be stored in the house. Could Robert Corning be her husband?"

"You have a key?" I said.

"There's a car repair shop at the other end of the building from the Snarky Owl," he said. "They have an al fresco café for high-end patrons, and a separate powder room. They're closed. Just before you arrived, I picked the lock. No harm, no foul."

"You can pick locks," I said. "I'm willing."

We gave the driver an address: the Safeway at the Skyline shopping center. We found a bench. Split a packaged bagel. Didn't want to break into Rhymes's place on empty stomachs.

"I'm moving out of the guesthouse," Stan said. "I gave notice."

"Don't tell me," I said. "You signed a lease with the Snarky Owl?"

"I'd be under the care of the county flood control district."

"That metal box with wires," I said. "When they glow, heat comes out?"

"Outside the tent there's a battery. Charge it on a gas generator. Siphon gas out of tanks in the parking lot. Perpetual motion."

What was wrong with the easy living of the guesthouse? What was right with a squatter's hutch that wasn't on any map? The set-up had a staginess, an adolescent thirst for being his own nut. He wasn't copying anyone. This was getting ever more to be a weird I couldn't explain: why I liked him. Exclusivity, without extravagance, nor decadence.

"Stan," I said, "what are you doing?"

"Getting Blake out of my hair." He sat upright and touched my shoulder, our knees touching. "I met someone else. I had to do it my own way."

] *Chapter 12*

THE STRATEGY was proposed and adopted at the edge of a parking lot. We split goodies in two bags and made our way to Travis Rhymes's place via the pedestrian underpass. By the time we were inside, the back door shut and locked, we were adjusted to what light there was, easing our way off kitchen linoleum onto hardwood. Our phones provided plenty of light to move around safely. Next to the kitchen was a mudroom, and in it were two boxes labeled ROBERT CORNING. There must be more. We could grope our way around individually, room to room, speed things up. If it turned out there were boxes all over the place, we'd spend the night in the guesthouse and dig out what was Bob Corning's the next day. Stan was possessed with the confidence of a psychic.

Along the long side of the next room were rows of boxes stacked three deep. We scanned the top boxes of stacks within an arm's reach, all but one stack marked as belonging to Arthur Ashen. Were the boxes underneath also marked ARTHUR ASHEN? We're here. Give this a whirl. Underneath an ASHEN was a ROBERT CORNING in black marker, sealed head to toe with transparent cellophane tape, and six more in the immediate vicinity buried in Arthur Ashen's stuff. Rhymes's collection had its own corner, plays he'd presumably written on his own, or that he and Bob had produced together.

I turned my phone light off. Job half done. A deep breath held a feeling: finally, a high card had turned up around here. There remained the promise of a civilized one-night stand, and how it might transpire. I could undo a button of my jacket: a silent signal? My left hand crawled up his back to a shoulder, well within the bounds of courtship, leaving open access for his right hand to cup the far side of my jeans where the fullness of the bottom joined the top of the thigh. The boxes could wait for transportation. They wouldn't be on their way in the next hour, that was for sure, anyway.

Let some or all of this happen where we were, standing up, *au naturel.* I planted a wide open kiss and palmed the bump in his pants. I scraped a shoe off and pulled a leg out of my pants, faced away, bent forward and took hold of some wallpaper.

"I forgot my panties," I said.

"That won't be a problem. Can you sell torn panties on eBay?"

"Top dollar will require a storyline."

We went at it. Let's say we were knowledgeable.

I had Corning's books. Stan had sampled me. Released in silence was the togetherness question. Would we bump into each other again? He popped the question: he pointed up; i.e., there was a second act on a round bed in the third-floor loft, not *the* act, but what comes to mind after all that brain chatter stirred up in the chemistry of the hormones was there on the surface.

We went upstairs to the loft. I took care of the love child in the bathtub, while Stan warmed the bed. In the dark I heard, "Are we staying the night?"

He was on his side. He would in a moment make himself useful. I dropped a damp towel from my shoulders to the floor. While I pulled the covers over my head, I established a leg over his hip. All sorts of invitations there. With his lips nibbling my neck, an arm plunged between my thighs. A hand grabbed a cheek, then clamped the other, in no time hitting on a rhythm giving each its due, while the forearm agitated the bush.

I caught his wrist and pulled the attached hand off my butt, and pushed it from between my legs. He caught on I was up to something, scooted an inch backwards, on the assumption I was laying claim to my half of the bed. Not exactly. We needed room for a stable platform. I put my head on a pillow above his, located his jaw between a thumb and four fingers, and supplied a nipple wiggling to the warm place. The word I was prepared to introduce if needed was, *suck*. Unnecessary.

The oral tendencies upstairs underway, I gathered his arm two-handed, placed his hand on the keyboard, my middle finger on his, getting the pressure and motion on the clitoris up to where I could let the whole assembly take off on its own. One step at a time. Leave the mechanical thing to him. Tune in to whatever a heaving breath articulated.

As I was coming down off the hill, the final moan settling into an endless French kiss, I was awake enough to an awareness he was ready to enter again. In the rising pitch, his tempo, my tempo, was a sudden, "Ohhh, yesss!" Perfectly irrelevant, I told him to come in my hand.

I washed my hands and wiped him off with a wet cloth. The third act didn't quite bring a finale to the swing of things. I French kissed his cock. Make of that whatever. I went downstairs and brought up a bag of nourishment. I pulled the drapes open on the window facing the street, and one by one passed packages across, streetlight announcing each brand.

I got a tear in a bag of Cheetos with my teeth and widened it. We lay on our backs munching. He got one of my Cheetos, and I got a piece of his popcorn. "Watch out for kernels," he said. He was throwing them into the dark. Something to step on.

After a long time of whatever thoughts we were not sharing, I decided to break the silence. Was he thinking of another woman? I guess I cared. How to put that?

"You're keeping your distance," I said.

"I try to understand things." He twiddled my nipple. "I didn't notice I was keeping my distance."

"I was wondering how to get you hard whenever I need you hard," I said.

"Do I dare reveal the secret code?" he said.

"What unlocks the love slave?"

"Simpler than that," he said. "A girl wanted my attention. She was on the university track team. She'd seen me training. She made inquiries, found out I was a high school sprinter. She was thinking of a run at the Olympic team in twenty-eight. In exchange for some coaching, I could have companionship with her."

"How is that deal coming along?" I said.

"We had a few coffee dates. We talked. Eventually, we had to have a talk. We talked about my position at the university in relation to undergraduates. Out of some effort to shut everything down between us, I opened up. I didn't know there was anything to open up about. But there it was, a naked confession to an undergraduate: I preferred older women. I said sorry, she didn't attract me."

"Blake was younger?" I said.

"Forty-three, if you calculate from her yearbook. Right off, she caught on: she could manage me. My exuberance for pulling her pants down, for example. Too much hands-on from me and she'd find a reason to skip our meetings. She'd enforce a cooling-off period."

"Blake was your first go with eldercare, then?" I said.

"She had something —something that years gave her, whatever it was. What I once took seriously about boys and girls, she'd been there and moved on. Weird, though, how it all started. All I was doing was tossing crumpled orange debris in a waste receptacle at the Space Center."

"You were out of a job, maybe for life, and she offered you the guesthouse all of a sudden. You wondered?"

"And then she disappeared. The next day the living was free, and I was on the porch waiting for a sheriff demanding a year's back rent."

"And then I showed up," I said.

"The 'It' was sure there. I'm moving a cubic yard of mud, and this elegantissima blonde number is watching me. The next day she walks right into the guesthouse without batting an eye, alone, unarmed, breaking bread with an axe murderer. Women don't do these things."

"And then they do…if they want something."

"You had me guessing there. I began to reason. Not all gorgeous dames are killers, if I may suggest statistical exculpation. And I described you to Heather Nelson. No matches."

"Whoa. You described me to Heather?"

"If you were me, you would, too. I imagined you and Blake in some fancy teamwork. I was the salami. Unbeknownst to me, my job was to keep the water and electricity running, as if the occupant were still on premises. Now why would that be? Might some misfortune have entered Rhymes's life? And then two and two made four. I'd be the guy in the place the cops would expect to find Rhymes's killer when they got around to explanations. There would be no Blake. She cut and ran when Rhymes went missing. That's not smooth. There's a crick in there.

"Then there you were, admiring a mud castle. You didn't look sex-starved. What in the world does she need with me? It's where reason took me. It's what stumped Einstein. How can this be? I pondered. I needed a theory of everything. It's why I hung around Heather in Lodi."

He was moving a hand over my bottom, swooping possessively, cheek to cheek. Not squeezing. Just enjoying terrain mapping.

"About what we're up to," I said. "Putting Einstein to one side, or not, where are we in the theory?"

"How pairings occur in nature?" he said. "Oh, boy. Affinities. Very unknown."

"You said you thought I'd be back."

"Something wasn't getting answered," he said. "You'd be back for it."

"I trust you. How do I understand that?"

"Dull enough to make some sense?" he said.

"Oh, aren't you sweet. What makes me so innocent?"

"You're up to what you say you're up to," he said. "Blake wasn't."

"What's this damsel locked in a castle business?" I said.

"She's always where she should always be."

"How far apart were the two murders?" I said.

"Twelve years, about."

I held the half-empty bag of Cheetos off the side of the bed and let it drop. "Logan's redheaded Hispanic playmate?" I said. "She did both?

"The jury couldn't believe it. It's what put him away. Heather's on Logan's side. She puts the murders together. Impressive grade of mind. It would take a genius to fool her. Logan's a flat earth guy. A trouble for him, and in some minds the clincher, was there simply was no other suspect."

In the morning I went to the office, picked up the keys to my car, got it out of the garage, and met Stan at the front of Rhymes's house. We loaded up Bob Corning's boxes, and tossed around names of places where we might drop in to honeymoon. We dropped the boxes off in the alley by the lower level of the English Department, and packed. We did Santa Barbara one night—didn't particularly want to see any more of the crowded tourist scene along the main drag, and found a three-night booking at a ranch house in Atascadero.

] *Chapter 13*

CHRIS FARBER, my librarian, was on the hard oak kitch-en chair in the middle of a quiet dignity, having twice now ignored a request to talk about feelings. Today is business, the business of breaking up. Or getting ready to get that going. I thought we might highlight old times, what can be toasted to of eleven years.

He'd returned recently from a three-week stay in Larkspur. Before that he'd been on a visit to Florida, considering a perma-nent stay. A good time there was not had.

"Fran's eye hit the west coast about five miles above Saraso-ta," he was saying, "a category two, less than it could have been, gusts easily cleared the shore. We heard a shriek. Ran upstairs. The sheet metal roof had peeled free at an edge. Most of the bolts held, but the opening was there. Water was coming sideways into the master bedroom. We got two holes drilled in the metal. A rope through them went under the bed. We got on the bed. That pulled the corner shut. We threw bedding and clothes out the upstairs window. Carpets soaked, power gone. A living hell getting the mattress through the window. Everywhere: floating washing machines."

"You survived," I said. "Second thoughts about relocating?"

"Something's going on in the Gulf of Mexico. I'm not going back to find out."

A half-pound of mail bound in twine lay on my desk. He'd come from my post box.

"Today is my last day." He leaned forward, pushed the mail to a corner, separating what needed tending to from what might be postponed.

"While you were away yesterday, there was a message from a Mistress Eleanor in Chicago. She'd appreciate a face-to-face at your earliest convenience—to be precise, a meeting between your realtor and her realtor. She's ready with an offer for the English Department."

"She had a dollar number?"

"She dangled the word 'cash,'" he said. "What she understood was garbled. She thought the English Department was already vacant, ready for new occupants."

"I was perfectly clear," I said. "The English Department was henceforth not ever again what it was, and it was not known when it would become what it would be."

"The precision in your ambiguity…that's what made your whippings so…enriching."

"Look, I'm not ready," I said. "Best, don't reply."

"Moving on, also yesterday: Lee Gilbert, Investment Images, San Jose. His secretary called. Pretended to know you as an English tutor. She quoted your web page: the promise you would continue meeting established clients. You saw Mr. Gilbert this past year, twice. Wanted to know if he counts as a regular. Does he need a new code for the gate?"

"I gave him a referral, a professional in town," I said.

"That's a no," he said. "O-kay. That's that."

"Oh," I put an index finger to my cheek. "Before I forget. Seven boxes are just inside the basement door. Would you call a Ms. Robert Corning in Texas—Austin—no, wait a second, leave the boxes. I'll call."

We were rattling along at speed, like the good old days.

"Oh, yes," he said, "a news item. A man in a delirium wandered from Visitacion Valley to the Stonestown Galleria articulating the mannerisms of a zombie rubbing its chest, apparently resuscitating a heart."

"This has to do with me?"

"He had a chastity clamp on his penis," he said. "Your name and profile were engraved on the shaft. His only identification. The U.C. emergency center called your number. I answered."

"Jesus! Graham Bogard!" I blurted.

"He had a lucid moment. In it he said you own his penis. I told them that's not a joke, exactly."

"I'm not his wife. You told them that, I hope."

"Although there is a contract with you," he said. "The chastity ritual on the wedding night?"

"They got the clamp off?" I said.

"I'll bet this will be in the papers. I looked today, but nothing. You know, it's San Francisco, nothing to take your breath away."

"He was here for his thirtieth birthday," I said. "He wanted a dozen strokes for each year of his life. I talked him out of it. He was fine when he left, but when is it ever not a passing phase?"

"Not necessarily absolutely," he said.

"Not necessarily absolutely what?"

"An item in the papers," he said. "Tabloids come out once a month. It'll get around. His company is in the papers, though. They announced a government contract for the development of an AI warming predictor. They can prophesy coming high temperatures. They're smack on to two decimal places the last two years. Apparently the curve is no longer linear anywhere. It's too late. The company can reliably claim his breakdown had something to do with weather."

"Or I wasn't available."

"Not for insurance purposes. And there's a Mistress Melissa" he said. "Requests an audience. Jade let her go. She may want a job. Says, though, she's looking for advice. Times must be bad.

Jade has a deep well of concern for women at a loss finding a paying spot in society.

"Coincidentally," he said, "Robin called. He didn't say what the Melissa problem was. He did mention a Travis Rhymes. A woman who didn't leave a name left instructions for Jade to stop being interested in Travis Rhymes's whereabouts. Robin said to pass that on to you. You would know what to do. Leave Jade out of it."

"I saw Melissa in action," I said, "if not in ecstasy, having her shoes buffed."

"The caller left a number," he said. "And another thing: a message from Brendan Hopkins. William Emmon left his house on Grant to a stranger, an Adele King. She says she never met William Emmon. She's worked up. She insisted Hopkins put her in a meeting with someone who knew Emmon. Hopkins would be pleased to offer your help."

I dialed Hopkins. I put the call on speaker. Hopkins's receptionist took down the reason for my call, which, I explained, was that a few days ago when the Emmon money reached the hand of Joanna Dempsey, aka Jasmine, at pretty close to ten after eight of an evening, she examined the check, asked the right questions—such as who William Emmon was supposed to be to her—and made a rational decision, as I saw it, taking possession of three hundred and eighty-some thousand without a blink.

"And with that," I said, "the last wishes of William Emmon, transmitted through my good offices that night, have come to an end." I hung up.

Chris went on. "Not one of your clients, but regardless, a disordered gent in Marin, he converted ten thousand dollars to dimes and threw them at a bunch of neighbor kids on his lawn from a balcony. The human angle was: 'Your tough luck, you should've been there.'"

"Could he be arrested?" I said. What else to think?

"What would you think of a pied-à-terre in Larkspur?" he said.

"You're moving to Larkspur?"

"There's thinking of moving, and there's moving," he said. "This is a three-corner bank shot. Think, Big Abe, St. Louis, fifty-four, the shootout with No Name at Wheels Pool Parlor."

"Moving is that tough?" I said.

He put a long silence into what had already been decided. The smile said, "What a shot."

On three walls of the office were vintage photos of Hollywood vamps, unknowns with whips, so not publicity shots, images letting the newcomers get their bearings: the English Department wasn't a used car dealership.

Chris removed a plate and saucer from the table to the kitchen sink.

Pride of place on the fridge in those days was a picture of a masked woman flexing a cane in a run-down motel corridor. She's in a thinking lean, her back against a wall, a shoulder flopped over a door frame, nothing if not a high fashion photo shoot.

"But can I afford a Monet?" I said.

"Ovaltine?" he asked, with his back to me.

"Sure," I said.

He filled two mugs with milk, set spoons on paper towels, unscrewed the cap on a jar.

"A dominatrix decorates her fridge?" he said. "A cause for wondering what Andy Warhol would do for a title. Can't get there."

He held out two mugs. "Brooklyn or Cape Cod?"

I took the mug with the iconic bridge.

He pulled a chair from under the table for a space to stretch his legs. "Our first meeting, the interview, you asked what I expected to get out of a job working for you."

"You fell silent," I said.

"You opened a door and there was a junkyard of books you wanted alphabetized. 'Another blonde bean-brain' is what I was hiding."

"I don't recall the remark."

"Have to say, when you opened your checkbook, I was suddenly in the mind of Sebastian Flyte: *Et in Arcadio ego.*"

We drank in silence. He clinked my cup and drained his.

"My last day. If you think of me, I'll be somewhere having a life. Call. I've done Florida. Larkspur? A place to call home? At the moment a befuddlement.

"Incidentally, this Travis Rhymes character, he's in our records paired off with a Bob Corning, once the Jennie and Ronald Brandt Professor of Contemporary Literature at UCB. On the shelves we have a heading: *Stepmothers for a Moral Awakening.* The collection of plays in which Rhymes and Corning released their squirrelly selves is *The Minutes of the Meetings in a Cabin up by the Bohemian Grove.* All on the shelf below, row B, level two, filed as 'Wild Midnights.'"

He leaned over a section of newspaper folded to a crossword. "'Woman with a Fan,'" he said. "Five across. It's deep."

The rough sexual tastes, forged here, were already in the back of our minds. The love developed in perversity survived here.

"You need a governess, Chris. I know how. Drop by once in a while."

"If I only knew what I needed. But anyway, about Adele King, why not shake the hand that shook the Pope's hand? The Kings are muckety-muck Catholics. Hopkins says she'll be on the Amalfi coast this Christmas season. Hang tight and take the meeting there. Be received with all expenses none of your concern."

"I met someone," I said. "It might work. Bring someone, show off your bridge skills."

] *Chapter 14*

I PLOPPED INTO the office chair and called a number, introduced myself to Melissa, first and last name. This was official.

"Are you looking for a job?" I said right off. Five minutes of back and forth eliminated.

"Not any job," she said.

"Of course not. Suppose I describe the job I can offer. You tell me. Okay?"

"What's the job?" she said.

"I don't hire over the phone," I said. "When can you stop by?"

I called Jade. It turned out Jade hadn't fired her. They'd had a talk, during the course of which it came to Melissa to dismiss herself. She was in the "I'm always wrong" business, operating in the domme business. She wanted out. She showed herself the door.

She buzzed at a quarter to five. A scraggly cut fell over a deep green waterproof coat. A haircut in a hurricane: a jagged blonde, the phrase these days. Early twenties. An adult appearance, not the kid I remembered seeing. She unbuttoned the top three buttons of the raincoat and slid a scarf off her neck into a pocket.

I held out a hand showing her to the door to the office. Her hands were in her pockets, pulling tight as much of the coat as could be bunched in front. I stayed out of motherly responses. Dispute this "always wrong" business, and she's left with the void.

Chris had left a notebook opened to a blank page. I put a hand on the notebook. "I need someone to transcribe calls."

"I don't get it." she said. "I transcribe calls? Wouldn't it be easier to listen yourself?"

"I won't be at this number." I said. "I'll be doing something else."

"Have the calls go to your mobile," she said.

"I would prefer the calls go to this number. I want a human at this end when calls come in. You know, a polite, receptive inter-action, like what you were treated to when you called."

"I spoke to a Chris Somebody," she said.

"He won't be here either."

"What happened, if it's okay to ask?"

"Today was his last day," I said.

"I've never done this before," she said.

"Saving yourself a year of secretarial school," I said. "Hands-on learning. It's a mixture of 'who cares' and 'what's the worst that can happen?'"

"I want to do a good job," she said.

"Excellent. So. Clients who've been with me a long time will call or, less often, text," I said. "You'll get requests for appoint-ments. They'll want some chat, expecting your predecessor, Chris Somebody. They'll miss him. He made them laugh. They'll ask for his private number. This is your opportunity to change the subject. Emphasize the English Department has closed down. You're filling in.

"Chris has left you a list of names, clients who will get a call-back from me. All others? Answers begin with 'unfortunately,' introducing unfortunate facts, such as Mistress Elizabeth has retired. No details. Keep it short. Narrow the scope of all calls, is what I'm trying to say. For meetings, let me do the scheduling."

"How long will the job last?" she said.

"Hard to say," I said. "That's not all. I'd like you to do a bit of research for me. You up for research? Public records?"

"Like what?"

"The name of the previous owner of this space we're in is William Emmon. Ingrid Halder was the actual owner. Emmon held the paper. That's no matter. You'll never encounter Ingrid Halder. I'd like it if you could look into any connection Emmon had with a woman named Monica Parker, or with her father. Find his Christian name, if you would. Actually, for that matter, dig up anything you can on any Parker related to Monica.

"Same thing for Emmon and a Joanna Dempsey. She calls herself Jasmine now, but the important connection is between Emmon and Dempsey's father."

"What kind of connection?" she said.

"A traffic accident, a financial connection, anything. A property owned in common. Take down anything that shows up. They might have lived next door to each other. Make a note."

She nodded.

"I called Jade," I said. "She likes you. Robin likes you. Anything else I need to know about you?"

"Ambition? A sportswriter. I won Glencoe Elementary School's fifty-yard dash three years in a row. Beat all the sixth-graders."

"I've been exercising the power of recall for the name of an actress. She was in *Match Point*, a tennis movie."

"I look like Maja Sierpinski, the tennis player," she said.

"Botched that, didn't I? But got the tennis."

I indicated the door to the stacks. I pulled back a velvet curtain from a foot-high, two-step dais. Two filing cabinets stood on opposite sides of a reading chair and ottoman. Behind these was a coffee center, shelving for current reading or reading suspended and on its way to forgotten. From the slight elevation, she looked back into the room she'd entered from the vestibule at the far door.

"I heard about this," she said. She bent her neck back. Her interest followed thin wire cables that ran from above the chandeliers that down here reached different heights between shelves.

"There isn't a ceiling," she said.

"There were two floors. We didn't need a ceiling. The shelves would rise into that space. Guy wires hold the tops stable. The ceiling way up there runs out of light coming from down here."

A book was broken over the arm of a chair. She took a tissue from a box, closed the book on it, and shelved it between bookends on the coffee stand. "Scott Fitzgerald," she said. "Read *Gatsby* in the tenth grade. Fancy, but…I don't know."

"Someday we can hold a seminar," I said. "Who do you like to read?"

"Anything. Well, not the Greats. Anything else when I have time."

"A tour? Upstairs are three rooms," I said. "Where it happens."

"I'm out of that," she said.

I pointed. We went through a narrow passage between stacks to a trapdoor in the floor of the bathroom. I pulled the door open, flipped a light-switch, and mentioned a chore in the basement.

"There are seven liquor-size boxes of reading material down there. I can get them up the steps and hand them off to you. You slide them out of the bathroom."

"That's it?"

"That's it."

I lowered the trap door and scratched my hair. She had her hands n her pockets.

When I reappeared through the trap door the boxes were lined up along a wall.

"You read Wodehouse?" I said.

"I could start."

"Not part of the job," I said.

"What's it part of?"

"You quit your job at Jade's," I said. "Why'd you start?"

She was squinting, the puzzled look, not sure where I was going.

"I was running out of money," she said.

"Boring, isn't it?"

She laughed, the sound of a bark admitting disgust.

"I'd expect you'd get sick of hanging out with a goofy aristocrat and his manservant," I said. "Wodehouse found some humor in them."

I took her to aisle 2, put a light on coordinates 7H, walked my fingers to a couple binders: *Rumba Nights*. Author: Bob Corning. Production: Travis Rhymes. *Rhythm Section* was the sequel. Corning and Rhymes.

"They had some fun with a French countess and her suitors," I said. "Ran four seasons in a cabin along the Russian River. Two-act plays, French farce tangled in S.M. satire. The money shot left to the imagination."

"The money shot?"

" 'Thank you, Countess. May I have another.' "

Either that summed it up, or it was nonsense.

"Have a look at *Tales of the Unbreeched*. It's in the stacks, two copies, by Anonymous. We get requests. There's a note in it: not to be lent out. Free-wheeling Bertie Wooster stuff. Bob had fun till the muse who guided his imagination had enough of him."

I excused myself and took a private call from Stan in the office.

"I'm in Lodi. Heather's in the hospital. Wait and see. I understand what went on at Rhymes's house now, and why you won't find him. Tell you when we meet."

I went back to see how Melissa was faring with Bertie Wooster.

"How are your living arrangements?" I said. "You getting by?"

"Five girls sharing two rooms. I'm in a closet."

"That bad?" I said.

"Surviving."

"I have an empty room as of today," I said. "I'll be selling someday, but you can have it till then."

"What do I do for it?"

I thought of lots of things and nothing in particular. "Nothing."

I drove Melissa to an apartment house in Berkeley. She was in and out with her life's belongings in fifteen minutes.

Melissa put her things in Chris's old room. I got off my feet in the kitchen, and imagined Chris and me clinking glasses. An hour later there was a knock on the door. Melissa peeked in smiling. "I borrowed *Devilment, a Day in the Life of a Countess in Moscow*. You didn't tell me she was MI6. Thank you."

"You're welcome."

A text arrived from Stan at almost midnight.

May have a job. Find out in Berkeley tomorrow. I'm okay. Maybe we can talk about me moving in with you. I can carry my weight.

] *Chapter 15*

I ARRIVED AT the café at three o'clock. A cold afternoon, gray, Stan in a well-watered-grass green T-shirt sitting in a back lean against a wooden rail, doing some nodding with a dark-haired woman in an open parka. They were alone at a table pinched off in a little peninsula in the outdoor patio. She was leaning a black sweater and pedant over the table. She was older than me. An observation as I waited in line to order at the counter. I was behind a customer having her troubles. There wasn't much left of the pastry display. Take it or leave it selections at this hour.

Outside I caught Stan's attention sliding butt sideways through tight spaces in the main island of tables. Stan pulled a third chair to his table between him and the woman in black, and apportioned table space for my cup. Sophia Reynolds and I exchanged smiles on first and last names. I sat and let my presence as the intruder establish itself. Stan didn't speak. Sophia's hand went up as if to catch the attention of a guy passing on the sidewalk. An apology to us. She had to go. She was on the move as I said, "Nice meeting you."

"Professor of history," he said when she was gone. "She has a prodigy on her hands. Philip Reynolds, a legend by the Bay. Sits in on graduate seminars. He was in my class last year. He wants to work with me. Get into research."

"You have a job?" I said.

"A hundred an hour is on the table."

"What does that mean, 'work with you'?"

"Contribute to the well-being of math."

A booth emptied inside. We went in. A woman zipped a laptop into a canvas container, tied it in a backpack, and buttoned herself up in Alaska wear. Stan ordered ice cream to justify our occupancy. Mint chocolate chip my choice. The kid in me born with a need to pick at little rascals hiding in food. I put my hand on Stan's hand, which had fallen palm up on my side of the table.

"A new wrinkle," I said. "My librarian moved out. I hired a replacement. She moved into his room." I waved a spoon at his nose. "You've been busy"

"I got a call from the hospital in Lodi. Heather Nelson gave them my name."

"You're all she had?" I said.

"I was all she wanted. I stopped by the house, collected some of her things. Dropped them off."

"Who will care for her when she goes home?"

"The hospital wanted someone with a power of attorney. Didn't know whose problem that is. Will she go home? Circulation stopped in her lower legs. I recall she said her parents aren't in Lodi, but she didn't say where they were. Up in the air, where she dies. I said I'd come up and hang around for a day. Out of thin air, Blake showed up at the house. You won't believe this: Garrett Logan is dead."

"The guy who was framed for the Wilmot murder?"

"Shot in his garage. Blake was hiding out with him. She got up to make breakfast, looked around to see what he wanted. There he was, flat on his back, the trunk of the car open."

"She's sure he was dead?" I said.

"She grabbed her keys. Came straight home to her house in Lodi."

"She'll report it?"

"She was sitting on a sofa when I got to her place. I mentioned Heather and the hospital where I'd been. She didn't care."

"If not her?" I said.

"Yes. If not her."

"Heather must be glad you were there."

"Looks like Heather's on her own," he said.

"You and Blake? Old home week? Like you'd never parted?"

"Who killed Logan was on her mind. Should she clear out?"

"I have an idea," I said. "You could stay with her."

"It was an offer," he said. "She asked me to help her find her father's killer. That was her deal with Logan: She'd find the whore who framed him, and that would be Joe Truesdell's killer too. And probably Logan's and Henry Wilmot's as well."

"Justice for her father is all that's left worth salvaging of this life?" I said.

"That's all there has been for most of her life. There was her father at home, and then there wasn't. Then there wasn't a mother. Then the father's father was gone. The father's mother is in a nursing home. Logan plugged a lot of holes for her."

"How about you filling in?" I said.

"She was never misty-eyed about me," he said. "While we were talking, it came back to me, the tough depth in her expressions: she won't let herself need anyone. Not for long."

"That's what captivated you?"

"There were other times. She could seem like someone fallen overboard in the middle of the ocean. But she'd realize what she was drawing out of me, and that look would disappear, and when the boat docked, there she was, her feet up, sipping a tall cool one under an umbrella."

"A survivor," I said.

"That last call I had with her," he said, "that call when she let me know the guest house was unoccupied, that day the bottom had fallen out of her world. Logan was all there was left. She's been living with him in secret since that day. They had a house outside Lodi."

"Logan was in prison, I thought."

"What I thought. Logan dead would have been a blessing, but he wasn't in prison. Blake gave him the reason to get out."

"She told you this?" I said.

"I was curious about that last phone call she and I had. I told her she sounded scared. I asked what had happened. What happened was Logan had a scheme. She went along. She was a fucking idiot."

"Two fucking idiots?" I said.

"Logan was a dope who always had to be right. He was no less confused than she was. But during the years she was visiting him in prison, the holes in his ideas didn't get any scrutiny. It's like women who marry men on death row. The absence of the most obvious qualities you look for in humans isn't important. You can carry on perfectly reasonable conversations with them. You can even sleep with them."

"She slept with Logan in prison?" I said.

"Worse. She spent years searching the S.M. community looking for a reheaded Hispanic dominant. The woman would have to be older. Surely retired by then. The search went all over the place. There are plenty of Hispanic sex workers. They're asked to get into fetish stuff. Some do, some don't. So she found women who generally fit the description. She'd visit Logan with photographs. They didn't trust the prison postal system.

"Time goes on. One day she heard that a guy in the S.M. community by the name of Travis Rhymes was married to a woman named Carmen. Sounded Hispanic. She brought that to Logan. That got a ping out of him. He knew the name Travis Rhymes in the S.M. community. Why his wife would want to frame him was beyond Logan. Same for Rhymes.

"Anyway, now Blake had something to go on. To Carmen's misfortune, she was born in Argentina, and she had once played dominant roles in a playacting group with Rhymes, but not as a professional. Blake brought that to Logan. This was their first lead."

"Back up a second," I said. "Who is this Carmen?"

"Just Rhymes's wife."

"Blake didn't know what she was before they were married?" I said. "Didn't need to, I guess."

"Logan didn't recall meeting Rhymes, but he knew the name and knew where Rhymes might be known. He gave Blake some places she might try. One of them was a coffee shop along the Russian River. Rhymes and his wife were remembered there. Carmen was fond of sexy wigs. Some of them were red. That last fact popped a cork in Logan's head."

"That's what got them going?"

"Blake went around looking for photos of Carmen." Then he said, "Oh." His elbow went on the table, his cheek in a tripod of thumb and two fingers. "The Fanon I found in the guesthouse. I brought it to the hospital. Told them what they could get for it. Help out with Heather's expenses. They wouldn't take it. It's not theirs to sell. I took it back to the house. When Blake saw it, she couldn't believe it. It had been sent to Logan in prison. Logan was sure that whoever framed him had sent it to him. It was his one correct hunch in this entire idiot plan."

"So Logan decided Carmen Rhymes was the woman he was after?" I said.

"Blake never got the photo of Carmen, but his suspicions of her were enough to get Logan to go after his parole. It's when Blake had her first doubts. She decided to get a good look at Carmen before Logan found her. That's when she made the effort to get close to Travis Rhymes. She met him at this S.M. business I told you about. They hit it off. She made herself marvelous at what he liked. She was one more mistress, and he had all these properties all over. One of them had a guesthouse. Now and then he would drop by."

"Logan got his parole?" I said.

"A full confession was his way out. He was up for parole, knew what they were listening for. He had to confess to a murder he didn't do."

"Be that as it may," I said, "he got out."

"Travis and Carmen lived separate lives," he said, "but they switched off and on in domiciles. One day Carmen showed up at the Woodminster house. She saw Blake outside on the porch of the guesthouse and introduced herself. Said she'd be around for a couple of weeks. If Blake was up to it, they could get together."

"Oh, boy."

"You got it. Blake told Logan."

"Why, in God's name?"

"She felt guilty about it," he said.

"And so Logan killed Carmen?" I said.

"Almost. Blake called Logan, told him where he could find Carmen. Logan arrived with a gun tucked out of sight in the back of his pants, cool and calm until he met Carmen at the door. Blake said that Logan asked Carmen if she remembered the book she sent him. He showed her the book. She said she didn't know what he was talking about. Blake told me she knew then by the way Carmen denied the accusation that she was telling the truth. To Logan, though, it sounded like a guilty answer. He pulled the gun. Blake pushed the gun to the side. Carmen slammed the door."

"Carmen survived." I said.

"No shot was fired. Logan ran around back. The door was open. They thought Carmen must have run to a neighbor's house and called the cops. Looked that way. Then Logan did a crazy thing. Instead of running to his car, he insisted they wait for the cops. He put Fanon on the kitchen counter. That was his evidence."

"The copy we found there," I said. "How did it get to the guesthouse?"

"Blake had no idea. Must have been Logan but, then again, that's just logic. She could have forgotten. Anyway Blake pointed out to Logan that if he was going to find the right woman, he had to stay out of prison. And here he was carrying a gun. She insisted they had to keep looking. How else would they find who killed her father?"

"She convinced Logan to go back to Lodi?"

"The first good decision of the day arrived in the nick of time. They went into hiding together."

"If Carmen could describe Blake reasonably accurately to Travis," I said, "the cops would have a person to start looking for, and they'd have a place to look."

"Yeah," he said. We looked at each other.

"That didn't happen," he said, "or the cops would have found me in the guesthouse."

"Nice chick," I said.

"It looks like Carmen and Travis had the hell scared out of them. They went into hiding too, with no clue who was after them. You don't believe the police can protect you from an unknown assailant. I don't know how their imaginations kicked in after Logan's attack. Maybe they already had stuff to be scared of."

"After all that, did you ask Blake why she would tell you the guesthouse was vacant?"

"We got around to that. She said she felt sorry for me."

"You believed her?"

He nodded. "I never understood why she wanted to be with me."

"You could talk about mysterious things like you knew what you were talking about?"

"She did like bedtime stories."

"You told her about the Fanon in the basement?" I said.

"It proved she was right. The murders were connected."

"You said she asked you to help find out who killed her father, Joe Truesdell," I said.

"I told her to stop looking for Hispanic whores. She'd already decided that was smart."

"You tell her who to look for?"

"We were sitting in the front room. The Fanon was on the coffee table. I told her that was her best bet."

"What do you think?" I said.

"Logan brought it with him to Rhymes's house. He planned

to stuff it down Carmen's throat. I told Blake it was the wrong throat."

"You're all she has," I said. "Whether or not Logan is dead, he's dead to her."

"She's by herself. Logan alive and kicking was something to hang on to. Carmen's age alone told Blake that she couldn't have been the one who killed her father. That link was always her reason for throwing in with Logan. Logan was innocent, she believed. Just as strongly, she believed her father's killer was the same as the woman who framed him. Heather Nelson agreed with her. Agreement between them was so rare that she took it as gospel."

"Once she knew Carmen couldn't be right," I said, "why tell Logan?"

"He'd meet Carmen, see his mistake. That would get Carmen behind them. Then go get the right Hispanic whore. Back to the plan. It took that encounter with Carmen to tell Blake she never had a deal with Logan. He let her believe they'd turn their evidence over to the cops. That was the deal, as he let her understand it. But he would have killed ten women to get the right one. Heather said that what convicted Logan was appearances. He looked like a guy out on parole for murder, and shouldn't have got it."

"You were impressed that Fanon kept turning up at all these murders," I said. "You told Blake that was her best bet—but where should she take the hint?"

"Heather said she could never put Joe Truesdell, Henry Wilmot, and Garrett Logan in the same world. But that's what you have to do. It's like any mystery. You're forever telling yourself this idea or that hunch can't be right. You glide over an entire problem. Nothing catches you."

"You told her?"

"I wanted out. She understood."

] *Chapter 16*

I FETCHED THREE big Amazon boxes from a storage room, and filled them with a closet full of clothes still on the hangers. Stan's luggage went in that closet. The walk-in closet stayed as it was. We pushed the boxes into the hall. Figure that out when Stan needed a hanger, if that ever happened. A light gleamed at the bottom of Melissa's door when we arrived. Still on when we snacked in the kitchen, but not when we knocked off for the night.

We were up late in the morning. If Melissa passed through the kitchen for breakfast, she washed and dried up, put her stuff away, and disappeared. I found the light on in the stacks. Heard what I imagined was somebody hard at work, and shut the door. When I came back from the food mart, voices were in the kitchen. Melissa was telling Stan how to understand how it was that something couldn't happen regarding seven bridges in this town she called Königsberg. I emptied a shopping bag, making my presence known by opening and shutting the refrigerator, moving things around in cabinets making space, expecting a reaction, an acknowledgment of my presence. I mean, it was the first time we were all together, and shouldn't we, well, how about a hello? It was my first experience with the super bonding nature of the mathematical search for truth. These two had bonded. The rest of the world didn't exist.

I spent an hour in the office returning calls, sorting mail—two bundles this morning. Melissa was at her ease with Stan, and I set aside a minute for a freshly experienced sense of her, a mix of surprise and relief that she didn't feel she was expected to treat me as the mistress of the domain.

When I came back to the kitchen they'd pushed their chairs back from the table for a good old discussion of the inevitability of an extinction level event: the human horizon. Where there had once been seven bridges, now there were five. The puzzle was reduced in complexity. What wars are good for.

I washed and dried my hair in the afternoon and offered a hand in the kitchen. Melissa would have none of it. A generational recipe for a sauce that enhanced French toast to a hallelujah steeped in a religious hymn would remain a family secret. When appreciation fell to a human friendliness, Melissa said to me, "Sounds carry around here."

"What kind of sounds?" I said.

"People talking in bed," she said.

"We keep you awake?"

"I kept my ear to the door. You said I'd never run into the name Ingrid Halder?"

"Did you?"

"Is there an Ingrid Halder?"

"Was," I said. "The previous owner of the roof over our heads. She installed me, held the paper two years, then gave it to me."

"There's a gap, then, in public records," she said, "where there shouldn't be. This property was purchased by the Arcadia Land Corporation, two years after the repeal of the Volstead Act. Listed as a storage unit for alcoholic beverages from thirty-five till ninety-nine. That's sixty-four years preserving stale air."

"The location was hardly prime commercial real estate," I said. "It was underground, for one thing."

"In seventy-five there was a large transfer of wealth to a

William Emmon," she said. "A certain Petra Weber made William Emmon the owner of the Arcadia Land Corporation."

"You did some digging," I said.

"You asked. Who is William Emmon?"

"Was. A front for Ingrid Halder," I said.

"The 1950 census has a William Emmon at 613 Merrivale Road in Mineola, an unincorporated community in Lowndes County, Georgia. He was eight years old. A rural community. Wouldn't expect he left home with much at all."

"William Emmon is the name in which Ingrid owned everything."

"So Petra Weber transferred a fortune to Ingrid Halder. When did Emmon become Ingrid's soul-mate?"

"I'm not sure I understood the story when I heard it," I said.

"Anyway, you asked me to find a link between Monica Parker and William Emmon. From what you're saying, the link should be between Monica Parker and Ingrid Halder."

"Must be," I said.

"So the link is there, you're saying. But it's…what? Invisible?"

"It's not something I can imagine," I said.

"Why would it be visible between Emmon and Parker?"

"William settled money on Parker. It was his money. Ingrid was dead."

"I can figure Emmon and Joanna Dempsey," she said, "in the abstract, some of it right, some wrong. Give me three chances around sex and it's mostly right. But give me all the chances in the world, and I still can't get Emmon anywhere near Monica Parker. And you asked about their fathers."

Melissa reached between us for her coffee cup, just something to twist in circles. "Were the amounts Emmon gave to Monica Parker and Joanna Dempsey the same?"

"To the penny," I said. "A quick decision, it seemed."

"Quick or not, they were equal in Emmon's understanding of his responsibilities at the end of his life."

"What are you thinking?" Stan said.

"It's asking the question another way, but it might help if I knew why they were equal. And why weren't there more winners?"

"You might keep going with that," Stan said.

"Emmon paying Dempsey for sex?" Melissa said. "A little late?"

"Logan's ears popped," Stan said.

"What are we talking about?" I said.

"Where his ears popped?" he said. "I'll bet it's a little corner of the Arcadia Land Corporation where Logan's pay-in-advance kidnapping adventure happened."

"Remind me," Melissa said. "Logan was the guy who tried to murder Travis Rhymes's wife?"

"You heard right," Stan said. "You overheard who Rhymes's wife was?"

"She looked like the redhead who framed him," she said. "Sorry to interrupt. If you would, please."

"Logan said the redhead took his watch," Stan said. "It wasn't till the cops asked for an alibi that he had to provide a travel time on the road. Sort of difficult, keeping time riding around in the trunk of a car."

"Would he know he had to?" Melissa said.

"He came up with 'about an hour.' Couldn't say less or more. The cops added an hour, explored north to Sacramento, guess after guess, railroad crossings, gravel roads, potholes, anything with a jolt in it. Of course the redhead could have zigzagged through Lodi before hitting an open road. Could end up anywhere."

"You mentioned a little corner of the Arcadia Land Corporation," Melissa said.

"It was in prison that Logan thought he remembered his ears popped. The redhead must have driven him into the foothills. That means she took one of two routes. One was Highway 88, which separates from Highway 12 up near Clement. There wasn't time to get to Martell, or to anywhere past Highway 49. That meant searching the few roads off 88 and 12. After Logan was released on parole, Blake told me she drove him around in the trunk of his car, to see if they could figure out where the redhead had taken him. On the way to higher elevation, his ears popped.

"Within sight of Clearwater Road there was this vacant motel on a rise at the end of a sharp up, down, up. Then a left, and there they were, in the back parking lot of the Wanderers Inn. When Blake got Logan out of the trunk, there was a distant sound of cars moving fast, but not a steady traffic. He thought he remembered the exact sound of a car passing along the main road on his previous trip. His imagination, I'm sure, but he knew he was in the right place: an isolated dwelling near a sharp rise after a right turn off a highway. This is where he was having his fun while Henry Wilmot was killed."

"When his escort unloaded him, he'd see where he was, wouldn't he?" Melissa said.

"He was blindfolded."

"He paid for this?" Melissa said.

"Good money. Asked her for another session. Kept her number."

"But what about the little corner of the Arcadia Land Corporation?" she said.

"The inn is shuttered. It's still there, across from a gas station and convenience mart, isolated for half a dozen miles either way. Logan looked up ownership. Eight hundred acres north of Highway 88 purchased in 1948 by the Arcadia Land Corporation. There was an office in Sebastopol. Logan dropped by. Nobody in the office reminded him of the redhead."

Melissa left the table. She came back with an open laptop. "Clearwater Road, paved in eighty-four, developed for access to the Wanderers Inn."

"Aren't you the scholar?" I said.

"Buy me a real computer. I'll show you how to look this stuff up."

"We've established that Emmon took over the Arcadia Land Corporation in seventy-five," Stan said. "Logan was held on land owned by Emmon, as a front for Ingrid Halder. He's involved in a coincidence that doesn't interest me enough to tell Blake about it."

"Then why did Blake drive Logan around searching for where he was held?" Melissa said.

"She told me she had doubts about his story. They had an agreement. If he ever got out, she'd help him search for the real killer."

"William Emmon didn't kill anyone," I said. "Neither did Ingrid. I knew them. This is ridiculous. And who murdered Logan? You can't blame William and Ingrid. They were already dead."

"When Blake found him," Stan said, "she got out of there."

"She didn't see Logan get shot?" Melissa said.

"That's what she said."

I stood up. Melissa beat me to the sink. "Wash them by hand?" she said.

I sat and clinked a spoon on the side of my cup, not asking for silence. "I have something to tell you, Melissa. You can serve family recipes to your heart's content."

"Total agreement," Stan said.

"You might want a second opinion," she said.

"I am the second opinion. And a deep well of good intentions in there."

Stan screwed the top and bottom of the coffee canister together, looked at me while tapping the side, "Another pot for the road?" He settled into a rigid posture in a chair at right angles to the table, like we were talking to the refrigerator, and what we were saying was about the refrigerator. He poked at the uneaten servings of French toast. "Anyone?" Heads shook. "How about going thirdsies? We all suffer equally?" Groans.

Melissa was shaking a damp dishtowel. I pointed to a curtain rod. Hang it there.

"If you explained all this to Travis Rhymes," Stan said, "plus a solid reason why his worries are over, you could maybe get the Woodminster place at a steep discount."

I laughed. I mean my head bounced in my hand.

"You going back to Lodi?" Melissa said to Stan. "Help Blake cope?"

"Blake?" he said. "I didn't go to Lodi for Blake. I went for Heather Nelson. I might see her once more. If I get a call."

"What can you do?" Melissa said.

"I don't know. It's the usual numbness you can feel sympathizing over the hand someone else was dealt. You can't do a thing for them. You're afraid that after they die, you'll live with their stuff, thinking that fortunately you're not in their shoes. I walked away after leaving a sympathy message. You know, I'm a decent human being. When Blake was seven her mother picked her up from school and told her her father was dead. There she was, seven years old, and there wasn't anyone called her father. When I heard about that, I understood that lost look underneath the cheer. I saw it once, then I saw it all the time."

A silence lasted a minute. Stan broke it. "Sharp lady, Heather. Some good conversations with her. She was so proud. She knew how to construct a perpendicular from a point not on a line to a line. She was going to show me. I was game, but she winked: I was in the know. She liked people who didn't reduce what they know to talk."

"Heather followed the Logan trial?" Melissa said.

"She put a good grade of thinking into the case. She knew Joe Truesdell inside and out. How any woman got a fist around Joe's cock? She didn't believe it. Joe wasn't the target. Or, he was, but his murder was intended to punish someone else."

"Why not murder the someone else?" I said.

"Heather said Joe's father was involved in some trouble. There was a girl he deflowered, and a kid, Joe's half-brother. Long forgotten water under the bridge, you'd think."

"The motel makes some sense," I said. "And the redhead. Joe's last night is forever a scandal. The Truesdell name is tarnished. Were they church people?"

"There was a Bible among Joe's stuff in the basement," Stan said. "Along with the Fanon book. Blake said only she and Logan knew about the copy of Fanon Logan received in prison. Neither knew about the copy in Joe's stuff, which was put into storage in Joe's parents' basement. Nobody knew. Still, Heather had a hunch the two cases were connected. The trouble with that kind of hunch is that you don't get a next step to follow."

"Strange that the step was there to follow, though," Melissa said, "if you could see."

"But maybe the twelve years between murders were designed to unlink the two cases," I said. "There's nothing to dilute the evidence against Logan."

Melissa and I retired to the office. She was rearranging this and that thingamajig on the desk, when she brought up the play: *The Man Who Would Not Be Known.*

"Bob Corning was good," she said.

"Bob was my first brush with object relations theory," I said.

"This man in the play," she said. "You couldn't predict his actions, nor what he would say, not even get a feel for his tendencies. He had no observable nature."

"The man who would not be known?" I said.

"A dominatrix got through to him, though."

"And there's Joe in the motel room," I said. "The redhead got him in there. An art of persuasion we dommes have. They say you can't teach it."

] *Chapter 17*

I'VE BEEN AS clear as I can be. That's regarding the first time Brendan Hopkins asked that I have a talk with some woman Emmon gave his house to he didn't know—which didn't sit easily with her because she didn't know him. Sounded familiar. Only this woman didn't say no, or yes, to the offer. She postponed a decision, while she kept on and on at Hopkins for the name of someone who did know Emmon, for the sake of finding out what reason Emmon had to pick her, a complete stranger, for such a gift. And whose name would that be? Hopkins reached me with a new pitch: she was old money. Used to getting her way by offering extravagant compensation—Hopkins employing just-between-you-and-me persuasion. So there was a very generous offer for a meeting. I wasn't dug in so hard afterwards.

"Abarbanel and Hopkins," a woman's voice said. "How is your day going, Ms. Cromwell?"

"Excellent," I said. "And yours?"

"Fine, thank you."

"Brendan Hopkins, if you would."

"What would the call be about?"

"I'm returning his call." I said. "It would be about what he called me about."

"Mr. Hopkins is looking forward to speaking with you, Ms.

Cromwell. He's in a meeting at the moment. Can he return your call at this number? It shouldn't be long."

"Mr. Hopkins asked me to speak with a woman named Adele King, who inherited William Emmon's house. If you would, please ask him if Mrs. King's father was murdered. Also. Find out when that happened, and where. No rush, but as many particulars as possible would be appreciated. Very likely it happened a long time ago. Yes, I'll be at this number."

I had a shower and took a look at what needed surgery. I got a couple thumbnails on a pimple, but couldn't eliminate it. The red came out redder. Had to be touched up, Neosporin and a band aid.

Melissa was in the office retrieving messages. A space heater in the well of the desk was in action. I hung a jacket over the back of a chair, latched the heel of a bare foot on the seat and got going on toenail polish.

Melissa shut off phone messages. "Daedalus Hainey," she said. "He's asking if he might swing by with his recent book of poetry. He's using a pen name. He asked me to keep it confidential."

"Everyone knows what I know about Daedalus," I said, "but not from me. He's in town?"

"He says he's footloose on the facets of the earth."

"These rhymers. Nothing's simple."

"His editor caught a bug. Life's suspended until she doesn't sound like a frog. Could you meet him in the riding outfit? You'll know which one." She pointed at a yellow pad. "He left a number."

"What's the score?" I said.

"Three so far in the coming week. A Margaret would appreciate a chatty hello. A Jack's on location in Utah. He can send a private jet. Nate is not sure about meetings from here on. He asked for Chris Farber's contact info. I said what you said to say. I'm new here. When you're free he would like to hear your voice. Be strict with him. His words."

A call came in. Melissa stood and said I might want to switch chairs with her. She recognized the caller. I sat at the office desk and pressed speaker.

A man's voice. He asked if he was speaking with Elizabeth Cromwell. A silence followed, then a woman identified herself as Adele King, and said, "My father's birthday is coming the end of January. Why would you ask if he was murdered?"

"It would fit a pattern," I said.

"Our infant son was kidnapped thirty-six years ago. We haven't seen him since. Would that disturb your pattern?"

Hard feelings in her tone, having to say to a stranger what she had said, I imagined.

I understood from Hopkins that she wanted to hear my version of William Emmon. Get it over with. Describe the pattern.

"William Emmon asked me to split a considerable sum of cash between two women," I said. "Neither woman ever heard of him. Subsequently, I learned that both of their fathers had been murdered. That was long before the daughters received Emmon's gifts. I understand that in his will Emmon left his house on Grand Avenue to you."

"You must have wondered." Mrs. King said, "as I have wondered, what was his motivation?"

The flat uninflected cadence of the remark left the question hanging, not a question, but an offer to toss back to her some platitude I could extract from a mind-reading journey into William's thoughts. She was listening. Hang up or not, a decision she was leaving to me.

"Emmon wasn't dumb, but honestly, it was beyond him to plan a murder, let alone a murder that he might want to get away with. Same goes for a kidnapping. That's all I can tell you about William Emmon that would have any relevance to the house he gave you."

"You knew him?" she said.

"It's a question I've been asking myself."

"Were you two involved romantically?"

"Nobody who knows me would ask that question; nobody who knew him, either."

"Nobody who knows me would give me their house," she said.

"The house he gave you was purchased with his partner's money. Every cent he had came from her."

"That amounts to a hill of beans, Ms. Cromwell. If she gave him money for a house, it was *his* house he gave me. His name was on the title."

The hill of beans was that Ingrid might have told William to put Mrs. King in the will as inheritor. I didn't have to think. Not a chance. That was not Ingrid. Mrs. King was right, but I couldn't explain it. I could agree with her.

"Agreed," I said.

"Of course. Who doesn't agree with me?"

I took a few breaths. "Mrs. King, it would seem this was a cathartic act taken as William planned the last steps of his life. Why he thought he owed you, I haven't the slightest clue. I don't believe it was related to your son. If it helps, I never saw him with a child. If there was a child in his background, I'd expect the name would appear in his will."

"I know his background, Ms. Cromwell. Thank you. I'm curious. You said a woman gave him every cent he had."

"His name covered ownership for her."

"What was she up to that required cover?" she said.

"Didn't ask," I said.

There was a pause for a whisper that went silent.

"Would you have her name?" she said.

"Ingrid Halder."

"A middle name? Initial?"

"You're not going to find anything about her. I'm just curious: Your father is alive, but did you ever happen upon a copy of a French novel by a writer named Frantz Fanon?"

"Oh, God…" After a pause, "I'm having a hard time, Ms. Cromwell. Please excuse me. I'll call you back."

"I'll be here," I said.

Melissa's face had turned to an expression so appalled there wasn't a muscle she could move. A Michelangelo converted to a perpetual woman-with-a-question on a pedestal.

"Her baby was stolen," she said. "Emmon had something to do with that?"

A light on the phone blinked. I connected Adele King.

"Are you available?" she said. "I have your address."

"Not here," I said.

"The Fairmont?" she said. "I can have a car pick you up."

"You're where at the moment?" I said.

"This is important, Ms. Cromwell." It took her a second. "You cannot know. At least I pray not."

"Okay," I said. "The Fairmont is a short walk. What's good for you?"

"The Fairmont has a helipad," she said. "Give me an hour, if you would, please."

A MAN IN a dark suit was leaning a palm on the hotel desk as I entered the Fairmont. When he saw me, he picked up a piece of paper from the desk. He looked at me and put the piece of paper in an inside pocket while launching his full height into action. We met, exchanged identification, and that was it. I was the right blonde. I was his assignment. He would get me to where we were going. He stepped aside and held his left hand out from his body to an elevator behind him. He punched a sequence of seven buttons on a digital pad, and we entered the elevator. When we got out on the fifth floor, he followed me down a short hall past six opposing pairs of colonnades. The hall ended at a memorial to the creation of the United Nations. Behind that was a kidney-shaped pool with tropical fish and smooth rounded rocks of varying sizes. Behind the pool was a short hall that connected to another building. A second elevator stopped at a door marked S3. It opened to the kind of room that did justice to anyone coming and going in a helicopter.

Beyond a surrounding wall of slightly bluish-magenta glass was a good chunk of the magnificence you swoon over when you're talking about what you're paying for up here. Mrs. King said my name, her name, and welcome to the Fairmont, no fanfare, her humble abode. An Asian woman in silk opened a door to the patio. At one end of the patio were four chairs facing a glass table. Around the perimeter was an ornately sculpted iron railing. It couldn't be sturdy enough. Not for me. I took the chair furthest from the railing. Mrs. King took the chair to my left, perhaps to keep herself out of a distracting background.

"We have a red," she said, "and a list to choose from, as you wish. Coffee is ready. Anything to eat?"

"I've had breakfast," I said. I moved my hand, "Nothing, thank you."

"Thank you for coming, Ms. Cromwell."

"I'm sorry to hear about your son, Mrs. King. I can't imagine."

"This book by Frantz Fanon," she said. "Please, if you would, I'm interested."

"There is and isn't much to tell," I said. "Two murders in Lodi happened about twelve years apart. This was a long time ago, thirty years or more. A guy I know found a Fanon among one of the murdered men's belongings. The book wasn't noticed. Had my friend not previously encountered a copy of the same book left behind in a guesthouse where the daughter of one of the murdered men was living, he wouldn't have cared to notice that the title didn't belong among the murdered man's books."

"A second copy means what?" she said, and answered, "Oh, yes, there were two murders."

"Fanon is an odd book to leave behind," I said. "But again, one copy is odd, so what? You don't think even to bother checking its value in the book market. Hefty price tag for a book left behind. Eventually, we understood: a book, a murder."

"The daughter," King said, "she connects to the other murder in Lodi?"

"Very good," I said.

"I've been at this a while," she said.

"A long story," I said, "wrapped in mysteries."

She let the silence go on a while. "Our son Conall's carriage was on the walk at the back of the house. The nanny was in the den watching television. She could pull a knee onto the couch, twist her torso, and see the carriage. She did this often, she said. But when she looked into the carriage during a commercial break, she lost the ability to think, or never had it. She found a book, but not Conall. She assumed I had come home, picked up Conall, gone off for an errand, and left my reading behind. She brought the carriage inside. The book was in a foreign language, so she shelved it with the travel books. She washed and dried Conall's blankets while waiting for me to come home. This was in 1988, before cell phones.

"She had been under instructions to remain with Conall at all times. No exceptions. It occurred to her, while waiting for me to come home, that I would be displeased with her. She might be terminated. After an hour she checked the crib in Conall's room. She looked for Conall in places that could only be places to look if he could walk off seeking a little privacy for himself to read the newspaper. Thorough, she was, doing everything she could to invoke a miracle that would cover her mistake.

"We were in a gated community in Newport Beach. My husband's parents gave us the house while he was serving in Washington, D.C. The girl had a boyfriend, a gardener/handyman in the colony. It's how she got her job. I got her name from friends of my in-laws.

"Who do I blame? It was my fault. I hired her."

She looked in the direction of the Bay at the catastrophe that was, as far as she had decided, her fault. To talk, or not to talk? Talk she did. She summoned herself to return her thoughts to my presence.

"I was a kid myself, a young mother. I learned too late you can hire someone and look them in the eye and tell them in utmost seriousness, 'Don't put the baby in the oven to warm him up'—for what it's worth. My husband called the police when he got home from work. Conall had been gone four hours by the time I got home."

I couldn't say that I couldn't imagine what she'd been through any better than I said it the first time. That was done. Anything else was uncalled for after thirty-some years.

"This is all once upon a time," she said, "when I looked like Napoleon in a storm on the shores of Elbe."

I got a quick look from her. I got the Napoleon thing, or I didn't. She continued.

"I knew my effect on those who graciously listened, Ms. Cromwell. They stepped up to the task when needed. I got smart. I developed a pain in my ribcage. This inexplicable pain was my loyal companion. I kept a button open in a blouse and a hand inside to hold my ribs together—in the presence of company. That display of hysterical suffering rid me of them. Then the pain disappeared. I'm a hermit now. I have my faith. I'm not desperate to endure friends."

I was working out a sentence that would get it across that her grief touched me. I couldn't get that sentence together. But the old body language must have. I must have indicated I wasn't just a passive listener.

"I appreciate your presence, Ms. Cromwell." A second or two passed. "I don't know that a word covers what I see in you. 'Maturity' is too… 'Humanity' is closer. The word I'm searching for, I believe, is…'hallucinatory'…now that I've met you."

"It paid the bills," I said. "What do you hallucinate I can do for you?"

"I might have said 'police' earlier," she said. "I meant FBI. They're impressive when the stakes warrant it—President Reagan stayed with my husband's father on visits to California. They wandered around together—the two of them, mostly, but there was this other fellow who arrived a day late. He wandered around unsupervised. He's in Sausalito these days, retired. I'd like to invite him to join us."

"Now?"

"That's a yes?"

"Sure." I said.

"She put a middle fingertip to her phone, waited, and said, "Ms. Cromwell is with me at the Fairmont. It's fine."

She held the connection open. She said to me, "You're busy this afternoon?" She held the phone vertically to let me transmit my answer directly.

"I'll have to make a call," I said, "but okay."

She listened and hung up. "He'll leave in a minute. It'll be a while. May I bore you?"

"I've never been up here before, Mrs. King. It's my pleasure."

"It's about the theft of my child. I haven't told this to anybody. I would like to tell you."

"Please go ahead," I said.

"A crucial few seconds went by in the moment my son was taken," she said. "I used to see those seconds any old when. A woman is carrying my son. She disappears around a hedge. I see what the babysitter never saw."

She pointed inside. "Refreshments. Sing out."

I was fine.

"It wasn't until the next week—*week!*—that Donald Sterling—the man you will meet—found the ransom note tucked inside a green book in the travel section. If not for him, I wonder."

"Would anyone have ever noticed the book?" I said.

"Donald tracked the babysitter through every step she took after the kidnapping, second by second. She remembered she had taken the book out of the carriage.

"Why take it?"

"She thought it was my book. Needless to say, the ransom drop-off was late. My husband placed the ransom money on a table in a tent. The tent was in an alley between two dilapidated rows of houses in Venice.

"The Venice in Los Angeles?"

"Thank you. A while later the tent burst into flames. Two hundred thousand in old bills, non-sequential serial numbers, and so on, burned up. For some reason the ransom note specified a thousand-dollar bill and a five-hundred-dollar bill be included.

We received a note subsequently that we had not complied with instructions: the FBI had used money with embedded threads that could be traced. We never heard a thing again."

"The gang wasn't after money," I said.

"The FBI focused on the political angle, at least that's what they shared with us. It helped exonerate the babysitter and her boyfriend."

Mrs. King raised her hand. A woman came from inside the glass partition. "I'm having a coffee," Mrs. King said to me. I included myself. "Two coffees, please."

"The gang picked Conall to satisfy its cruelty," she said.

The coffees came with a tray of things in gold wrappers with little flags that described them in Italian. Containers of three kinds of milk were lined up with five kinds of sweeteners.

I got my coffee going with the silvery clink of a miniature spoon. Mrs. King waited until the appreciative look after the first sip. She told the server we were fine.

"You should know," she said, "I haven't recorded our conversation."

"A fact not taken for granted, Mrs. King, even when told."

"You don't seem to be a person who would hit anyone," she said. "Of course I wouldn't know what trait would show in a dominatrix."

"The gift of surprise is useful," I said.

"I'd like to read up. Any suggestions for a book that peels the cover off your profession?"

"Plenty of instructional texty stuff on basic etiquette. You know: be polite, take a shower, be on time; if you can't, call, let your mistress in on your inescapable dilemma. An outline of human decency."

"Fiction?" she said.

"The stuff to my liking isn't published. You're welcome to camp out in my private library. Any special interest?"

"The English Department. Why that name?"

"I'm an eighth-grade dropout," I said. "The name boosted my sense of self."

"Back to Donald Sterling," she said. "The house next door to us was for sale. It was viewed by two women on the day of the abduction. The realtor's statement to the FBI was that the prospective buyers were with her the entire time of the showing.

"Of course anything could happen, and the investigation had to go in every direction at once. Donald liked the possibilities in the next-door house being for sale. He took the realtor through the viewers' visit, prying for gaps in memory and things that might have happened in the gaps. One of the women was on crutches. She had a cup holder attached to the side of a crutch. She accidentally dropped the sleeve of a sweater in her coffee. She had to use the bathroom, rinse the sweater in cold water. She was in the bathroom only a minute, the realtor was sure. Donald suggested they retrace their steps from that day. At the end of the second time around, he asked the realtor how long they had spent in the kitchen. She couldn't say. But she could say that the woman on crutches a week ago had been in the bathroom at most a minute. She said that twice. But she wouldn't get pinned down on this kitchen business.

"In fact, there was a second door to the bathroom. Steps from there went to the back door of the house, and a path led through a hedge to the place where Conall was asleep in his carriage. Donald went through the hedge to the place where the buyers had backed their car in—where Donald had left his sedan. He opened the trunk, counted off five seconds, closed the trunk, went back up the steps to the bathroom, and checked his stopwatch in the master bedroom. It could have happened this way.

"After dinner he dropped by the home of the babysitter to see if a woman had spoken to her recently about a babysitting job. Possibly this woman offered her some terrific wages, perhaps as much as two dollars an hour over the rate she was used to.

"The babysitter said yes, a woman had offered her a job. She and the woman talked about her current work and the procedures she followed in the care of an infant. The woman gave the girl twenty-five dollars as an advance. She left her a name and number, and a promise she'd call.

"Donald called the FBI agent in charge. He thought the babysitter dodged a bullet. If she'd been in the backyard at the wrong instant, well, there it was, she wasn't. The timing had to be perfect, an aspect of the case that Donald decided was essential in some respect to the meaning of the book we had found, the Fanon as you call it, a ruthless crime that had been designing itself in a mind. A revenge.

"Donald says he has reason to believe that Conall is still alive. Ms. Cromwell, you are the first person who might give Donald something of interest to deal with. But we're very familiar with blind alleys."

I raised my cup to say with a silent gesture, "Very good coffee, Mrs. King."

] *Chapter 18*

DONALD STERLING was shown out to the patio with a bottle of beer in hand. Was this that kind of gathering? I supposed so, if I understood the beer. He was five feet and another four to five inches on worn sandals, blue wool socks, a man with a flavorless smile that must have been with him all his life, like the very smooth skin that gave him a college kid's face into his sixties. Fine pink hair combed high on the crown put a faint part on the left. A large head was one abnormality in his appearance. Another was that he carried a slight underweight build, but stuck out in front with a pregnant bulge. No exercise plan could make that tummy go away. A narrow leather belt held his pants up over the tummy. He had large eyes. A glasses case showed a row of stitching above a breast pocket in a black-and-white striped shirt. A fleece-lined olive coat was under his left arm. A portion of a gray wool cap was visible in a pocket. He was the kid known as the Genius from an early age, and wherever he went to school, he looked like nobody else, and he certainly did not look FBI.

He held his lips to Mrs. King's temple, while a left hand tenderly made its way along the back of her hair, a no-fuss, no-upkeep cut that fell in a thinned white cascade straight to the shoulders. A brown barrette fastened a sweep of hair against the side of her head, uncovering an ear that was turned to me, as if she hadn't got into the hearing aid racket. Part of the isolation?

I met Sterling on my feet with a hand waiting. "Donald Sterling," he said. He bowed and gestured with a nod for me to sit. He sat opposite and settled his beer on the arm of his chair. He got a thought going, twisting the base of the bottle between a coordinated clockwork thumb and middle finger. He made a full circuit of the bottle lining up his opening pitch.

"Are you in a hurry, Ms. Cromwell?"

"There's tomorrow, and the day after," I said. "Let's count on them, if we need them."

"You can imagine our gratitude. I'd like to emphasize our appreciation by saying that Mrs. King is eager to compensate you for your time. Please don't hesitate to accept. If I might add a special remark, the appreciation goes much deeper."

I nodded to Mrs. King. "I'm happy to help," I said.

"Help, Ms. Cromwell, I can sure use it. Any help you can provide."

"Happy to help," I said to myself.

"How about we start with William Emmon and why he left his house to Mrs. King."

I let a few seconds have a rest. "He's not your kidnapper. He can't be. Listing his prominent characteristic: He was under the control of a woman. I mentioned her to Mrs. King: Ingrid Halder. William couldn't organize a picnic. Ingrid wouldn't ask him to organize a picnic. If Ingrid organized a picnic, she wouldn't involve William in the details. He would screw it up."

I set my hands as if I were holding a basketball in front of my chest. I was holding the big picture.

"William Emmon was given a job," I said. "Drive Ingrid from Miami to L.A., drop off the rental car, hand the ticket he'd been given to ticket-takers so that he might board a flight back to Florida. He didn't make his flight."

"He distracts easily," Sterling said.

"Ingrid provided him a decent allowance. To his credit, he

was generous with friends. Women found him attractive. Enough that he found himself to be a man of value."

"How do you know so much?" Sterling said.

"I had lunch occasionally with women who said nice things about him. We agreed William was well adjusted."

"English Department material?" he said.

"I think I said this: He's not your kidnapper."

Sterling looked at his beer, a frustrated man about to employ profanity.

"You mentioned the Fanon book to Adele," he said.

"We have to go back a ways," I said.

His fingers were interlaced. He lifted his thumbs. I told him the little I knew of the murders in Lodi; the frame from Logan's point of view; Carmen Rhymes and her escape by the skin of her teeth; Blake, Stan, and Heather filling in the few details that clarified the picture; the two copies of Fanon; the recent Logan murder.

I told him there was more that I knew about, and no doubt more that I didn't, but he was looking around baffled as it was, like he was saying over and over to himself, "Never in a million years." I saw an unbelieving man when his glance fell on me.

"When I was a kid," he said, "my mother's sister walked me home from nursery school. It saved her a lot of time if we took a shortcut along a stream that was lined with all manner of foliage. From time to time I would see a flower of particular interest. I'd stop to peer at it closely. My aunt would tell me to stop my dawdling, and I would say, I wasn't dawdling, I was looking at flowers. She did not put up with this. She was doing my mother a favor, so let's get going. One day she quit explaining. She said, 'If you don't get going, I'll make you sorry.' She broke a switch off a tree and whipped my legs. That did settle things."

This might be an accusation. This could be a confession to some twisted attachment to *things*.

"You're hitting close to home," I said. "What for?"

"As an older kid," he said, "I was free to leave the house on my own and be with flowers. As it happened, I had a talent for art and was given materials to practice with. I could draw flowers. I could draw anything. I could have become a professional artist. That was not to be."

He studied his bottle, a compassionate study. "I've been living with failure too long."

"A great failure?" I said. "Or working things out as best you can, like the rest of us?"

"Intolerance, Ms. Cromwell. It turned inward. This cop's disease. Art. For some, it's a wonderful hobby. In me photographs of bodies produce gnarled emotions. They engender a feeling that the soul of the subject has been spoiled, deformed."

"You're experiencing your unwanted sadism," I said. "Your aunt has some answering ahead of her. You ever have it out with her?"

"She knew I hated her."

"It might help if we discussed a few of the things you hate," I said.

"Excuse me," he said. "Let's set the bar a bit higher."

"It was set higher," I said. "We weren't near getting over it. Remember? My opinion was that Emmon didn't do it. Ingrid didn't do it. And now they're dead. And you got us off on a bitch who stepped into your life without a shred of care for treating a child any better than she was treated."

"Mind if we review the bidding? I asked you why Emmon gave his house to Mrs. King."

"Okay, I skipped the intermediate bid. I jumped to game. They didn't do it."

"And the old-time frustration welled up and started beating the hell out of me all over again. It is a fact: Emmon gave his house to Mrs. King. I confess, I'm not satisfied with where my talent has taken me, Ms. Cromwell, I apologize. I'm not competent to understand that fact other than as a confession that they did do it."

"I heard I was the bitch of the moment," I said.

He smiled the smile. Success. The bitch caught on.

"Do you enjoy art, Ms. Cromwell? I mean, do you create?"

"I've snapped a few photos."

"I've contributed to the successful prosecution of nine murderers, Ms. Cromwell. But that's what I miss: creating."

He put his empty bottle on the table between us. I didn't catch a signal, if one was needed. The bottle was removed and another put in its place.

"Emmon owned the Arcadia Land Corporation," he said. "Six months before he died, he transferred the corporation to three gentlemen with whom he had no previous contact. That is, I can't find any indication that he knew them."

"Ingrid was in charge of the corporation," I said. "When she knew she wasn't going to be around much longer, she instructed him to put the wealth where she wanted it put. That's how the three gentlemen got what they got."

He raised his bottle. "She told you that?"

"It's how they worked," I said.

"Okay. So, Ingrid instructed Emmon to leave the house to Adele?"

I opened and shut my eyes, agreeable-like. "I wouldn't say no. But Ingrid had hired a woman who lived in the house with them. William threw her out the day after Ingrid died. He was pleased with himself, is what I saw. It's possible, then, that when Ingrid was past caring, he might have changed the will. That isn't something he would have done when she wasn't past caring."

"Brendan Hopkins took his orders from Ingrid?" he said.

"Her orders would go through William. If Hopkins ever met Ingrid, I'd be surprised."

"We can't know, is what you're saying."

"If one of them had a guilty conscience, it was not Ingrid."

"Thank you," he said. "I was getting lost."

I stared at him as calmly as I could, to keep a level stare from going rogue, prompting me to confess he could be right about Ingrid and William. I was wrong. Who knows.

"I can hope Ingrid said something," he said, "not directly to you, but a remark dropped, say, in your hearing that caused you to turn it over in your mind afterwards. You might remember something of the sort. Properly understood, it could be a secondhand confession. If convincing to the right people, it would close the case."

"Look, she hadn't dropped things in my hearing for years. I was invited to her funeral. I was surprised."

"But you attended," he said.

"It was only an hour's drive."

He ran a palm over his brow, smoothing an exasperation with me.

"There were two women who took Conall King," he said, "a well-oiled operation. One of them had a tattoo: *sub aquila*. Indicated the bearer served under the eagle—figuratively, service in the military. The real estate agent saw it on her forearm. Her sweater was wet. She pulled her sleeve past her elbow."

"A great clue," I said. "What came of it?"

"You needn't take your shirt off," he said.

"I've seen Ingrid with her shirt off. No tattoo."

He put his hands together at three pairs of fingertips. "I could ask the Bureau to reopen the case," he said. "I've asked twice before. Wore out my bona fides. Would you agree to sit for a formal interview?"

"Let's get formal," I said.

He threw a "thanks" at me.

"How did you and this Ingrid meet?"

"I was about to stick a foot off the curb into Noe Street. A car was turning off Market. A man and woman were in the backseat. William and Ingrid. Another woman was driving. She knew what to do."

"What does that mean?" he said.

"The driver cut me off. She lowered the passenger window, asked if I was available. It's what I was in San Francisco for. I was seventeen, fixed up to look twenty-something, up from L.A. to meet a woman who could use me. The driver held an envelope. I could have what's in it. Was I willing to answer a few questions? No obligations."

"You knew the answers?"

"Was I available for a couple of hours?"

"That's it?"

"The note in the envelope described a one-act scene. I could do it. The bullwhipping would be easy. I'd been doing long whips off and on since I was fifteen. The role-play would be in the style of a commedia dell'arte. I hadn't read any classics, but at seventeen I was familiar with whipping as fundamentally farce. As far as an observer would experience it."

"You opened the envelope?" he said.

"I wasn't a rube."

"The driver was running the show?" he said.

"She did the talking—the director. I agreed to meet them at a leather shop on Stafford Street. She introduced me at the shop. She made the arrangements. There was a back room where customers could try out the merchandise."

"Would they still remember her?" he said.

I shook my head that they would not. "As I discovered, the shop was in William's name. He hired the employees."

"And now he's dead," he said.

"And the address is now known as the address of the English Department."

His eyes went to a place over my head. They calculated there, and met my eyes when they were finished. "You now own this place where you and William…whatever. Congratulations seem to be in order. Could I just express a *wow*. How did you manage that? Take all the time you need."

"Ingrid invited me to come to the desert with her," I said.

"Who was the driver who propositioned you that day? Anybody give you a name?"

"Never heard."

"Please, go on," he said, "if you will. Sorry to interrupt."

"You won't find Ingrid under any name," I said. "She want-ed it that way. The doctor who cared for her during the last six months, I'm sure records of their meetings don't exist."

"Died of what?"

"An aggressive cancer, I heard at the burial."

"No record of a birth in the United States."

"She came from Munich."

"No immigration record on her?" he said.

"From what William told me, no."

"What can you tell me?"

"I can tell you what she told me. She was born in East Prus-sia in 1945. The Russians were charging all over sacred German soil, plenty of revenge on their minds. The German authorities in their district initially wouldn't let the civilian population flee. They called it defeatism, which undermined army morale. They had a point: why defend people who are running away? A neigh-bor carried her across the Elbe. They linked up with a friend of the family in Munich."

"Stories of pursuit and evasion in those days are everywhere," he said. "Halder was her name back then?"

"I doubt it," I said. "Ingrid, though, that might be right. Her parents died in the final months of the war. The German people who remained after the war were driven out. It's no longer Ger-man—Poland got it."

"You two had conversations," he said. "Good friends?"

"We camped in the desert a few times. Pointed at patterns in the Milky Way as we were going to sleep. She said she wasn't happy growing up in Munich. Munich gave her the open, softer dialect of a southern region, plus exposure to a wide range of refugees; the bonus was an opportunity to develop her appetite for imitation."

"You had it too?" he said. "The appetite?"

"Getting into a strict character, it puffed me up."

"Amazing life," he said.

"If I hadn't met her, I don't know where I'd be."

He was rotating his bottle again. "She admired you, but excuse me for being blunt, it's quite a step from that to handing you a property in the center of San Francisco."

"I was gorgeous in those years. I took it for granted that's why people liked me. I had to unlearn simple truths, too."

"What do you believe? I mean if Ingrid *was* in on this kidnapping, somehow, somewhere?"

"I see what you're up against," I said. "Leaving a French book at a crime scene? Honestly, it wouldn't occur to her. I won't swear, but I don't think she knew French."

"It wouldn't occur to *you*. It occurred to someone. Why wouldn't it occur to her?"

A question I couldn't answer.

Sterling was leaning back, his nose in the air, sharp as a bloodhound.

"February forty-five," I said. "The ship they might have been able to escape on was torpedoed. One of a dozen roads not taken, thankfully."

He set his bottle on the ground. "I don't see the weave here. What knits this Ingrid together? Well, of course, God only knows. Incidentally, the driver was the first woman you remember with Ingrid. You ever see her again?"

"No, but there was a second woman," I said.

"Please don't think," he said. "Go ahead with that, if you would."

"I'm wondering if the driver was the woman Ingrid met in Inyokern?" I said. "William said they drove around the desert like old friends. She was a French teacher."

"What desert was that?" he said. He had his phone ready.

"Mojave," I said. "There was a military base."

He got going on his phone. "Naval Ordnance Test Station China Lake," he said.

"There was a school near the base," I said.

He hummed a bit of Beethoven, and said, "Burroughs High School," and did something with his eyebrows. "Go on."

"She was a French and Spanish teacher at the high school."

"Just a minute," he said. He considered choices on his phone. He made contact with someone. "It's me. Doing great. You? Great. Yes. There was a French or Spanish teacher at Burroughs High School. This was at or near the Naval Ordnance Test Station, China Lake. Just a minute." He looked at me. "Year, years?"

"Sixty-two, sixty-three?"

"You heard that?" he said. He went back to humming a piano concerto, moving the fingers on his right hand, playing. "Yes," he said. "Spell that, if you would. No, got it, perfect. Of course, I may very well do so. See you."

"Gabriella Brucolli," he said to Mrs. King. She shook her head with her eyes closed.

We sat there silently till Mrs. King asked what kind of music I listened to. I said I was good just now. I didn't know what the question was leading to. A baker's dozen of pastries were set up with coffee.

"I have an address for a Gabriella Brucolli in Inyokern," Sterling said. "Ingrid flew in? It's a military base."

"No. What William said was a boat picked her up near the Bahamas, offshore. Dropped her in Florida. William took her to California."

"In Florida, he say where that was? A city?"

"Miami? William worked for a group that moved women from place to place. Instructions were to drive her to L.A. The itinerary was programmed: how fast to drive, where to stop for meals and sleep. Do nothing to attract the attention of cops. Don't talk to the lady. If the lady talks, answer as briefly as the question requires, and shut up."

"Something else," I said. "William had a regular job dropping girls at parties. The Ingrid job was special. So William was special to someone."

"Lot of customs people have troubles making insurance payments on their boats. Money still buys a dark ride into Florida."

"There was some mix-up at LAX," I said. "William was

supposed to pass Ingrid off and catch a flight back to Florida. The guy who was supposed to meet Ingrid didn't show up. William and Ingrid took a train to Mojave instead. The French teacher met them there."

"Why not drive to Mojave?" he said.

"Something had to be done with the car? Dump it. Or something. I don't know."

"The gang wouldn't like it," he said. "An unexplained change of plans…a worrisome development when an employee disappears, not to mention a unilateral change of plans from a heretofore reliable employee. But if the party who had paid for the goods was satisfied? Let's go back to the French teacher. The teacher met them. Then what?"

"The three of them drove from Mojave to Inyokern," I said.

"Munich to Inyokern." He nodded at the sound of that. "Not the sound of a vacation itinerary, more like a mission."

Sterling moved some pink threads on his head. I cut into a three-colored chocolate cylinder. I kept the delight quiet, like I belonged up here.

"Emmon was expected back in Florida," he said. "He didn't say what he did with the plane ticket?"

"You should have some of this," I said.

He rubbed a hand over the back of his shoulders and squeezed a few lumps out of the side of his jaw. Then he caught his windpipe between a thumb and finger, and looked at me a while caressing a cheek full of air. He held up an index finger, and let it fall.

"This driver," he said, "she wasn't a hired driver?" he said.

"William said they met as friends, but hadn't met before."

"Emmon screwed with an organization," he said. "What a simpleton."

"William was given a simple job by an organization that didn't know it wasn't so simple, as they would have known if they'd dealt with Ingrid over stakes she cared about. She figured William better than the organization."

There's a fondness for the desert in some people. Ingrid and I had our fun at a few old mining sites. I found an old *Saturday Evening Post* with an F. Scott Fitzgerald story covering cracks in the walls of an abandoned shack. We entertained each other by role-playing dominant and submissive, acting out aesthetics while naked. Ingrid didn't sign things, including her body. As for a tattoo, Sterling wasn't any closer to Conall's disappearance. William and Ingrid as some new style of Bonnie and Clyde? I wasn't sure one way or the other. The motive for these crimes? If they were in Ingrid's heart, they weren't on paper. Nobody would ever know.

As I left, Mrs. King was not standing. What I saw in her look? A long haul was finished? Conall was dead.

Sterling accompanied me to the street. The look he was giving me was a new one. He was nice about how he did it, subdued.

"I'm looking back more and more at close calls," he said. "I escaped peer pressure in school. There wasn't anything I could become in order to conform to a prevailing norm. What you see is what they saw. I was a dwarf until my growth spurt. I got big feet and big hands out of it, and a decent analytical apparatus. I came close to throwing in with painting. All the way. A hand reached down and stopped me."

] *Chapter 19*

I T WAS PIZZA NIGHT at the English Department, four of us at the kitchen table. Stan was swilling purified water. Otherwise we were a beer ad, beer currently the coin of the realm, passed from the fridge by me and Melissa to Donald Sterling, who waved off the hard stuff, but indicated that when he could no longer focus, an offer would be considered.

Three weeks earlier a boy of ten or so had rung the bell at the Truesdell home, delivered a first edition copy of *Les damnés de la terre* to Blake's hand, and didn't leave a whom to thank. She mentioned the title when she called Stan to ask if he would help with Heather's arrangements. Heather passed.

Stan was reassuring: Fanon was not a warning. Logan's shooting was a follow-up act, a signature verdict from the group who had originally targeted him, a response to his parole. Logan got out of prison, but he did not get off. The killer took care of that. The killer was done. Otherwise the killer would have dispatched Blake the same morning as Logan. The book dotted that final point.

Stan had discussed the protective power of mistrust with Blake. Play dumb with strangers.

"Play dumb?" Melissa said.

"In case I'm wrong," Stan said. "In the murderer's imagination

Blake might have seen the murderer from an upstairs window, or driven past the murderer's car on the mad dash from the Logan house. Or someone was just getting around to another Truesdell. They would try to lure her to an unsafe environment. But I'm not wrong. They got their Truesdell a long time ago. They don't need another."

Melissa looked at a fingernail. That's a relief.

Stan also thought we might have caught a break. He had called Sterling. They agreed the latest Fanon was a mistake, reasoning that the killer might have purchased it recently, the kind of error that leaves tracks. Sterling would look into this. At long last, an opportunity to get himself into the field. The old gumshoe.

The kid who delivered the book to the Truesdell home was the first consideration. Post offices were covered by security cameras. Send a book, use a kid. Key question: Was the boy still alive? Taking care of that, the killer would eliminate a connection. Alive, would the kid be a local from the neighborhood? This killer and that mistake? Sterling didn't think so. Canvassing wouldn't be the better use of his efforts to turn up a lead.

"I met with a book dealer in San Francisco," Sterling said. "A national directory keeps records of traffic in rare books, but not perfectly; some go unrecorded; some are recorded secretly. Dealers in Atlanta, New York, and Philadelphia have sold *Les damnés de la terre* in the past six weeks. Another eleven sold copies in the four months prior. Names and addresses of buyers were recorded. As in any specialized commodity, there's fraud, and secrecy. I tossed a coin here. I wasn't poking around in the market in stolen books.

"I got what I wanted by asking. A first edition of *Les damnés de la terre*, thirteen and a half by twenty-two centimeters, about four and a half by a bit less than nine inches, was sent from Unwerth Rare Books, Philadelphia, by snail mail, and delivered to the mailbox at 428 Cedar Lane. This address was at the T where Laverne Road runs down Miller's Hill and ends at Cedar Creek, just outside Lodi. A young couple in residence. Fanon readers? Hardly, he thought. This was the lead he wanted.

"The mailbox was a metal drum built in a stone wall that runs along the driveway to the garage. The wall is across the street from a grove of trees that borders Canal Park. Continuing in the same direction, beyond the park, is the Canal Shopping Center."

Sterling had sketched a diagram of the area, showing where the killer likely hid his car, and where he waited to intercept delivery.

"Moving at my speed," he said, "I recorded twelve seconds of exposure breaking from cover, reaching the mailbox on Cedar Lane, and returning to cover. A young runner could cut that in half."

Sterling handed out diagrams, stacked an extra on a cracker box.

"You say a young couple lived at the house," I said. "Suppose they were expecting a special delivery. They might be outside waiting."

"Think it through," Sterling said. "I looked them up. They're lawyers. They have ways of receiving mail where they work. It's certainly possible one of them would be under the weather on the day of delivery, they're home, but then not likely waiting outside in winter weather. I checked, though, to be sure. They never received the book."

Sterling held his hands apart, clapped them together, and looked at us one at a time, as if to check that what had needed to be established to this point in the lecture had been. I drank off my water. I was good. A shadow between Stan's eyes might have been an awareness that Sterling was a capable man.

Sterling turned his diagram vertically. He held it bottom edge to the table. He spoke from memory. "You see the area numbered *four* at the edge of the Canal Park? I found tire tracks leading to there from the main road. They go to a turnaround at a clearing. There's nothing there. No structures. Might have been a picnic spot way back before the park was spiffed up. The trees are bare, but even if you glanced that direction from the main road, it would be easy to miss a car in there. You might not see anything gray. You see this red line? It's out of sight from the main parking area, but follow that line and you get your feet soaked. At the end of the line, pick a tree along a wire fence, and you're out of sight. The number *five* is a hole in the fence."

"Cigarette butts?" Melissa said.

"None. No footprints, either," Sterling said. "Irregular pebbly ground. You wouldn't take this route to the park from this direction. Walking, you'd take the shoulder facing traffic along Cedar. Advanced caution every step of the way."

Stan put a finger on the map. "This *three*, what is this?"

"A possibility," Sterling said. "The *one* is the main shopping area, the Home Depot, Staples, Ross, and Costco down here, loaded with security cameras. They cover the parking lot across from the park. Up here at *three* is a dead end. You could pull up here, and not be seen changing your plates."

"You're not going to find this sucker," Stan said.

"Not practicing the simple art of murder, not this one," Sterling said. "They haven't killed Ms. Truesdell. It would be our last chance to exploit a mistake. But Stan's right, there's no chance. Logan's murder was not a Gen Z escapade."

"Logan's killer might possibly know about me if they'd kept the Truesdell house under observation," Stan said. "But I'm not looking for anyone."

"Easy to cover your tracks when nobody's looking," Sterling said.

There were actually five of us present: the four of us at the kitchen table, and Mrs. King waiting outside the office door for a food delivery from the Fairmont. She couldn't pass anything I had on the premises through her system. Alone, and proud of it, she could nevertheless hear us.

"Sustenance tried and true from the Fairmont," she said.

"Let's pass the hat," I said.

"I'm paying, Mrs. King said. "I have more than all of you put together by multiples of thousands."

"Make that exponentials," said Stan. "And I'm impressed."

"I beg your pardon?" was heard. "What are exponentials?"

"*Au contraire*," Melissa shouted to the open door. "You're

wearing luxury lingerie, *Il brivido della frusta*? Well, I am. And don't tell me you've ever heard of it."

I mimed: "She lost her son."

Melissa whispered, "I'm sorry."

Mrs. King said, "Well, I know enough Italian to know what I want to order at Taverna dei Migliori. That's in Amalfi, incidentally. I can leave your name with them."

"I would appreciate you leave my title, the Baroness," Melissa called back.

"As long as I'm playing with house money, I'm in," said Stan.

I said, "A dog starved at his master's gate, predicts the peasants will be irate."

Sterling pondered, "A propos of…?"

"A propos of Tennyson," said Melissa, "or worthy of him."

Mrs. King's shipment from the Fairmont arrived in cylindrical hatboxes, the tops supplied with glass handles we pulled slowly upwards with a hissing that released a vacuum ending in a suction pop. A menu was passed around. Bread rolls and porcelain plates were stacked on the table. Contents of glass cups were identified in a fancy handwritten script on foil covers that peeled off without tearing, if you were careful.

"Risotto alla Milanese," Melissa said. "Canary yellow. Takers? Braciole…pappardelle with white Bolognese. Too late. First dibs."

Two rows of individually wrapped coffee cups went next to the urn.

Melissa swallowed and raised her cup, "Vive le wow!"

Stan retreated to the upholstered arm of a chair in a corner, and lined up his dinner selection on newspaper spread out on a tray. He leaned an elbow on the back cushion, happy as a clam in isolation.

I stashed risotto in the bread box and pulled a chair to Mrs. King, who had joined us at the table.

"Can I get you something?" I said.

"A few breadsticks and a coffee, please."

She dipped a stick in coffee and bit off the tip.

She was getting into the motions of clearing a space on the

table for her coffee. That would free a hand for a proper greet. I gripped her wrist softly. "Don't bother," I said. "I'm glad you can be here."

I graded a bluish stone on her ring finger. She dabbed the wedding band with a thumb. "My husband and I are separated. We used to meet on a whim…a suggestion in a Christmas card: *Let's get together somewhere.*"

She unwrapped her legs and stretched a good five feet ten of herself. "Bread? Save you a trip."

"Think I will," I said. "Thanks."

"Ciabata or sandwich bread?"

"Umhh," I said.

"Big holes, small holes?"

"I'll have the holes you're having," I said.

"Stan," she said. She nodded at the guy over there.

Stan was considering something coming out of the ceiling. "Isolating the long-term possibilities of a breakthrough idea from the day-to-day ideas," I said. "The days win, he tells me."

"I envy you the way you looked at him," she said. "You looked at him twice while you were talking to Donald."

She went to the counter and extracted a hunk of bread. She pulled crust chunks apart from around the air holes. Kept pieces tucked between her fingers.

"You're in Carmel?" I said.

"These thirty-some years. Came up with my father's sister. She took me to Dodgers games. I was very upset when I first experienced the intentional walk. I don't understand to this day the intensity of my reaction. People should go to jail."

Mrs. King draped a leg over a knee, curling the toe around a calf. I noticed I was imitating her buttoned-up posture. I took my turn at the smorgasbord, returning with a farro salad on a wide plate. I used my knees for a table.

"You ever had an enemy?" she said.

"Don't know how to answer that," I said.

"A mortal enemy. You or them."

"I've received sick stuff," I said. I stuck my fork into a collection of miniaturized ingredients, picked out some red pepper and waved the air with it. "Compliments to the chef. Thank you, Adele. Very nice of you."

"I have a mortal enemy out there," she said. "For many years I hid from danger. Imagined danger? Didn't take a chance. Plenty of the hidden me is ensconced in Lady Weary's castle. I once posed a conundrum to an employee: was the point where a river entered the sea the eye of the river or the mouth of the river? It was time for the talking cure. Four days a week on a couch. In less than a year the doctor died of exhaustion. Then water coloring, punching it out with daytime demons on my own two feet. Here I am. I mingle tonight to show myself I can."

"I'm glad you're here," I said.

"Donald took some colleagues to Inyokern, reconnoitering. Set them loose posing as a pair of Seventh Day Adventists on their rounds sharing scripture. They stopped at a home built by Herbert Brucolli in 1926. The 1950 census listed a Gabriella Brucolli, age fourteen, in residence. A woman wrapped in blankets was in the backyard."

"The Second Woman?" I said.

"That's what Donald says.

"He'll take this to higher-ups?" I said.

"And you'll swear on the stand that Emmon and Halder are as clean as the driven snow," she said.

"I see your point. What will the higher-ups say to the statement that a man named William Emmon gave you a house?"

"You two are the higher-ups," she said. "Donald believes in you."

It was going on two weeks since Jade was buried. She had come downstairs to see Robin an hour after bedtime, not feeling well, not doing badly, returned to bed and made it to within an hour or so of first light. Robin had asked for a pow wow down the road, topics he would like to run by me. He needed an extra hand.

] *Chapter 20*

MELISSA'S BRUSH with destiny was all ahead of her. (More about that soon enough.) Stan was already motioning he was heading to bed. Sterling had twirled his last beer bottle. He'd be going to Carmel by chopper with Mrs. King. She insisted we drop by any when.

Stan was brushing his teeth in the bathroom, thinking about something that enhanced a vacant look. A mind open and not open. I was frittering with a battery-operated airport clock in the corner of the bedroom, still on daylight time, way past the occasion to set it an hour backwards; i.e., we fall backwards leaving daylight time. The clock was next to an oil of Edward IV at the moment he was crowned in Westminster Abbey on June 28, 1461, an item left in partial payment of my services.

Stan came to the door to the bathroom, or reversing perspectives, to the door to the bedroom. I was bent at the waist in a robe, rummaging in a drawer for AA batteries, in some curiosity as to how I'd be steering him if I said he could help me fix the clock (engineering the initial steps of the mating ritual on our feet). Perhaps not much of a come-on, but for a guy with twenty-twenty vision, my ass better be enough.

The left hand was the leading hand. It went in small circles, sliding gently on the middle of my back, calling attention to nothing much. The fingers on the right were faster, bunching my robe at the hip. So the right side of the robe was rising. Leg began showing while he was kissing my neck. When the active hand was aware there was no underwear above or below the waist, the hard breathing loosened the belt, and the robe opened, and since this coming together isn't anything new in literature, I'll skip some and just say that when I was on my knees I heard my name called simultaneously with a knuckle rap at the bedroom door. The door was wide open, and I mean, why shouldn't it be?

A few seconds of token embarrassment is how we got started; the tumult demanded of French silliness lacked force. Melissa carried softcover manuscripts a step into the room. That's what this was about? Maybe six manuscripts, for God's sake. She piled the lot on the corner of the bed. The one on top was held open to a page with a monster paper clip in an upper corner.

I passed a question to Melissa, first silently and then aloud, "Could this wait?"

"Follow the paper clips," she said.

I tied myself back up in the robe. The covers were pulled back in a sharp edge, hotel style. Stan slipped under a sheet.

Melissa put her finger where the "read that" instruction applied. Saved me a question.

"That" was a list of three names in *Fiji Hill*, a play under the authorship of one Imity Anon. I had a look at the cast: Neil Logan, Upton Truesdell, Weldon King, and said I was finished. In another play, *Occidental Escarpment* appeared over the same byline, Imity Anon. Cast of characters: Oscar Dempsey, Michael Morgan Parker, Hamlin Townes.

"Could we do this in the morning, Melissa?"

"It just hit me," she said.

"You mean Logan and King?" I said, extracting last names from the cast, evidently the only thing to extract, remaining on point, unless this business could just go haywire.

She jumped to, "Upton Truesdell, Neil Logan, Weldon King," the threesome in *Fiji Hill*.

"I see it," I said. "You do have something there."

"*Occidental Escarpment*," she said.

"Grant you that. Hamlin Townes. Who's he?"

"A Lance Townes was murdered in 1982. Paso Robles."

"The paper clips," I said. "They're huge. Never seen them."

"In Bob's box," Melissa said. "All manner of OfficeMax stuff."

"Bob is the Bob of Bob's boxes?" Stan said.

"Elizabeth put me on to Wodehouse," Melissa said. "Said if I like him, I should have a look in Bob's box."

I tossed him *Occidental Escarpment.*

"Aha," he said. "What do we have here? A pen name."

"How do you know?" Melissa said.

"I see," he said. "What's in Bob's box? A trick question?"

"Bob wrote under his own name," she said.

"A man of many hats," he said. "Do you know how to reach Bob? Give him a call. Then again, would he admit to being Imity Anon?"

"I should have said, boxes," Melissa said.

"Remember the boxes we took out of Travis Rhymes's house?" I said.

"Yes, a hat in each box. Sorry. Many pen names, in other words."

"You're sleeping with this guy?" Melissa said.

"He had a nickname in high school," I said. "Member of steel, dumb as stone."

"With the girls, I hope," Melissa said.

With Stan between us holding up his end, Melissa and I were getting along.

"Fine. Imity Anon, whoever that is, has access to a list compiled from unsolved murders," Stan said. "That should be an officer of the law, or…a newspaper reporter. This is their speed."

"The first play was written in 1997, the fourth was 99," Melissa said. "Would names from such a list find their way into plays? With or without a pen name?"

"Do cops write plays, in other words?" Stan said. "What are you getting at?"

"Bob didn't know cops," I said.

"So much for that," he said.

"*Shabby Chic Bench*," Melissa said. "Hamlin Sears Townes, Lee Bachman. Arnold Townes came up," she said. "You want to bet something?"

"Relaxing in the loo, a bullet to the right temple," Stan said. "What about Bachman?"

"Haven't looked yet," she said. "Hamlin Townes reserved a private room in a gentlemen's lounge in Bakersfield. The woman he was with wasn't with him when he was found. To answer your question, the murder was circa May, 1987."

"Circa?"

"May 14," she said.

"So, Imity Anon picked his casts from newspaper articles?" Stan said. "He must have. Mustn't he?"

"A lot of searching for names that don't mean anything," I said.

"*Egress Warily*," Stan read. "What's in a title? I'm thinking, ask Bob."

"Bob has Alzheimer's," I said. "I spoke with the wife recently. They're in Austin, Texas. He's not expected to live long. It's why we moved the boxes from Travis Rhymes's place to the library."

"Not what he wanted to be remembered for?" Stan said.

"Not what the wife wanted him remembered for," I said. "She asked me to destroy the lot. Send her the bill."

"Would she know who Anon is?" Melissa said.

"If he was Bob's friend and also a guest at their home, maybe."

"Also?" Stan said.

"A random visitor at a department party, no," I said. "Actually, now that I think of it, he'd have to be close faculty, and even then...I can't think of a reason Bob would have to identify Anon as a fetish playwright. Not to the wife. Not to anyone. He wouldn't."

"Who you gonna ask where these names come from, then?" he said.

"Any suggestions?" Melissa said.

"In what sense?" I said.

"Send a note to Sterling," Stan said. "He can see if the other names match the pattern."

"They will." Melissa said. "*The Swing at the Gates of Eternity*". I'll have a look."

"I'm meeting a kid tomorrow," Stan said. "We're working on a problem. I need sleep."

] *Chapter 21*

THE LADY IN the campus safety office turned the green
sheet of paper in my direction. She circled a rectangle in
red pen, poked her pen at the window behind me, and x-ed the
paper at a spot that indicated a location just outside the window.
She connected the x to the rectangle with a continuous red arc.

"Follow Campus Road to your first right. Then a right. Park
heading into a space. Leave the green paper on the dash above
the steering wheel, facing up. Be sure to lock the doors, and if
the lot's full, please be patient. You're free to park until noon.
There's a half-hour grace."

Occidental College was built on a side of a hill. I parked,
changed shoes, and hiked Campus Road up and over a crest to
where a sidewalk passed downslope through a tunnel in a hedge.
It was a warm December day, but not hot. I got my jacket off and
tied the arms around my waist. A sweat had started. I pumped
my blouse to get some cool air next to my skin. I tucked the
university map in my back pocket, and took the right turn where
the sidewalk became two worn dirt paths. It was the only place
I could have missed a turn in a dubious excursion that I would
no doubt eventually be referring to as a waste of a day. Two days,
actually. I would be checking in this evening for an overnight in
the Hotel Bel-Air.

Where the right fork made its long roundhouse turn back to the campus was the Swing at the Gates of Eternity. I'd seen the tree, the swing, a sliver of the view beyond, on Google Maps. I didn't have to be anywhere soon. I left the path for bushes at the edge of a drop. On the other side were a couple of candy wrappers in bushy enclaves. The valley beyond included an arty mosaic of homes sprinkled in the not-so-far-off surrounding hills. The swing gave the same appreciation in motion that I'd experienced in still shots. The special effect of the usual in the unusual setting was a reminder of a child's swing set I'd seen in a long-abandoned desert camp.

At the bottom of the path I passed the so-called shabby chic shady bench. A bunch of boards under a shade tree, perhaps torn off a decent bench, were stacked haphazardly for effect. A metal plate on a rock stated I was on Fiji Hill. Around and down to a paved road was, from the parking lot to here, all of a quarter hour.

The Academic Commons was a name on a building. I entered that building to get further on to the Mary Norton Clapp Library. At the information desk I asked for directions to the library reference desk. I wasn't a member of the Oxy community. It didn't matter. I didn't need an account to ask a question.

At the library, three students on their side of a long, wide counter were into something with a woman in the inner staff area. On the wall across from her was a glass-enclosed historical display. A woman—a student possibly, but not of student age—holding a notebook in front of her chest, arms folded, like a student anyway, was having a look at a photo of a man in a suit and tie smiling with a shovel. The first shovel full of dirt. Where it all started.

"Are you in line?" I said.

"No, taking a minute for a look. I was a student here, long ago. You?"

"Just waiting my turn," I said. "I have a quick question."

The room was suddenly quiet. Two of the students at the counter had left. The third, a young woman, was waiting silently.

The lady on the other side of the counter she'd been talking to was bouncing glances around on something online, jotting data on a pad. She came back to the counter and said that what she wanted existed at the University of North Carolina, and nowhere else that she could find. The student could try interlibrary loan; if not, see if they'd make a copy at UNC. They wouldn't let go of the book.

I stepped to the counter. I waited for the lady to give me her attention.

"How can I help?"

"I'm looking for a writer," I said. "He wrote plays. The titles indicate he might have been, or might now be, on the faculty here. I only have a pen name: Imity Anon. He wrote four plays for a private audience. The titles are *The Swing at the Gates of Eternity, Fiji Hill, Shabby Chic Bench,* and *Occidental Escarpment.*

I took my hands off the counter and sagged a little. "That's it."

The lady, a senior employee but a good ways from retirement, perhaps fifty and some, turned her face to the side, shook her head a bit, and didn't say anything near to what I thought she would say.

"What's in the plays that interests you?" she said.

"I wanted to know how he chose the names of his characters."

The woman put a twirl in the pencil she was holding. "Not an easy question. You might almost be under the impression these were geography-based texts. But those wouldn't be dramatic works." She frowned. "These titles are dramatic works?"

"I'd call them dramatic. Not great works, but they'd come under that general heading."

"Odd titles," she said. "Then again: *A Streetcar Named Desire.* You wouldn't visit New Orleans to locate the author."

"Tennessee Williams was there," I said. "There might be a watering hole he was known at."

"A lot of writers have been through Oxy," she said. "A documentary on the movies filmed here was showing in Pasadena a few years ago."

"Anon was drawing attention to Oxy, or to himself in this place," I said. "Tennessee Williams was being cute?"

"You think so?" she said. "*Cat on a Hot Tin Roof?*"

"Hard to say how a writer points a way into a story."

"That's a shame you don't have Anon's real name," she said.

"I came along after the performances. Playgoers are scattered to the four winds."

"I like your guess," she said. "Your anonymous writer offered a gateway into his private life."

"Occidental has its memories," I said.

"For a lot of us."

"These plays," I said. "A Hollywood fellow was in attendance. Finding him won't be easy, and I'm not that motivated."

"What do you do?" she said.

"I *was* a professional dominant."

"Ah," she said. "Mr. Anon. I was wondering: the plays touch on the profession. Well, all I can say is that if he's one of the faculty, I can't think of how I might direct you. Sorry."

"Thanks for your time," I said.

A wide walk divided the campus. On my way to the car, I stopped at the student union for an early nibble. In the student store I bought a card for Stan—a toddler puzzling over a doughnut linked to a hook out of reach—and mailed it at the campus post office. I'd see him before the card would. I stood to one side on the stairs thinking about what I would have made of myself had I had four years at a place like this. What a gift. Not to everyone, of course, but it would have meant a lot to me.

As I was coming off the bottom step, a remote "Hi" sounded somewhere, no need to place it, it couldn't be for me.

A moment later a voice, familiar, or maybe not, said to my back: "I didn't get your name."

I turned, saw nobody, and turned the other way. A woman was pointing a finger at her chest. "We met at the library. I'm glad I found you."

"I'm sorry," I said. "Where did we meet?"

"You asked if I was waiting in line," she said.

Then I recognized the lilac blouse and gray and brown hair: the woman in the library.

"Your mind was a thousand miles away," she said.

I said, "Hi," an afterthought.

She looked at the sack I was carrying. "You're having lunch?"

"I was going back to my car," I said.

"I tried the visitor's center." She gestured to higher ground behind her: *up there.* "I asked two people if they'd seen a tall blonde in jeans and white blouse. That's all I had. I thought I'd missed you."

That blanked me. Missed me for what? Confusion must not have come across as a brush off. A minute was there for us.

"If you have a second," she said. "*Eagle Rock* was an unusual mystery of sorts. They made a movie out of the book. Wrecked the story, par for the course." She held up her phone. "I looked up the author, Nathan Lagersfeld. You might want a look."

"Elizabeth," I said.

"Margaret," she said. "At the library," she said, "while I was listening, the novel *Mildred Pierce* came to mind. After you left, that's what stuck. Or, I should say that's all I had. I wanted to talk to you. I needed a reason. James M. Cain couldn't be your writer, though. He died in the seventies."

"What's wrong with talking about *Mildred Pierce*?" I said.

"I felt silly, bothering a stranger," she said. "Then I remembered, there was a James M. Cain retrospective in the *L.A. Times* about five years ago. In the article I recall a comparison of the character Mildred Pierce to Ethel Ridgeway in *Eagle Rock*."

"James M. Cain. I like him." I brushed her elbow. "If you have time, let's have lunch."

"Where were you thinking of going?" she said.

"Where do people talk about Ethel Ridgeway around here?"

The intention of getting an agreement on track might have kept her from steering. We spent a little time affording each other an opening suggestion.

"Do we have time for me to grab something?" Her eyes walked up the steps to the door. There was a breath, not hard, not soft, a look I took to be a consideration of how long she would be asking me to wait for her.

"I'll be here," I said.

She went up the stairs to the student union, and in ten minutes came down with a sack, same kind as mine.

She was tall, almost as tall as me. She didn't make herself up. Her hair was brushed straight to the shoulders. No curls. Gray streaks were multicolored gray. The left side was clipped clear of her brow. A thin cluster of gray-whites made a line at her left cheek, covering an ear, the whole head at the moment being mostly pale yellow. A quiet blonde, but you wouldn't call her a blonde and leave it at that, the way I'm known as a blonde. The connotations weren't there, in spite of a body that set a fast pace. She would be energetic right up to a few years of the end. Her life had given her a face without lines, but the glow of twenty had gone out. In her eyes was a lot of caution.

"You know your way around Occidental," I said. "You're a graduate?"

"Class of ninety-three. Had a roommate with a condition. That got us a primo room in Haynes my last two years. Obama got our room after us. There's a plaque on the steps up there. If you'd like…?"

"Perhaps later," I said.

"I could climb out of the covers into an unforgiving morning; two minutes, and I was asleep on a chair in class. How's that for the art of not cutting class?"

"You teach here?" I said. "You look like faculty."

"I read on benches. A few kids say hello. They're being friendly, respectful to the old girl. If not yet, then someday I'll have acquired the ultimate reputation: the old loony. A divorce left me a house a mile and a half from here, on the other side of Figueroa. A pleasant walk down Yosemite. I go to the library for newspapers. But that's not the real reason I'm here. The campus has the pull of an endless book. Each day, another chapter."

On the way up the hill to the swing we checked that's where we were going. So I was returned.

"You could sit in the swing and be the sorrowing old man of the painting," she said. "I looked into eternity often, but I never hopped on. Afraid the ropes would break."

"Clever idea," I said, "putting a frail-looking swing at the edge of a slope."

"It was here ready for me when the second half of my life rang its bell. I looked up the Van Gogh painting. Poor Vincent. There's a debate now: did he kill himself, or did some angry farmer settle a dispute."

"The truth ought to stay that way?" I said.

"God, how stupid," she said, in a flash of anger.

"The things that upset us?" I thought. I was smiling faintly.

"I'm sorry for snapping," she said. "It's why I live alone. I'm easily offended. Please, don't you be too. You've no way of knowing what's important to me. I'm deeply sorry. It won't happen again."

"I offended you. We could look at it."

"Remarks are always hitting me wrong," she said. "I'm sorry."

"You know," I said, "a difference of opinion is in the conversation. Might be interesting to see where it takes us."

"I'm attracted to you," she said.

"You want to do what about it?" I said.

"We can't do it here."

"We can explore our thoughts here. Do I sound like a shrink? I talk like this."

"I'm not so nervous now," she said.

We got off our feet on the panoramic version of eternity, spread out the contents of a couple sacks, and toasted togetherness with a clink of paper cups.

"Nathan Lagersfeld was a movie writer most of his life," she said. "There's the writer connection you're looking for. You said you were a dominatrix? The subject matter of your plays might be of that sort?"

"What's *Eagle Rock* into?"

"A woman with a fierce fire to bathe in worship on a pedestal. Lagersfeld latched onto Mildred Pierce for the design of the decline and fall."

"What went wrong?" I said.

"Ethel, quite the elevated society dame in her own mind, on top of the world, becomes a mother."

"A tragedy guy," I said, "no onwards and upwards."

"The movie's claim to fame is its opening scene, so beautiful. The father in an Orthodox church, consecrating his newborn daughter above his head to the light of a stained-glass window. In the next scene we have a disagreement over the girl's name. The difference of opinion goes in Ethel's favor. The arc of the story."

"Oodles of quality time between Ethel and her daughter coming up," I thought.

I looked up Lagersfeld on my phone and scrolled to the novel *Eagle Rock*. "Catchy cover," I said. A woman, pulling on the second of a pair of leather gloves, was focused ahead of her on a point beyond the edge of the cover, apparently the point occupied by the coming recipient of her attention. Her hand was within inches of a whip fallen in a lazy S on an octagonal table. The table was loaded with tomes. The room was a library, the revelation therein being classical forms of sexual excitement in the classical places of learning.

A bite of tuna salad and two swallows. "Ethel whips her way to the summit?"

"She whips Charles Fregis. That's in the book. The movie wanders off, every which way. You've seen *The Great Dictator*?"

I mumbled and nodded. Go on.

"She's in a thrift shop, and there's a whip on the counter. In the book she buys it. In the movie, she shuts everything out. She grips it, twists it around, getting a high, like savoring an incredible experience she had once. She hands it back to the saleswoman with the line that cracks up the audience: 'I'd like you to show me what to do with this.'"

"Like Chaplin with the globe," I said.

"Like Chaplin with the globe," she said. "Although Chaplin knew what to do with it. Lagersfeld used to live right over here across the path."

"Thanks," I said. I clicked ADD TO CART. Expected delivery, two days. The superordinate wonder of the world: books falling from the blue sky.

We parted at the path. "We'll meet again someday." She waved and turned downhill. I picked the uphill where I'd left the path earlier.

] *Chapter 22*

IF I WAS GUESSING points of the compass correctly on Google Maps, what might be called the Occidental escarpment around here would be the landfall off the promontory northeast of Occidental college. As such the reference by Imity Anon would be where Escarpa Drive made a sharp turn, the point of greatest curvature pointing northeast. I picked up my car. It was a minute to where I pulled into a dirt cutoff at 1952 Escarpa—the address listed for Nathan Lagersfeld.

It was a pristine sky, and one of those days when the blue of the sky was the paler blue they can get here around the time of the Rose Bowl game over in the Arroyo Seco (meaning a *dry stream* in Spanish.) A low white fence along the edge of the asphalt sported red reflectors and rose bushes. On the other side were high trees close to the fence, and low trees not far beyond that looked like well-developed trees that were rooted a good ways below the high trees. A blue trash container and a brown trash container made off-kilter angles to the fence. The trash had been collected. It was getting on to afternoon. The owner hadn't taken the trashcans in yet.

A newish Honda was parked nose-out in a short driveway laid with planks. The driveway was level from the street to a pair of small windows in deep green trim shaded by green awnings.

To the left of the drive was a wood walkway supported on square wooden pillars bolted to cement pilings. Before I stepped off the drive, I went down on my haunches to get a look under the house: metal pipes supported on cement pilings a long way down. The drive, the house, the narrow veranda around the house, was what they were. Hard to say what you'd be insuring. If the thing fell, you couldn't expect to live to collect.

I tapped a brass doorknocker. No sound returned for a moment. Then a sliding door sound, and a glass set on a glass table? The door opened inwards. A man stood behind the screen door, taking his time making some sense of me. Might have been fifty. Might be six foot two. Might be two hundred, a little more rather than a little less. A muscleman T-shirt (Lisa's Gym) showed off muscles with bulges and a faded beach tan. No visible tattoos, no jewelry, no visible body damage. He was a man smiling whose mind was smiling. He couldn't quite formulate a question.

"Hi, I'm Elizabeth," I said. "If this is a bad time…"

"I am busy," he said.

"I was hoping I could meet someone who knew Nathan Lagersfeld."

His considerable shoulders sagged to one side. "Sorry."

"Anyone in the neighborhood, maybe?" I said.

"Never met anyone in the neighborhood," he said. "I would imagine, yeah, people knew him. He built the house. Long time ago."

I moistened the edges of my lips, easing a foot backwards, hardly sales technique, but I must have given off that vibe.

"What are you selling?" he said.

"Nothing. I just wanted to ask a question. This address is listed as belonging to a Mr. and Mrs. Nathan Lagersfeld," I said. "Might she be available?"

"She's living with her son," he said. "You know the area? L.A.?"

"Somewhat."

"Thousand Oaks," he said. "It's a drive, is what I'm saying.

A good hour and a half this time a day. I guess you know what you're in for."

"It was a long shot," I said.

He had been maintaining a hold on the edge of the door. He let go. He was forgetting he was busy.

"What's the question?" he said. "I could give her a call?"

"It's not that kind of question," I said.

"You lost me," he said. "You want to ask her yourself?"

I had come a long way. I put my chin on two fingers.

"If you're cautious about strange men, you can lock yourself in your car," he said. "I'll pass the phone through a slit in the window."

"You're being awfully generous," I said.

"If this is a scam, I'd like to see how it comes out."

He was a safe bet. I went in. He shut the door behind me.

Inside he whistled, a quick up and down. "Boy. If my lady showed up…"

"I'm just borrowing your phone to make a call," I said.

He shut his eyes, "Yeah, and she's had three husbands. You want to sit, or… Before you call, how about your question? I'm gonna hear anyway. You wanna sit? A beer?"

"Your veranda is fine," I said. "You mind?"

"You wanna jump? Kidding." He slid the door shut behind us. "Flies. It gets warm, and they're over here freeloading."

Down below, the tops of houses went under treetops up to hills and then up the hills, separated by gaps running crosswise. In one direction far off were the San Gabriel Mountains, or maybe the foothills thereto.

"I was sipping rum and Coke," he said.

"Thanks, I'm driving," I said.

"So what's your question?"

"Lagersfeld," I said. "Are you familiar with his work?"

"Couldn't go that far. Seen his name on scripts. I work with the son, Dan. This place was unoccupied, and I rented it. As you see, not bad."

"Lagersfeld wrote four plays," I said. "The names of his characters match the names of real people, names that came up under tragic circumstances. I want to know where he got the names."

When I turned back from the view, he was in a folding canvas chair. He put his glass in the drink holder and put a knowing look on me.

"My first guess: You're pitching a script," he said. "How'd you get this address?"

"You in any mood to believe what I say?" I answered.

"What can I say?" He stuck his fingers together and pulled his hands back and forth, emphasizing a struggle. "It's not your script?"

"Someone sent me," I said.

"Who's unhappy? I prefer you." He finished a gulp. "What's your offer? Better yet, forget that. What does he think I can do for him? It is a he?"

"Scam?" I asked.

"Pitch Perfect Solutions," he said. "Our racket. You compose your masterpiece, you turn it into a script, you send it to us, we promise an Academy Award–winning producer will seriously give it the attention it deserves. Don't forget our fee. Can't miss." He fished out an apple chip from his drink and sucked on it. "Back to how'd you get my name?"

"I still don't have your name."

"Alternatively," he said, "send us the book, and let one of our editors turn it into a script for the editorial fee—seven grand this week—and everything same as before. Can't miss."

"You're a scriptwriter?" I said.

"Scriptwriters never lie. And like that old scriptwriter in the ballad, they just fade away."

Down below there was a junkyard abutting a school parking lot. I pointed at a sign in the junkyard. "What's that?" I said.

He turned his head. "What's what?"

"That sign," I said. "Ulysses."

He stood. "That junkyard?"

"The sign. It's leaning on that whatsamacallit." I stretched my arm out, definitively pointing. "Ulysses, block capitals."

"Yeah, what about it?"

"Underneath," I said. "You see: Molly Bloom, Stephen Dedalus."

He went inside. Through the screen he said, "You want an apple?"

"How about a half?" I said.

"Sliced?"

"Thank you," I said.

Slices were lined up in a cereal bowl advertising Catalina Island. He kept his glass in his lap. "They had a Joyce festival here at Oxy," he said. He fiddled with his phone. "The Ulysses Centennial: February second, twenty-two. Missed it."

"Is that junkyard down there part of Occidental?"

"You got me there," he said. He gave me the left-eyed raised eyebrow. "The dope who sent you doesn't deserve you."

"I'm the best," I said. "Payment in advance. Don't get me on no flipping percentage."

"So no names," he said. "What was it you wanted?"

"A question for Mrs. Lagersfeld," I said.

"At least I'll get your name."

He dialed, put the phone on speaker. A courteous voice was slow. "Mrs. Lagersfeld speaking."

He reached his phone to a small table. I was on. "Hello, Mrs. Lagersfeld. My name is Elizabeth Cromwell. I'm visiting Eagle Rock in regards to some plays I believe your husband wrote. I was wondering…"

"He was just a kid," she said. "They were all just kids." A wavering voice on a swing. There was nothing else to say.

"Thanks Ms. Lagersfeld," he said. "Sorry to bother you." He hung up. "I know the rest of the story, if you're interested."

"Shoot."

"Nathan Lagersfeld's father signed for him on his seventeenth birthday. He left for basic training at Camp Roberts the next morning from Union Station. His father gave him six bucks. Money was never important again. He promised his parents he would come back. After basic training he joined the Army Air Corps. They sent him to the gunnery instructor's school at Las Vegas, Nevada. He was a very bright boy. They changed their minds. They sent him for navigator's training. When he got his wings, he was stationed at Wheelus Army Air Force base in Tripoli. At the base high school he found a lifelong interest in writing. Operation Tidal Wave went out to bomb the Ploesti oil fields. He was a navigator on a Liberator, the *High Flying Swallow*. August first, 1943. They ran into thick cloud cover. The strike force was under strict radio silence. The *High Flying Swallow* went off course. A letter came to the Lagersfeld home, the letter they dreaded. Nathan was missing in action. That's the way it remained until the second letter arrived. That one was from Nathan. He'd been found in the wreckage of his plane by Yugoslav communists. Hope that helps you."

"Thank Mrs. Lagersfeld," I said, "for her husband's service."

"Oh, I forgot. Nathan was born in Glendale, March 3, 1925, died April 20, 2017, the third of four children of Leo and Golda Lagersfeld, of Glendale, California. You'll need that, too. And he graduated from the University of California, Los Angeles."

"What are you working on?" I said.

"*The Swedish Snowbirds*," he said. "A young adult thriller set in Key Largo. Action packed. Tell your author I can get him a reading from Aaron Sorkin."

"I'll let him know," I said.

"For the record," he said, "Nathan's list of credits includes a collaboration with Tippi McRae on *Hell's Peak*, an MGM picture. He died of complications of emphysema. And by the way, drop me a line someday, David Labowitz. I'd like to know what this was all about."

"You got it, David."

] *Chapter 23*

I WORKED MY WAY down to Eagle Rock Boulevard and made a quick dash to a turn north back uphill to where I expected the stilts under Lagersfeld's place would appear on the Occidental escarpment. The house with the Joyce sign in the adjoining junkyard was a one-story/two-story wood-frame fusion that had seen its share of adding on. Everything else in the neighborhood was single-story stucco, very old fashioned in style but clearly a generation newer than the original style. No surprise that the house was set sideways to the main drag, its postal address attached to a short street oriented to some pioneer's esthetic when everywhere was flowers, now a short block that dead-ended at the base of a hill.

Large lots with houses set close together filled the curb under the purview of NO PARKING signs that eliminated a half-dozen perfectly good places to park. A dog took umbrage at my stopping in the access drive to a junkyard. The sun extracted a reddish hue in the dog's shoulders, but he was your basic short-hair black, shiny lean teeth, mean and no fat. I sat and thought about it: he may know a secret way out.

I pushed my car door open. That's all I did. The whole warning system went from a steady growl to a higher gear, a vicious gurgle showing willingness to tear flesh to shreds. To nature born. I might be convinced this breed could be raised with a kind disposition, but I'd have to be shown a live one who shook hands and left it there.

Forget about picking up some rocks. I pulled into a spot a block and a half away, locked up and snuck around unseen to the front door of the junkyard house. Didn't need to knock; the dog was on the other side of a flimsy door, at it again, the same racket vibrating the door. The racket was heard across the street. A man over there in overalls came outside. He left the front door open, stepped off his porch, and took a few more steps toward the street and let it go at that.

"What's going on?" he said.

"I wanted to ask a few questions. Is the owner around?"

He cupped his left ear, "The owner?"

"The owner," I said. "I'd like to ask a few questions."

Without letting go of his ear, he said, "I'm the owner."

I walked closer, stopping at the curb on my side of the street. "I was trying to get a look at the backyard. Your dog is one way against that."

"You woke him up. Good you didn't try to get your fingers through the fence."

"Some people try to calm him down?" I said.

"Read the sign: 'No trespassing.' He means it. What're you looking for?"

"I was up there on the hill," I said. "I saw a sign that says 'James Joyce' leaning against a pile of things. I wondered if you had other signs like it."

"You're sort of fuzzy from here," he said. "I can't cross the street without glasses."

"I'd be happy to cross the street," I said.

"Better than I have to go in and find my glasses."

He hadn't shaved, he hadn't bathed, he hadn't changed his overalls for quite a few meals. Been a while since he clipped his nails. No visible dog bites.

"You're good-looking," he said. "You're an artist. They used to come by for distressed wood. Needed it for their projects. What kind of project you doing?"

"I'm looking for an inspiration," I said. "I'm searching for signs with names on them."

"Inspirational names?"

"Not necessarily."

"You mean like a memorial, like a bunch a kids that won a championship?"

"That could do it," I said.

"Well now, they had a baseball field in Arcadia. They wanted it fixed up—some fresh bleachers, get the splinters out, a new fence in the outfield, tear the old clubhouse down for a place they could install new showers. The suburban Junior League. That was in the nineties."

"Anything before that?" I asked.

"With names?" He put a finger in his ear and rotated. "There was a bronze plaque on a stone down the left field line. One name on it. Served with Teddy Roosevelt, it said, a Rough Rider. He was killed on San Juan Hill."

"One name?" I said.

"Not sure if he died on San Juan Hill, or what. We left the stone where it was. Could still be there."

The whole memory seemed odd to him, as the past comes back in isolated bits.

"The name was in two places," he said. "He was also on a memorial to his regiment. I'm thinking the rest of his regiment must of survived. He was the one killed. That's why he got his own plaque."

"Where was this regimental memorial?" I said.

"On the other side of the fence," he said. "A sign. The construction people told us, take it."

"You wouldn't remember the names, I guess?"

He bowed his face. "The one soldier that was the same? No. Can't say I do. Might be Palmer."

"Could I have a look, you think?"

"Gone," he said. "Solid wood. Two girls wanted to make a door out of it for their studio."

"Local girls?" I said.

"Must a been. They came around, took things for inspiration. Artists."

I STOPPED at a service station to decide which way I wanted to enter the freeway. I looked up Arcadia. There it was: Parker Field. Okay, a Parker. Would this be named for the poor exuberant who fell on San Juan Hill? A much more likely Parker was the railroad tycoon in Arcadia history who named the city from a vision of heaven on earth, and, to the point, left a fourth wife remembered for her charitable causes in the compact Arcadia history brochure.

Rattling around in a collection of factoids in the Arcadia library, I found the Arcadia Land Corporation, an enterprise listed as belonging to a Colonel Dodd, then to a Petra Weber.

I knew the rest. The corporation descended into the hands of William Emmon, who ghosted the business for Ingrid Halder from a desk in Sebastopol.

I opened a text from Stan:

> *Finished today with the kid I'm tutoring. We got onto an unsolved problem. He wants to work on it. We don't have a chance, but his mother is paying me for something or other. We meet again Monday, next week.*

I started a text, erased it, and called instead. Stan picked up. We missed each other. I said so first, so he asked what I wanted to do about it.

"I'm sleeping alone tonight in the Hotel Bel-Air," I said.

"I'm looking at flights from Oakland to LAX." A pause. "God, this is makeable. There's a plane at half past five." Another pause. "A car gets me to the Hotel Bel-Air in under half an hour."

"I'm getting more and more fond of you," I said. "What airline you using?"

"Just a second." A pause. "I'm booked on American. Arrives six fifty-seven."

"See ya."

THERE were a dozen of us inside the terminal, waiting along the wall at the side of the down escalator. A girl of about six was informing a dog cradled upside down in her arms that he should be happy, Daddy was almost here. Stan was with two men at the head of the stairway leading the descent to the stepping-off point, where they recombined waiting for Stan. He said, "Elizabeth" to them and, "Gavin and Scott" to me. Recovering which was which, I said, "Scott," and got a smile back. Gavin provided his full name, Gavin Lowrie and, making full-body eye contact, it was a pleasure to meet me. Stan counted to three, giving me the opening to offer a ride; but, as I discovered, the three of them were waiting to see how a tentative plan, thrown together on the flight, might shake out.

"Gavin invited me to give a talk tomorrow at Caltech," Stan said.

"You want me to stay?" I said.

"Gavin wants us to talk to the math chairman," he said. "There might be a position open."

"I'll call tomorrow morning," Gavin said. "We can get an announcement out then. You'll get an audience. A few faculty, some grad students. I can reserve a room for you at the Athenaeum."

Stan looked at me. It was up to me. Gavin interrupted the look. "I'm sure there's a room available tonight. You'll be my guest."

I nodded. "I'd like that."

Stan's turn. Where from here? "The talk's at four, I guess," he said. "Would two nights be possible?"

Gavin looked above his head briefly, dialed a number, waited, and dialed again, waited. Third dial, an answer. "Hi. This is me, yes, great. Look, I'm at LAX with Konstantin Arnold. Yeah. Okay. He's giving a talk tomorrow. I can't reach Betty directly. Could you get a room for two guests? Yes, one room, tonight and tomorrow at the Athenaeum. A double. Konstantin Arnold. He's with a friend. And could Betty get an announcement out tomorrow? Yes, if possible." He looked at Stan and decided to leave a question open. "Title to be announced."

"So," Gavin said, "you want the corner of California and Hill. Pull into the lot from either side. Park anywhere that doesn't say, 'Absolutely no parking ever.' Plenty of spaces this time of year. The guy at the check-in counter will give you a permit. He has a list of places to eat. I should be on campus by eleven tomorrow. You have my number. Anything comes up, give me a call."

The kiss in the car just about answered his question: Did I want to get in the back seat? It did stop me from starting the car a minute.

"Any leads today?" he said.

"There's a baseball field in Arcadia," I said, "Parker Field. I was told there's a plaque on a stone along the left field line. It memorializes a member of the Roosevelt expedition to Cuba in the Spanish–American War. It might still be there. On the other side of the fence was a list of soldiers in his unit. That one was scavenged for the wood it was on." I put my hand on his pants. "I could go on."

"Not bad," he said. "You hit a single."

"What should I be proud of?"

"You connected to Arcadia. Nothing forced. Perfectly natural."

"You're cheering me up," I said.

"Names on the list, any more hits?"

"Spanish–American War. That's a classic."

He put his seat belt on. "Let's not forget what we were doing."

"Arcadia was once a major agricultural center," I said. "Save that for pillow talk."

] *Chapter 24*

I ENTERED California and Hill as the destination on Google Maps and asked Stan, "What's there?"

"One of the corners of Caltech," he said.

"You met your friends on the flight?" I said.

"An opportunity to quash the rumor: they heard I was dead."

"Gavin mentioned meeting the chairman," I said.

"An assistant professor took a position at Wisconsin for the fall. She asked if she could leave now. There's a position open if I want it. If I take it, I solve problems. It would be a couple quarters, and who's to say what happens after that. Gavin wants me to meet the chairman. He would have to sign off on an offer."

"Gavin said that *we* meet the chairman," I said.

"The chairman would want the opportunity to answer any questions you might have."

"You want the position?" I asked.

"That would be getting ahead of events. The chairman could decide, Stan Who?"

"If I'm understanding what's passing out there beyond the window," he said, "I can't see me living here."

Traffic was spreading itself out across lanes in each direction. I sped up going into a long curve. The voice that turns data into instructions told me to pick one of the two left lanes, get in it and stay there. The lane took a big swing in the direction it ought to, and ran into ten lanes that eventually plopped us into four lanes of a clogged freeway with a new number.

"Seriously," I said.

His hand rested kindly on my thigh. I couldn't very well shut my eyes.

"I'd rather keep our bodies in the same area code," he said.

What vehicles there were in the Athenaeum lot were bunched along the service landing of a Mediterranean-style three-story villa under terra cotta tile. I pulled into a row of empty spaces, turned off the ignition, and looked at chipped gray plaster, a real ancient wall, topped by a wide parapet, the decorative Greek touch.

"How'd your search go?" Stan asked.

"As expected, nothing much," I said. "I'm pretty sure I found the writer I was looking for."

"You'll make Melissa happy. She feels like Archimedes jumping out of his bathtub."

"A guy named Nathan Lagersfeld," I said.

"Where'd you get the name?"

"He wrote a novel, right subject, connects with material mentioned in the plays. I ordered a copy. Something may pop up."

"The names in the plays?" he said.

"It's weird," I said. "An army unit that served in the Spanish–American war put themselves on a memorial plaque that was junked. The memorial's a door somewhere. A fellow named Parker died for the cause. They put his name on a stone in a baseball field in Arcadia."

"Arcadia…as in the Arcadia Land Corporation?" he said. "Petra Weber's baby?"

He fiddled around on his phone. "Now here's a fact: California entered the union in 1850. September ninth. That's late in the year, but they managed a census that year."

"If I ever finish the eighth grade," I said, "I'll know that."

"I bet I knew this once: Lincoln ran in a four-way race in 1860. Lucky Abe. The Democrats were divided three ways."

Our conversations to come? They were calming phrases, an intimate touch without responsibilities for answers. I liked him for that.

"The Spanish–American war," he said. "I can't find a mention under Arcadia. Wait. Possibly this has a bearing: The war was going on five years before Arcadia became a city."

"We passed a grocery on California," I said.

"I'm starving," he said, and went on. "Not what I'd expect. I mean, a bunch of Rough Riders don't get a line in local history?" He looked up, eyes far off. "Arcadia had a racetrack at the turn of the century. It says here: 'A fun-loving population, an economy based on entertainment.'"

"Eat in?" I said.

Coming back from the market we picked up room cards. Stan took a piece of paper dangling from a strip of adhesive tape outside for the car window.

The room had two beds. Dropping our stuff on chairs and tables took a minute. I scooted onto a window seat. Stan took the side of a bed and opened his sack. We didn't need paper plates. The main course came in form-fitted plastic containers.

"Here we are," he said, "a Petra Weber in Sebastopol. The 1950 census. Not there in forty."

"Did we try Arcadia?" I said.

He heard the crisp click of a chip breaking in half. "What kind of chips are those?" he said.

"Yummy."

"What'll you take for a handful?"

I poured a handful for myself, then rolled the sack tight and tossed it.

"Bingo," he said. "Petra Weber in Arcadia in forty, thirty, twenty; not in Arcadia in ten. Where was she?"

"Try Munich," I said. "It's where she met Ingrid."

"Okay. Couldn't stand the old country. Arrived after 1910."

He was looking at a wall and moving his thumbs. "Here's something. Asians could buy marginal land in California. Europeans of good stock could throw an anchor, pick up land with deposits of precious metals."

I poured fizzy water and had a swallow.

"Explain something," he said. "How does a single woman transplant herself half a world away to California, and end up with a land corporation?"

"America," I said. "Wide open spaces and opportunity. An Arcadia."

"Do the open spaces include a basement in San Francisco?"

"It was a speakeasy," I said. "It made money."

"Anything can make some sense," he said. "Where'd the money that made money come from?"

"What's your theory?"

"It gets harder and harder to have one."

I refilled my cup and held it to my lips, sipping. I set that off to the side, and tapped an unwrapped éclair against my nose. A signal: I'm not sharing this.

"You did the search," he said, "and wound up in Arcadia, effortlessly, all very naturally. In physics, that's big. It usually means you better be ready to get knocked off your feet—if you have the guts to face consequences.

"Just a second," he interrupted himself. "What was the name of the second woman?"

"It'll come to me. How about Brucolli? Gabriella Brucolli."

He got his thumbs going. "Wait a minute. There was no Petra in Arcadia in 1910. We knew that. What does that mean?"

"Should I be looking for Cubans?" I said.

"I'm not pushing Cubans," he said, searching. "I'm pushing Arcadia. Arcadia, or bust."

"You're attractive when you're excited."

"Life is worth living at the moment. A hair shy of five hundred souls in Arcadia at the dawn of the century. Just a second. Wow. Brucolli. I suspected this. Nineteen hundred, a Herbert Brucolli."

He pointed a finger at me. "Okay, here's your Herbert Brucolli in the 1900 census: address the Dodd Orchard, Foothill Road, Arcadia, California. And here just might be one of your Rough Riders: Colonel Cameron Edward Dodd. And we got some other names, but no more Brucolli people. He was alone. At least it seems that way."

"No Brucolli children?" I said.

"Not by that name at the Dodd Orchard," he said. "Let's see here. Same gang at the orchard in 1910, minus Petra. Let's try twenty. Yes, saw this before. Mrs. Petra Weber Dodd in residence at that orchard. And guess what? We could have deduced this, you know, where her money came from. Our Lady isn't picking oranges."

"Is she producing offspring?"

"Good question. Okay, wait a minute. Go back a ways. There were two adult women at the Dodd Orchard in the 1880 census, Sarah and Mabel, both twenty-two years of age. The ranch also had a Marianne, age six; a Daphne, age three. Some boys: Randolph, three; Charles, two; Simon, one."

"Dodd was married to both?" I said.

"I would think he actually married neither. There might not be anything to see here. Dodd's a Mormon, say. When did California get the monogamy thing straightened out? Anyway, here's a few additions: an April, age six in the 1890 census, and a Loren, age eight. We did 1900 and 1910. But wait a minute, no Brucolli in 1920. But oooh, no Sarah in twenty either. And no April, and no Daphne. Now that is good. Here's a conjecture…"

"They all left with Brucolli?" I said.

"Not all," he said. "Daphne is still there. But how does Gabriella get the name Brucolli?"

"How?" My question was full of tasty éclair.

"It doesn't look like this Weber lady had any children, not with Dodd, not that they were recorded. And they would be."

"Didn't Donald Sterling say a Brucolli built the houses in Inyokern?"

"Yes, but I can't see how that makes Gabriella a Brucolli," he said. "But Brucolli did finally get himself a woman between 1910 and 1920: Sarah. Mabel stayed with Dodd."

I jumped ahead on my phone. I read off, "Colonel Dodd was in Arcadia in 1930, but no colonel in 1940."

"That's about when we'd expect him to check out," he said. "He died in the thirties. Let's try something. Okay. Lieutenant Cameron Edward Dodd. Service record says he was a soldier in the Civil War, Illinois cavalry regiment. The Colonel died in thirty-three. Yes, here it is in his bio: he died in 1933, Arcadia California. What would you guess? War's over. He heads out to the frontier."

"Could be." I said.

"He left a wife and family in Illinois maybe?"

"It doesn't seem to matter, does it?"

"I don't know, does it?"

"Okay, he went to California after the Civil War. Frontier duty wasn't necessarily the motivation in his blood, but he wound up a big-shot landowner with a gang of loyal followers."

"He missed Little Big Horn," I said.

"Good point," he said. "He wasn't a follower."

"I'm being funny."

"Funny can make a fine point: A man with ambitions doesn't ride off for excitement on the whim of some crackpot glory hound. He settled in California. We know that. When and where…well, no matter. No indication of gold fever. He planted his feet out here as an officer in the U.S. Army."

"A man with a plan," I said. More funny.

"Right on. But not the plan he would have had if he had arrived with a bankroll. He doesn't have enough for a startup in ranching or farming. He's betwixt and between. So what's he got? Well, what was here? Indian duty, settling the tribes on reservations, enforcing jurisdiction, riding herd on renegades."

"Dodd was a soldier," I said. "Joined up with what was left of his regiment."

"What did you say?"

"That I shouldn't have?" I said.

"But you did. Where'd the regiment come from?"

"That man I met living near Occidental. He was on a junk removal job for a renovation project: the baseball park I mentioned. They cleared a sign from the premises. Some artists picked it up at his yard in Eagle Rock for cheap, thought it would make a fine door. He said the names on the sign were a squad in the Spanish–American war."

"Could the family names of the victims of Ingrid and Gabriella be surnames on that sign?" I said.

"Doesn't seem possible," he said. "But you got there. You recall what you were thinking?"

"How I got there? I didn't get there."

"We were going somewhere," he said. "Where were we going?"

"Speculate. While Arcadia was cleaning itself up, Dodd sends for a European wife. He married education, culture. Imported some class for the Dodd Orchard."

"The first war started in 1914," he said. "Petra wasn't with Dodd in 1910, but she's the lady of Dodd Orchard by 1912 or 1913. Dodd already had two wives and seven kids by then."

"How did he bring Petra in as a wife?" I said.

He stirred figure eights in the air with a straw. "Sarah and Mabel weren't white women. No marriage."

"How do you know?" I said.

"Like you say, Dodd had a squad from his Army days. The gang stuck with him, reunions every summer, carousing, the good ol' days alive in the blood. The gang would put up with frontier behavior, but they wouldn't put up with white women treated like whores."

"The names on that memorial were from his old Army squad?" I said.

"It got old and forgotten, and torn down," he said. "Arcadia forgot a man with illegitimate children. Wouldn't want to own up to what was there to come to terms with: a white man's privileges on the frontier?"

"Okay," I said. "The children were there before Petra arrived. She has no questions?"

"There are always *questions*. What's Petra's question? Dodd had his pick of European girls with all the trimmings of culture, born to families of six or so, the dumpier of them lucky if they could marry an apprentice baker. She knew how men and women set up shop. If a young husband had means, he'd run through a mistress or two every few years. If poor, he'd find women after dinner in alleys. Either way, life-threatening risks. Dodd was in his seventies. A made man. Plenty of climate to offer a cultured lady."

"She kept her questions to herself?" I said.

"What did he tell her he wanted in bed? There's a question. All we know is they had no children. She took the offer. Dodd bought himself a dignified position in the New West. You're making too much of how things looked to Petra a hundred years ago. Her first morning, she opened her eyes to a view of orange groves and snow-capped mountains in the background, the California sales cliché. She put in her time quietly, and it was in time all hers. That's how I see her calculating. She must have been quite the impresario. A woman like her with Dodd in her corner would be in a position to avail herself of opportunities that create a fortune in land speculation. In time, with a shirt full and Dodd gone, she could walk back to Munich on water."

I caught up on my phone. I read off, "She was Mrs. Petra Dodd in Arcadia in 1930. She's Petra Weber in 1940."

"She reclaimed her name."

We bagged our trash in one sack and dumped it in a container in the parking lot. I got a heavy coat from the trunk. He was in a T-shirt, not impressing me.

"I'll show you something," he said.

I followed him to a brick walk at the front of the Athenaeum. Looking away from the Athenaeum, he pointed down the walk through a long row of trees as tall as the buildings on both sides.

"Straight ahead at the end of this walk there used to be an

administration building. It was a big building for the time. It had a fire escape you could see from here. At the end of lunch, the faculty would leave the Athenaeum and they would see the fire escape the whole time they were walking—all the time until they split right or left to return to their offices on the other side of the building. But nobody saw *what* it was. There was a famous chemistry professor here desperately searching for exactly that structure, but it was in his mind that DNA had another structure."

"I see it: The fire escape was a strand of DNA."

"They tore the building down," he said. "They wanted to put a pond in the center of campus, make it look pretty."

"An old building would be dangerous in an earthquake," I said.

"I grew up with a dog," he said. "From my backyard I could walk him to a park. Now, we both knew it was cooler in the morning and in the evening. At noon in the summer he wouldn't go with me to the park. It was too hot. In some sense he knew that the thing in the sky that dissuaded him from walking at noon went around the place where he was living. He was comfortable when he didn't notice it, when it was over there, or over there. So that's *what he saw*, which is exactly what I saw. But I could never ever get him to care that the place he was living at was in constant rotation, and if he thought about it, it would explain the apparent motion of the hot thing in the sky."

"He didn't tell you," I said.

"Conversely, my dog lived a happy life.

"You can bet Dodd did his due diligence with money barons," he said. "Bad reputations flock together, drink together."

] *Chapter 25*

I T WAS IN THE MOMENT when the light was showing around the edges of the curtains that Stan said, "You feel like talking?" We were in separate beds.

"I got a message," he said. "Gavin says not to buy a house."

"You got the position."

"The message would originate with the assistant chairman. He wants to meet you."

"What do you want?" I said.

"If I take the honorarium and walk, they'll say it's you. What else can they think? I'm unemployed."

"You don't want it?"

"I didn't sleep," he said.

"Seriously," I said, "we take off, and send the news from Fresno?"

"Think of the entertainment value," he said. "We'd be the dinner-table topic for days. I must be into whips."

"You're going to make me cry, Stan. This is too much like you."

We looked in on the self-serve breakfast. I paused at the headlines of complimentary copies of the *Los Angeles Times*, *New York Times*, *Wall Street Journal*. No auguries pronounced from yesterday's market retreat. The inside scoop: who knows? An older woman, backlit by a table lamp, chin on her chest, skimming stuff in a folder, was putting a briefcase in good order. I couldn't have felt more out of place with a baseball hat on backwards boosting axe-tossing at the Oregon Lumberjack Convention.

Stan nudged my arm with his phone. Gavin was leaving West-wood. Expect him at the math department around eleven.

The view from the front patio of the Athenaeum was grass and dorms, and a double row of olive trees. Tennis courts in a sycamore grove were deserted.

The sound of a handcart running on a metal ramp was coming from a loading dock. We turned away from the sound, then walked up California St. against the direction we'd arrived yesterday.

"The students here nurture a good clean rivalry *vis-à-vis* Mass Tech," Stan said. "That's the low-I.Q. institution on the east coast, its inferiority disguised in initials MIT."

"The ones admitted here claim superiority?" I said.

"Of course they applied *there*, but the rejoinder is, 'We all make mistakes; happens to the best of us.'"

"How long will the math department give you?" I said.

"They're doing me a favor. If I don't decide by tomorrow, it wouldn't look good."

"You're past the point of no return?"

"I'm committed to the talk. There's no point doing this and not doing a good job. Not wasting their afternoon will be appreciated. Can't say what damaged my outlook on working for a living, but giving a good lecture is also too much like me."

Stan and I did a loop. He explained the significance of some questions he would have put to Democritus. We went in opposite directions when we arrived back at the olive walk. There was a message for me at the reception desk that included a name, Claire, and a phone number. The fellow at the desk said that the woman who left the message had been waiting for me in the reading room, but she left not minutes ago, leaving a new message: She would be waiting in the parking lot, a dark green Camry.

I went out the side door of the Athenaeum and, sure enough, there she was, a woman leaning against a car. She created a smile and turned it at me as I came down the steps. The car she was leaning against was green. She was showing a gray-bluish hair tint. A silver crucifix filled the valley of a pert chest, a woman admitting to faith at fifty.

"Welcome to Pasadena, Ms. Cromwell." She put a hand out: "Claire."

I stopped within reach. We connected. "You're from the math department?" I said.

"Sort of. You're invited to a smallish get-together, you and Eleice Berthou—Gavin's wife—and me, sticking my nose in, off and on. How about the why on the way over?"

"You'll have to fill me in."

"How about somewhere private?" she said.

"If we keep our voices down," I said, "this is private."

A pause, then she said, "As you wish, to get us going. There was a family discussion, Gavin and Eleice. Gavin hoped that you and Konstantin could make it a foursome with them tonight. That was the hope. Christmas shopping for the relatives was the cause of the argument. I? I can't not answer patient calls during the holidays."

I unwrapped the sentence. "Eleice is your patient?"

"Eleice is struggling with her marriage."

"You lost me," I said.

"Eleice is excited to share a few hours with you."

"Gavin is where?" I said

"Unaware of his wife's struggles. As she sees her struggles."

I needed a minute to let this stuff quit vibrating.

"The English Department," she said. "Eleice is very curious."

A nuttiness began to run through the stare I was giving this Claire. A force of will squeezed the insulting tone out of it, leaving confusion.

"In all honesty, Claire, I didn't expect this."

"Of course not," she said.

"Things are uncertain at the moment. I have to decline."

"Ms. Cromwell, I apologize. I don't cure people, I care for them. I try to find them people they can get along with. Anyway. I like your hair. You do Lana Turner beautifully—very, very hard to pull that off. I see why you're famous."

"I'm not on billboards," I said.

"Eleice was all wrapped up in the injustice of a wifely duty: She *must* meet a math guy, as a *favor* to Gavin. Per usual, it rubbed her the *wrong* way. She bitched at me. She kept bitching. I have a family. It is my Christmas too. I couldn't find the off-ramp. Eventually I asked: Who is this Elizabeth Cromwell? She didn't care, but she shut her fat mouth while I looked you up."

"I can get that," I said.

"I noted you worked from the thick end of the whip. Interested me, too."

"And that shut her up?" I said.

"Generated speculation. She wanted to meet you, a possible career, but on her terms. None of Gavin's business."

"Why put up with this?" I said.

"Why do I do what I do?" she said. "I told you, I like cheering people up."

"You're terrified what she'll do," I said.

"What do you know that I don't?" she said.

"I haven't been thinking about that. Gavin's oblivious?"

"Not entirely," she said. "Doesn't want a showdown."

"He believes in marriage?" I said.

"I wouldn't know how to answer that. When I tell her you're under the weather, she'll look for her cat, and in the fullness of time decide the cat doesn't want to be found, that cats are found when they're ready to be found. Things happen when they happen. She forgets names at parties. She asks friends questions she would ask strangers. Could they use a handout, for example."

"Better she doesn't stay with Gavin?" I said. "How cheerful can she be with him?"

"She has this way of explaining things to herself."

"But the lack of cheer is getting worse?" I said.

"She is in the vicinity of losing her mind, yes."

"Twenty-four-hour care?" I said.

"She comes from privilege. The overhead's covered. She saw Gavin alone in a concert hall playing a piano. The overwhelming brilliance struck her dumb. Wedding bells pealed over the land."

I took a few steps towards the center of the parking lot, a large deserted space. I'm not sure why, but I reversed myself and spent some time opposite Claire, a step further back than before, letting a foot settle down. We matched facial expressions: all in a day's march.

"She married a mathematician," she said. "Not a relationship, but he holds up his end of the structure—the bright shiny structure these days is a whorehouse. Her words."

We nodded goodbyes. She got in her car, backed out and put the car in drive, and stopped. "You're too good for a mathematician. Save yourself."

She rolled her window up, used the same smile she greeted me with, tried and true, and disappeared at the bottom of the drive.

] *Chapter 26*

I WAS SITTING on the Athenaeum steps watching for Stan, expecting him to enter the night somewhere at the far end of the olive walk. I had my eyes cupped in my hands, straining for the slightest sign of motion in filtered lamplight. But Stan was Stan.

A hand cupped my shoulder. Stan sat down next to me, collected a thigh, knee, and shin within the grasp of an arm, the other hand polishing my kneecap. I rested my cheek on a shoulder in a plain magenta T-shirt.

"How'd it go?" I said.

"Success. They both clapped."

"Anything else?" I said.

"You want to go somewhere?"

"What if we have a kid?" I said. "We're not exactly not trying."

"Figure ourselves out?" he said. "Speaking of the Rubicon, you see that Fellini movie?"

"The one with the Rubicon?" I said. "It'll come to me. You hungry?"

He relaxed his armlock on my leg. "Gavin has a problem at home. He can't make the dinner. Fine by me. They want me to stop by in the morning, get the housing thing behind us. Taking over the lease would be neat."

"You don't want to?" I said.

"That would be neater."

We made another raid on the supermarket. Returning to our room didn't appeal. Dinner on the coast was too far. There was good enough light in the Athenaeum parking lot. We pushed our car seats back, spread napkins in laps and, our relationship young and fresh, exchanged samples of each other's nosh. Two bites into a egg-salad sandwich I brought up the position, but not directly.

I fed him a chip. "You've been thinking about math. Do me any good if I ask?"

"When we're in bed again. It's why I want to get this Colonel Dodd guy buried and forgotten. I know what happened: He and his squad slaughtered some Indians who weren't playing by the rules."

"You looked this up?" I said.

"I dropped by the library, looked up Indian massacres in California, post–Civil War. There was a relocation in Eastern California. How many died in the journey? The historical accounts are mute."

"Okay, there weren't any massacres," I said, "but there was a slaughter."

"Massacres can start out as fair fights," he said. "One side gets the upper hand. A white flag is just grist for the mill."

"A slaughter would certainly get its footnote," I said, "wouldn't you say?"

"It didn't make it in history," he said.

"Well, go on."

"The frontier was bountiful for an officer with connections," he said. "Dodd doesn't pepper your imagination with a lot of personality bullet points. Not a complicated figure. He was ambitious. He needed money for connections, which he didn't have. What he had was a reputation as good as money: his good name, a name that sells a service, a tough fellow in the saddle who gets things done. He's an officer, and no reason yet to act the gentleman. Some Indians broke off from their tribe. Went their own way. Got in someone else's way. They would be more than a few families. You don't need a whole regiment for a dozen families. A platoon is enough. It wouldn't be a crime in that environment. Merely keeping good order. Events of the sort wear out their news in a growing country becoming its better self. They get lost. I can't see it any other way."

"Can't see what?"

"There aren't reasons for things. That's for scholastics. There are human upheavals. They create backgrounds for the appearance of who you would think of, and who were thought of, in their time as necessary people."

"Dodd," I said.

"And Petra Weber," he said. "Don't need a picture of her. Beautiful, as in powerful, and wealthy and charming, and clever as necessary with powerful men. Careful with favors. She built an undreamed of fortune. Our story. The orchestra of myth-makers."

"The slaughter?" I said. "How do you see it?"

"How Petra saw it. I'll get to that. Dodd kept a couple of squaws for himself. Sarah and Mabel. Spoils of war."

"He could have bought them?"

"No," he said, "because we know the ending. Work backwards to the murders. It all fills in."

"What about Petra?"

"Dodd had no idea who he married. Petra decided pretty soon after arriving in Arcadia that what she had married into, she liked. Dodd Orchard was a new center of parties, barbeques, reunions, weddings, birthdays, the California social economy knitting itself together around the ownership class. Dodd and Petra. From the beginning, visitors see a winning team. In ten years, Petra is the centerpiece of the Dodd end of the network. You want to talk to Dodd, see Petra."

"She signed the checks," I said.

"She made the deals," he said. "She showed him where to put his X. Her hand was the hand shaking hands, the Dodd business evermore growing into a minor empire. You can be assured, Dodd was in complete admiration of his acumen."

"He married a winner."

"The society ladies set up the society morals they grew up with in the East," he said. "Allowances were made. The New Dodd is accepted. Petra makes a fortune. Life goes on. But Dodd's world splits up. Remember, Sarah and her daughters April and Daphne and Herbert Brucolli split off. I'm sure Petra launched that escape. She showed them how that could be done."

"She owned property in Los Angeles?"

"Might have, but she had money. She could support them, and there were the times. Jobs were there for them during the war. They could support themselves."

"A very destructive act," I said. "Petra's throwing a lot of hate into Dodd's face."

"And telling Dodd she's curious to see what he intends to do about it."

"I'm curious. I don't see it."

"Had to be," he said. "In the beginnings in Munich Petra investigated life in this new land. She surely anticipated a hard land, the law operating on the edges of its limits, decent customs operating tightly within clans. Sticking a fist in Dodd's gut? We're not talking about revenge, an eye for an eye. Not at this point."

He rolled up a sack and squeezed air out of it until it was easy to control, flipping it back and forth, hand to hand.

"There were these old-timer summer reunions at Dodd's place," he said. "Things got bragged about."

"And Petra heard," I said.

"She can piece a lot together if she laughs along with them. But she knows English, German, Latin, and French. We know that. Toss in classical Greek."

"How does that help?" I said.

"She's not afraid of languages. She's curious about the language she's hearing between Sarah and Mabel and their children. And she's the one with responsibilities—the boss. She sat the two women down and learned their language. She behaved towards them as towards friends. Eventually she put her heart out to them. She asked questions in their language. In time—I think it must have been Sarah who broke down—the story tumbled out.

"Okay," I said, "Petra learned about the slaughter."

"As Sarah experienced it," he said. "The fact is forced on you. There couldn't be any other guess that explains the things a guess has to explain. Can you imagine, the first time in forty years Sarah sees it all again, her people cut down all around, some dead, some left dying, crying, twisting into still shapes in the ground, and these strange men with strange tongues, and one of them forces her onto his horse. She could hardly realize that, riding away from that slaughter, she also died, that she'll never see life again. It will be extinguished. In the coming forty years a new shell of existence will wrap her up in a human appearance, human functions, children, and responsibilities that provide pathways that fill up days, that fill up years. And now this woman from another world has come to be with her in the orchard. She has arranged a moment to be alone with her. She could have chosen the moment to be alone with Mabel, but she chose Sarah. She knew Sarah's language. It was the language Sarah's people used when she was alive, and this woman is asking her questions about things that had slipped away. What comes back? It would be a remark about a thing that hadn't slipped away. Maybe it was a string of beads, but the string has a connection. Other things may have connections, but if the wall of not knowing what's on the other end of those connections stayed strong, then the little talk in the orchard would have ended in a shrug. And that would have ended Petra's attempt to know.

"But we know that didn't happen. The life from long ago pushed the wall over. The controls loosened, and all this remembering beads and stuff stopped being words. The sounds of remembering were no longer coming out as words in her language. Petra stopped hearing a narrative. Sarah broke down into the experience of a girl in the middle of a slaughter."

Petra sees," I said.

"She sees all those 'good old days' she heard about at the

reunions," Stan said. "Now she knows who they were good for. Then the beginnings of a cleansing act: Petra recorded all this stuff in her notebook—but in Latin, in case Dodd found it."

I put up a hand. "That's why Ingrid hired Aubrey: Petra's notebook. Aubrey knows Latin."

"If you're willing to put up with another guess, Petra's Latin, handed down to Ingrid as a description of despicable acts to be avenged, is an expression of rectitude; and in Dodd's case, an eternal condemnation. There are certain things a man must not do."

"If he is to remain human," I said.

"Not in Petra's eyes," he said. "Did Ingrid ever say how she met Petra?"

"She never mentioned Petra," I said. "But they must have met in Munich. Where else?"

"Where else? Right."

"Where was Brucolli in all this?"

"The opportunities wars provide. People who hated people have new options. Petra set up a plan with Brucolli. He was gone by the time of the 1920 census. So were April and Daphne, Sarah's girls. They cleared out. Plenty of work in L.A., and that's where they went. April married a man named Henry Penrose. They were living in Inyokern with a daughter, Beatrice, in 1930. And Beatrice had a daughter, born in 1936—and that daughter was Gabriella Brucolli, the woman Ingrid and Emmon met in Inyokern.

"Gabriella was in the Inyokern census."

"Yes. Nineteen-forty with Beatrice, no husband listed; a daughter, Gabriella, age four; and Henry Penrose, husband of April Penrose, Sarah's daughter. Remember, Brucolli built the one house, plus two more—for family. The occupants of one of them didn't match family names. Sarah was in the other one with some woman, a caretaker you'd think."

"Why did Mabel stay with Dodd?" I said.

"Poor health? Attached to Petra. Petra protected them. Ran

the Orchard as she saw fit. Gave Dodd his orders. Shut up and like it, or she tells her story."

Stan twisted sideways and looked at me. "Your loyal chum, Ingrid; I can't see her with you."

"I told you," I said. "Ingrid and William picked me up on a street corner. The next day she took me to the desert and looked me over—for what, to this day I don't know. Was I worth her time? On the next trip to the desert she killed two men who stumbled into our camp uninvited, drunk on the prospect of using their power on a woman. They gave every warning they wanted to play rough. And they would get what they wanted. Once they had what they wanted they would have to make us promise not to tell on them. Or they would see to it we couldn't tell on them. It was either wait and see or don't wait and see. Ingrid stepped out of a shack and shot them. I didn't know it was going to happen. There I was, though, and I'm not saying she was wrong. I pitched in on the digging and gave them the heave-ho. On the ride back to San Francisco, she was at ease talking about the peace she found in the desert."

"All the while letting you know she was referring to her comfort with you?" he said.

"We were comfortable."

"You're an accomplice to murder."

"Comfortable I'm alive."

A minute passed going over the scene for the hundredth time where Ingrid and I left the two creeps buried in the desert. I had been thanking my lucky star for all the years I'd been one of life's winners.

"No doubts why Ingrid set me up in the English Department," I said. "I'm mystified why she let our friendship unravel."

"You must have pulled in," he said. "She saw a danger."

"I didn't want it to happen again that I was compromised by someone's actions."

"Hard to guarantee and keep a few friends."

"The woman I met in Mojave, Monica Parker, she said she wouldn't go into the desert without a gun. I understood instantly.

She wouldn't hesitate if she were in danger. She said she didn't have friends. I understood that."

"I may understand William now," he said.

"William was loyal, but he made it clear I would need to draw a line with him. Cheating on Ingrid was his act of rebellion."

"Cheating, meaning…?" he said.

"Fucking someone else and leaving her out of it."

"You whipped William?" he said.

"That's how they introduced themselves to me," I said. "It was their scene. I didn't realize that in a few months it would be my career."

"Ingrid set you up in business," he said. "Generous."

"And do you see her now?" I said.

"Any regrets about the desert?"

"I don't like to think about it," I said. "You full?" I lifted a nearly full tin of nuts.

"Thanks."

He nibbled into a walnut half, hypnotizing himself.

"You want to ask me something," I said.

"Someday it'll burst out of me, a torrent."

"For now?"

He put his hand out slowly. A fingertip caressed my thumb. "She could have killed you after you dug the grave."

"No witnesses," I said.

"You dodged something," he said.

Suddenly there was Ingrid with a gun in her hand. No sound-track. What else was wiped clear of that night twenty-five years ago? A danger I didn't see?

"She got me right," I said. "She gave me financial security: my own personal cathouse. I never turned her in."

"You can coast from here on," he said.

"Coast? An older woman and a younger man. A woman has a problem with a fact like that. Here's a nightmare: When I'm an old bag, you'll be half my age."

"Scary."

"This could become a long bit of sniveling," I said.

"Something shorter, then," he said. "Petra and Ingrid met in Munich. An older woman and a kid. They clicked. Did Ingrid speak Latin?"

I conveyed a no sound: Not to me.

"English and German, then," he said. "We've been referring to Gabriella as the 'second woman.' That's our sequence: Gabriella got Sarah's story through Petra before Petra met Ingrid."

"Beatrice never told her daughter Gabriella about all this?" I said.

"They all knew Grandma Sarah had some knowledge of something, but they never asked."

"It's hard for me to see Petra going to Inyokern to get a kid to throw in with her version of Murder, Inc.," I said.

"I'm not saying that," he said. "I'm saying Petra was the important influence on Gabriella. Look at her career. Gabriella's a linguist, a college grad. Where'd that come from? And what about a girl growing up tormented, tormenting her mother, demanding to know who in the world she is? Mom doesn't know. Mom never asked about 'those things.' Leave the past to the past, there's nothing anyone can do."

"Too painful," I said. "I'm aware."

"There's always some secret between parents and children. Reliving the pain the one time that Sarah let it out with Petra, that broke the ice, you know, and led to the decision to leave Dodd. Only the start, though."

"So it was Petra who told Gabriella?" I said.

"A child's in torment. Beatrice might have asked Petra for advice. Petra would have been the wise old matriarch. She owned everything. Supported a lot of people. What to do with Gabriella? Beatrice handed the decision off. Petra figured out what the trouble was, and made time to find the moment with Gabriella. After the deluge of the monstrosity in her heritage, the emotional crosscurrents would have been awful."

"Dodd's blood runs in Gabriella's veins," I said. "Bringing back the past *was* a mortal blow."

"Blood was spilled," Stan said. "Petra took names. It's all there in Latin. Not so faint tremors in Petra's journal of *The Wretched of the Earth.*"

"Petra took a blood oath," I said. "The Fanon book: a blood debt passed through generations. Hearing of the slaughter from Sarah, Petra returned to California with a copy of Fanon?"

"Not then, I don't think, but it shows you where Petra was unknowingly steering herself. The misery running in Gabriella, *that* was the second nail, but not the turning point. Gabriella was still a kid. Maybe ten years old? Petra merely hated Dodd before. Afterwards, a whisper would have driven her over the edge. If she could have found the edge."

"She found it," I said. "If someone's open to killing a dozen people who never did a thing to them, they've taken up Fanon's thesis all by themselves."

"On the way to Munich, Petra stops at a bookstore in Paris. The tipping factor."

"But she couldn't get at Dodd's gang," I said. "They were dead by then."

"Fanon got them over that hump: the oppressors aren't just the ones with the guns. The oppressed don't stop with the first-born. They wipe them all out, the children of the children. Only way to cleanse hate. And there's an introduction by Sartre. Permission doesn't come any cleaner."

"Petra encountered Fanon when it came out?" I said. "That would be sixty-one, sixty-two."

"Ingrid arrived in Inyokern in sixty-three, if I remember you right."

"Ingrid was coming to someone else's fight," I said. "She could have changed her mind once she got into the magnitude of what she'd have to do. It's a lifework."

"Fanon wasn't just wrapping himself in European colonialism. The first application arrived in Algeria, but he makes it clear the prescription is universal."

"How did Petra get Ingrid into this?"

"Try this," he said. "I'm calling this proof. Pretend you don't know the end of the story. The pieces are a crazy quilt. Petra bankrolled a heck of a bill to sneak Ingrid into the U.S. You know that. She's not playing odds that Ingrid and Gabriella just might forget her version of what has to be done when they meet. Ingrid emerged in discussions with Petra in Munich. She tells her of Gabriella's despair that she will never cleanse her soul. Does Ingrid want to throw in with her? From there on it was just a plan with the details to come."

"The torch was passed," I said. "The blood debt boiled over."

"Ingrid brought copies of Fanon with her, courtesy of Petra," he said. "That they would leave a Fanon at the scenes of their revenge was already in the plan. Must have been. Initially that wouldn't be more than an intention between them to implement. Getting all the *i*'s dotted was a lot of ground to cover. They'd have to consider long-term tactics."

"And another thing you said: Ingrid wanted a German translator."

"Ingrid kept a journal of their crimes," I said.

"One of Fanon's goals is to make the pride in their revenge known. Ingrid kept bloody details. Glorified the details."

"Aubrey's going to publish the journals," I said. "Ingrid's instructions."

"Leaving a Fanon at each crime was cute. Aubrey will publish a full account."

"There's something else that's not a question," he said. "Petra was a wealthy woman when she made the decision to live her last years in Germany. Remember Mabel and her kids? Petra left operating control of a fraction of her fortune to one of that bunch. That can be looked up. That individual doled out support to the family as needed. Before her death, Petra turned the estate over…to whom? We know that at some point a large chunk went to Ingrid. When you met her, she was very well off as owner of the Arcadia Land Corporation. There are more corporations covering the portions of Petra's wealth that she gave to the others."

"They're connected to the murders?" I said.

"No, I'm sure not. Gabriella and Ingrid kept Arcadia Land to themselves. What confused me is the part of Petra's estate that went to Gabriella. Gabriella handed her share over to Ingrid. And I know why. Dodd was the origin of all evil. Gabriella picked up the torch, not the money. Wouldn't touch it."

"Ingrid was Prussian," I said.

"There you are, leadership."

"Only eighteen," I said. "Young for the scope of Petra's vision?"

"Napoleon was an officer in the French royal army at sixteen. Some people are born for good clean violence."

I bagged my leftovers. We pushed our sacks into a bin. I opened a message from Robin. Contact him. He didn't say ASAP, but that's what he meant.

He answered my call: "When are you coming back?"

"Stan's with me," I said. "We're about to talk about our situation."

"People are fucked up around here," he said. "Past talk. Need to be beaten into compliance."

"How long can you hang on?" I said. "I'll get you a date certain. They can hang on to that. Call you later."

I was closing the connection with Robin when it occurred to me to look up late night flights to San Francisco. Not advised. It would deliver an unmixed signal to Stan. Most of it would hint at what I didn't intend. I got in the car and remembered the swing on the edge of the hillside yesterday. Then I thought: What were we doing in Pasadena? Let's go home. I almost put the suggestion out there for consideration, but my powers gave out. I was spacing out somewhere on the other side of the windshield when Stan brought me back.

"The call," he said. "You're bothered."

"I'll be okay. I just saw a swing on a hillside."

"Let's go home," he said.

"Really?"

"I'm not cut out for Caltech," he said. "I couldn't hold my own around here."

"That's official?"

"I left Gavin a message."

"This couldn't wait a day?" I said.

"We should check out."

"I may drop in on Robin," I said, "make myself useful, serve cookies and wine at happy hour."

] *Chapter 27*

WHEN WE REACHED I-5 we compared sleepiness. Right now the road home was moving. Somewhere in the middle we'd get gas, and Stan would take over driving. Stan got going on the steps of drifting off, asking if I needed conversation. Give him his three hours. He rolled his seat back, and, as if remembering not to neglect a good-night gesture, dropped a hand on my inner thigh. The weight of the hand shared attention with a spirit of harmony for my brothers of the road who picked 'em up and put 'em down to a different drummer, the big wheelers overtaking each other at two MPH, a recreational van here and there barreling along at fifty.

"The funeral for Ingrid," a voice said. "Who was there?"

I looked at the dash. Half past ten. "We'll be at Kettleman City in an hour. Gas, but it's expensive there."

"We could save a few bucks," he said. "Stop closer to Oakland, get held up and shot for a few bucks."

"Her three sons," I said. "And a daughter."

"Which guy had the daughter?" the voice said.

"Joel?" I said. "Joel Cabot."

"Can you picture him?" he said.

"Northern European."

"The daughter?"

"Had an adult disposition. Confident. Friendly remarks to me and William without being spoken to, praised for pitching in with a shovel, a real trooper, and proud to be invited into a solemn proceeding, dressed in black."

"How old?"

"About twelve. She was the only one who spoke with William, drawing him into the group, though he had no kinship and obviously wasn't one of them."

"It fits," he said. "The other two so-called sons were not white.

"How old was the European?" he said. "Don't bother. You found Mrs. King's son." A finger was wiping his eyes. "Switch seats in Kettleman City? Think of it: paying top dollar and getting shot in Kettleman City."

"Ingrid never had kids," I said.

"A foster kid would fit," he said.

"I assumed Ingrid told William to get me to the burial."

A hand smoothed my thigh. "Ingrid never lost that thing for you," he said.

"She wanted me."

"She gave up on you wanting her," he said. "You kept growing up on an ambition to...what would you say it was?"

"Not be a dumb blonde."

"You grew up and kept at it. Nature made Ingrid complete before she was eighteen. What do you think? What did Ingrid need the girl for? What more of her life's work was undone when she died?"

"How many knew what she and Gabriella were doing, do you think?"

"A very short list," he said.

"The brothers?" I said.

"Ingrid and Gabriella brought in William, and there was everyone else. Take no chances. All it would require was one doubt that a blood debt was owed by blameless descendants of murderers, and blooey. Anyway, aside from Joel, the other two sons came through Mabel's line. They were out of it."

"And Joel was out of it?" I said.

"He'd be one more conscience they don't need. Ingrid was the prime mover. Gabriella was the incarnation of revenge. A good team. Fanon would be proud."

"Is it past Ingrid's vile aptitude that she hoped Joel would produce a devoted fanatic?"

"Hey, always a future."

"The girl said her mother was buried in Minnesota."

"I don't want to think about what was in store for this kid," he said. "Ingrid? The burial site was on the property?"

"There was a grove of trees. A mansion was on the other side from where we were. You could hear dogs barking. I really wasn't thinking that day. I'm thinking we should go over this again before contacting Sterling."

"A fire bell in the night," he said. "It's his job. We want to get this out of our system."

I looked up Donald Sterling, dialed, and put us on speaker.

A pleasant voice referred to my call as an unexpected and welcome surprise. A true gentleman.

"I'm sorry for the late hour," I said. "I hope I didn't wake you."

"Sitting down to breakfast at the Rome Cavalieri. Thanks for not calling this afternoon. You tried to reach Adele? Rome for Christmas. Incommunicado. Back on the third of January."

"We found Mrs. King's son."

I held the phone flat between us. Quiet on Sterling's end. He took a heck of a breathing space to catch his breath.

"Okay, I'm ready," he said. "Have a name?"

"First name: Joel," I said, "last: Cabot. He has a daughter— Catherine."

"What connects him to Mrs. King?" he said.

"I was at Ingrid's burial. Three men introduced themselves as Ingrid's sons. Joel was one of them. It's not possible the other two were her biological children. It was the joke they shared, calling themselves brothers."

"You knew them?" he said.

"Never met any of them before," I said.

"They invited you," he said.

"That was William. He was there, and Joel's daughter. The six of us."

"A wake? And where?"

"I was invited to the house afterwards. I didn't feel like it."

We paused a moment. Sterling said a few words directed at someone on his end. I heard silverware piled on plate sounds. He came back on the line.

"Did you ever encounter Ingrid with a child?"

Stan made a signal. I made a signal back: I'm done.

"Mr. Sterling, this is Stan. You have a pen handy?"

"Go ahead."

"Here's what you need to do. There was an officer in the U.S. Army, a guy named Dodd."

Stan said to me, "Dodd what?"

"Cameron Edward Dodd," I said.

"Cameron Edward Dodd," Stan said, "served in the Civil War, eventually owned a ranch-slash-orchard in Arcadia. Before he became a property owner, he and a squad of troopers chased down a group of families of the Paiute tribe, and slaughtered them. Dodd kept two girls for himself. Some of the others may have kept females too—the spoils. The Dodd women appear as Sarah and Mabel in the census records for Arcadia beginning in 1880. You'll see the names of some offspring, too. Anyway, Dodd joined the first families of Arcadia around 1912. He brought a wife, Petra Weber, over from Munich. You know the name. No children listed from that marriage. Anyway, Petra learned Sarah and Mabel's language. To the point, she learned of the slaughter from Sarah."

"A slaughter?"

"That's what started all this. Here's what you do. Petra built up a sizeable estate by the time she went back to Germany. Some part of it eventually went to Ingrid, but in William Emmon's name, as the Arcadia Land Corporation. Ingrid had Emmon transfer her property that was in his name to someone when she discovered she was dying. I don't know who it went to. You can look it up. Joel Cabot would be a guess, and the other two so-called sons who were at the funeral. Not much had to be decided when she faced her end. All she had to do was replace Emmon with a new boss. Emmon got the house on Grant and whatever he squirreled away. That went in his will to Mrs. King. He was in on the kidnapping.

"Getting back to Dodd. Here's where your going gets tough. It's not super bad, though. I'll tell you why in a minute.

"Remember, Dodd kept two Paiute girls from the raid for himself. Ingrid was fueled by a symmetry to snatch Mrs. King's son. In their minds the whole murder thing she and Gabriella cooked up was a mirror image of Dodd's raid, except they did it in slow motion. More fun. The old saying about revenge served cold. And slow."

Suddenly, Stan said to me, "Would she have a child with Joel? I mean, Catherine?"

"Absolutely no way," I said.

"Okay, Elizabeth said I had a ridiculous thought."

Out of the silence, Sterling said, "You were going to say?"

"Joel's daughter. I have some ideas there, too."

"You were about to say something else," Sterling said.

Stan bounced his head to get something right. "Dodd treated the two girls he captured pretty well—that is to say, comparative-ly. There were some rotten situations he might have left them in, if he wanted money. Instead they were his personal breeding stock, and everybody had a roof over their heads. The point is, with Joel at Ingrid's burial, what do we infer?"

Silence. "Are you there?" Stan said.

"I'm here," Sterling said.

"You want to say something?" I said. "We're not being polite."

"Keep being rude," he answered.

"Sorry for the lecture," Stan said. "Only way I know how."

"If I might interrupt," Sterling said. "Dodd's raid. Who would have guessed?"

"You got that," Stan said.

Sterling sighed. "A hundred and fifty years ago." A pause. "I interrupted. Please go on."

"Nature called it quits on Ingrid at eighty. Joel had a house and a decent bundle. That's it."

"One of the things we thought we might be up against," Sterling said. "We wondered why Conall's DNA didn't turn up. Most likely, he was dead. That was always worst case."

"Joel must have investigated where he came from," Stan said. "You're right, he's been ditching his mom. He must know he's a King."

"If I go back three or four generations," Sterling said, "I'll find a King serving under Dodd?"

"You might not. There was a memorial Dodd set up in Arcadia with a list of his gang. Elizabeth had a lead on it, but somewhere back when somebody didn't like the looks of a memorial over-looking a baseball field. It was taken down. You would have found a King on that.

"As I was saying, here's how you find Joel. The original fortune was Petra's. Half, say, or less, by some proportion, went to Gabriella, which slid over to Ingrid by agreement between the two of them. Put that aside for the present. Now, the other half was put under the name of some other corporate entity. You'll find the name. I'd expect one original owner, the boss of bosses on Mabel's side of the Petra inheritance. That was surely split into new companies, as each generation came along. Anyway, you can follow all that in public records. Somewhere in there is a group that Joel is linked to. Save you some trouble if Joel doesn't use his name publicly, but no reason why he shouldn't."

"Thank you," Sterling said. "I'm here at an old boy's detective refresher course. A couple friends. I speak for everyone: stay alert, good advice."

"Another thing," Stan said, "Joel could have been raised by someone descended from Mabel, Sarah's sister. Maybe on the land where Ingrid was buried. We'll send a map of where Ingrid was buried. Elizabeth says, try the house on the other side of the trees. We're driving up from Los Angeles. We'll be asleep tomorrow."

"If Ingrid raised Joel," Sterling said, "where would that have been? Where was she born?"

"Her birthplace was a farm in a Teutonic community of East Prussia," I said. "It's Poland now."

"But she didn't raise him," Stan said.

"She dropped in on him, maybe?"

"I doubt it," Stan said. "She kept herself secret. No vulnerabilities."

"Petra thought of everything?" Sterling said.

"Think of a lonesome man in Miami who can't forget this hot girl fresh off the boat. Let's assume he was hooked on Ingrid's looks, like Emmon was hooked. Hard. Emmon doesn't return. Mr. Lonesome gets curious. A stranger would then come looking for Ingrid, an unknown unknown. He gets lucky. He describes Emmon and Ingrid and someone remembers something. Ingrid wouldn't see it coming; the worst possible surprise. She couldn't protect herself.

"Originally, I think Petra put a stopper in that hole. Emmon would drop Ingrid in L.A., where she was supposed to meet up with someone who would shepherd her through a continuation of her journey. Petra gave the fact of the continuation to people in Miami. They wouldn't know where Ingrid went off to. Same for the guy with the hots for Ingrid." Petra had no idea Ingrid would keep Emmon for herself. A risk she didn't think about."

"The hole was plugged pretty good, though," Sterling said.

"Ingrid added a twist," Stan said. "I think the hotel idea was her invention. She gave Emmon the works. He disobeyed orders, tore up his ticket. Then they're off to Inyokern."

"It's a big step for a guy to mess with an organization," Sterling said. "They don't bother coming after him, but he knows he doesn't work in Florida again. On the trip across the country, Ingrid might have already been into means and accessories, how to put someone down and nobody's the wiser. Would she and Gabriella be safer with a third hand? And where do you get people you can trust in a murder plot?"

"Would Ingrid know William would kill?" I said.

"We don't know how these people make up their minds. Bring William to Inyokern. Talk it over with Gabriella. Try him out. If he doesn't work—well, but he did. William was a lucky boy. She was a killer-to-be on her eighteenth birthday."

"The swing at the edge of eternity," I said. "He jumped."

"What about this eternity?" Sterling said.

"A thick fog," I said, "of succor and sorrow."

] *Chapter 28*

A TWO-PAGE fill-me-in notice arrived from Sterling the last day of January. With Stan's roadmap, finding Joel Cabot was all of a lone investigator in the Waldorf Astoria on a laptop, an over-and-done-with search in a late morning. The assistant to the chief operating officer of Arcadia Land Corporation, a Miriam Walken, excited herself with coded hookups (*The dye on this Tuesday's garment will be ochre; The shepherd gathers his flock the third Wednesday of May*) with Joel Cabot, sole owner of Elite Fencing, an outfit dedicated to property beautification, main office in Santa Rosa, branch office in Petaluma.

A few weeks ago Sterling assembled case documents in a briefcase. They told a very short story, held together by a sixty-two-year-old woman and a thirty-seven-year-old man, and an assertion: It was at least eight trillion to one that the woman was the mother of the man. Sterling took his story to Washington, D.C. It was the one true fact he knew of pertaining to the King kidnapping. Adele King was the biological mother of Joel Cabot.

Sterling asked if we might jump the gun, a get-together, a me-and-him on our own.

I was volunteering at Jade's. I was off at two. Sterling was double-parked. I got in the back door, got out, got in the front seat. He had given his driver the day off. First hint.

He looked at me and said, "Sorry for the trouble. Just take a minute."

"I look tired?" I said.

"You look marvelous, Ms. Cromwell. Always."

"Stretching the adjectival budget, Mr. Sterling?"

"Understatement will do that," he said. "I'm willing to put a signature on that statement. Take it to the bank. Manager will provide interest. Anyway: toasts and heartfelt appreciations. Adele and I would like you and Stan to drop by. Per Adele's absolute insistence, she'll send a car."

"I don't believe Stan wears a tie," I said.

"Dress for the occasion," he said. "From Adele, a plea from the heart."

A car pulled up and stopped. The passenger window went down. The driver flicked a finger like scraping a piece of dust off a wall.

"I think that fellow wants to talk to you," I said.

Sterling rolled his window down a crack. "Did you want this space, sir?"

"You're in the way," the voice said.

"Have a look in front of you, sir. There's nobody in your way. Your path is free."

"Take some driving lessons," was the last of it. The voice drove away, having run out of instructions.

"He might have had a gun," I said.

Sterling tapped the glass: "Bullet proof."

A pause. Sterling's first sound was a laugh that floated on a statement that he considered funny: "For forty years there was a fortune backing me. I used a hell of a lot of it living any damn way I pleased."

"Not tweaking the lifestyle today," I said.

"If it ain't broke…you know," he said. "Two quick subjects to cover, Ms. Cromwell. Another minute, if I might?"

"Take your time," I said. "If we can find a space, you're legal around here for an hour and a half."

Sterling shrugged. Where did I want to go? I didn't feel like going someplace. We found a spot nearby on Noe St., up from a corner café, a coffee option. On the drive Sterling wanted me to hear it from him: He couldn't not go the feds. It was their case. He couldn't keep me out of it. Expect them.

"The case is closed," I said.

"Not till the movie comes out," he said. "A couple years, anyway, they'll have an active case on their hands. It's the kind that makes them happy: it's solved the entire time, most of it. They'll make the announcement, assign credit where credit is due."

"They met Cabot?" I said.

"They had their meet," he said. "Adele found her son. Cabot gave them a DNA swab.

"I suggested the feds start a file on that soldier, Dodd," he said. "I gave them what I had on him. They do it better. But the Dodd gang and the massacre? I couldn't verify a shred of it. They'll need your help."

"The principals are dead, except Gabriella."

"Bad shape, there," he said. "Her caretaker wheels her out for air. I have films. Had a doctor look at them." He paused for a verdict. "They won't get anywhere with her."

"All this evil goes to the grave," I said.

"Depends on the writer—writers—who want to make a buck. Some of them are pretty fair hands with evil. There might not be a last word, though. A last word is always vulnerable to a bit of tweaking from the next review of the evidence, including claims of new evidence. Take the Lindbergh kidnapping. It's not universally accepted that Hauptmann was solely responsible, or responsible at all."

"A crime of the wronged," I said. "Evil doesn't stay in its box."

"Adele's fate: it's a big case," he said. "Bigger than I ever could have imagined. Who the hell thinks of harvesting historical injustice?" He pulled the keys from the ignition. "Speaking of which, I'm thirsty."

Inside the café, we filled cups at the self-serve. He pushed my money away. He joined me at a table, setting five amaretto cookies in a sack between us.

"Forty years on the King case," I said. "Regrets?"

"A year or two." He shook a little yellow package, peeled off the top and dumped the contents in his cup. "It was at eight months, the first year, we got a ransom letter. Eight months! Late in the usual kidnapping timetable, but this letter had a photo of a blue baby carriage, a piece of the case not released to the public. We sat up. But I noticed that the foliage around the King house was a little higher than the foliage in the photos taken a day after the kidnapping. The substance of the letter fell apart. From then on, I was with Adele."

"I thought you went with Adele when she moved out of her house. Did I hear that?"

"Not from me. I met Adele at Mass the first Sunday in California. It was the early Mass, not crowded. She was alone in the front row, reserved for family at the time of the tragedy. I watched from the back pew. My job was to note anything or anyone that jogged a suspicion, but I knew the ritual and went along, up and down, sitting, standing, kneeling. A Catholic service is an experience during a catastrophe. It will connect you with terrible things you might have to face. When Adele passed me on her way out, she was the head of a funeral procession: she had accepted her child was dead. That he was dead was always my assumption. She must have seen me, and tucked away what she'd seen in my face, because she asked my name outside. We shook hands."

"She split from the husband?" I said.

"In due course," he said. "Anyway. The house and its contents were auctioned off after she left. The contents were photographed, and the photos turned over to an advertising team. The photographer kept a negative."

"It was the photographer," I said.

"He and his boyfriend. The boyfriend was the alleged Brain."

He dipped a cookie in his coffee and nibbled his way to

his fingers. He dried them off on a napkin and folded it into its original shape.

"The Brain waited a long time to go after the ransom money, months and months, which he lowballed at a hundred-fifty thousand on some principle his uncle taught him that a thief only goes for what he needs. He figured we'd overlook the auction, and pursue a neighbor who must have snuck through the hedge and clicked some shots. That was the last time a ransom letter had a plausible moment.

"A year later a letter from Adele landed in my box. She lived far more than I did that one year. Her face was older than I expected. She was aware of the change she was enduring. She sat me facing Monterey Bay. All these little boats and hang gliders were the backdrop behind her. She asked if I played cards. I did, expenses bought and paid for in nights of college poker. She had this guy bring out a couple decks. We played gin rummy, a penny a point. I won. After lunch she asked me to give her a number."

"The Bureau always gets its man is what I heard," I said. "Just advertising?"

"The King kidnapping appeared in the occasional Sunday supplement. The music would hit the fan for a time, die down and take it easy until the next article. Each month we'd get a dozen sworn sightings of the King kid. Adele wanted to feel her son was never forgotten. Someone would always be following a trail. You show me your forty years, I'll show you mine. Been in contact with departments all over the nations of the earth. If something came up that someone thought I might want to hear about, I'd hear about it."

"Lot of card games?" I said.

He turned his face past mine to the window. Something animated a smile. "I spent a philosophical afternoon with a priest as I was going off to college. I chose Columbia. I got in, my parents were proud. On the other hand, I was from solid Oak Catholic stock. He asked me, why not Fordham? I wondered if he saw something more than that I was Jesuitical material. Might I be of his sort, a fitter-inner among the celibate? We went at it Jesuit style, the number of angels that can fit on the head of a pin. It's never too late, and so on, and besides, they don't have to push the point, they're convinced: give them a boy to the age of twelve, they'll return you a Catholic for life. 'If you can do it, it ain't braggin',' as the Catholic quarterback said. I enjoyed diggin' my heels in."

"He wanted you?" I said.

"Physically? Didn't lay a glove on me. I told him he didn't know me. I was a G-damned independent. Then he pulled his ace: God will never give up on me."

"And?" I said.

"They've honed a powerful use of language. Ha, ha." He held up a cookie. "Along came Adele." He put the topic aside. "You worked with Catholics?"

"A sister of perpetual correction," I said. "Plenty of practice in that role."

"You took confessions?"

"When it was essential to the ritual they wanted me to follow," I said. "They were paying." I paused. "Anything you want to confess?"

"I became aware at the age of nine," he said, "of strange longings. I wanted to wear red panties. I also wanted to catch criminals."

"You don't seem to be brimming over with life's disappointments," I said.

He pushed his coffee to the side and put his forearms on the table. "The agents who came to see Adele, she informed them she doesn't want to meet Joel Cabot."

"Drop the whole thing?" I said.

"He knew he was her son."

"Too much for her?"

"The demands of dignity. She's so far beyond any way to express the thing: the forty years, their wasted passing. Bury him next to his rotten pseudo-mother for all she wants to admit to caring."

"Will she talk about it? That sometimes helps," I said.

"She'd listen to you," he said.

I could see it coming: a small ask, none of it prefaced by what Adele could offer in return. What Ingrid said of me to Cabot was unknown. That I was with Cabot at her burial was perhaps an indicator: I had an in with him. I could be a barometer of what to expect in the mother-and-son collision ("of fronts" to solidify the metaphor).

"A meeting, you and Cabot," he said.

The question sank between us. We got up and I followed him out to the car.

He turned the key. I didn't hear the engine, but the car backed into the street and followed Noe to a park, after which we zig-zagged to California St.

In front of the English Department, he was in control. "Send me a bill."

The silence went beyond the moment where I would have been expected to excuse myself. He understood I was giving him time.

"You're welcome to come inside," I said.

"And a fine flogging was enjoyed by all. And what's new?"

"I wouldn't like Cabot," I said. "I'd have to tell him that, and then tell him why I'm meeting him in place of his mother: I'm assessing his character? My profession never shouted 'character.'"

"Think about it, if you would, please. No doubts on my side. She needs to hold her son. She would even admit it, but she won't take the step. The son has to show up on his own. If he loves her, say so. She can't believe he never looked up his heritage."

"Give her time," I said.

"Time," he said. "Oh, besides the small matter of the last forty years down the sink?"

"I'm not taking this on," I said. "Sorry, it's this way. I feel terrible for her."

"Everybody does. What would you think of yourself, if…"

A civilized mourning became him on our previous meeting. Sterling was hard appearances now for the sake of handling a transaction, pitching me the strength of his sea legs in a hurricane. He could break down in front of me, but I'd have to help.

"Cabot knew his bloodlines," he said. "By thirty, surely. Adele is hard to meet if you're missing character. How much Cabot's missing glares to her."

He held his hands apart, some sort of mock-heroic effort at measuring a vacuum. "A fellow mortal, in all the integrity of nature," he said. "Rousseau. I do wish I could have seen you in action, Ms. Cromwell."

] *Chapter 29*

THE PRODIGY Stan was working with brought along a friend to show him real math, adding another kid to Stan's tutoring A-list. A girl overhearing people actually enthused by math asked Stan if he understood tangents. She was good at sines and cosines, but bad at tangents. She could pay. Income was growing. Stan was sharing expenses at the English Department. We were doing popcorn in bed with schlock films, messing with juvenile varieties of togetherness.

Stan was tutoring till five, if the four o'clock materialized. I went to the grocery to get something for dinner. I wasn't feeling the spring in my legs on the last slope, the steepest grade making my way home. Looking at life ahead at half a century was an endless image of coming run-ins with fifty. And then the years after. It's what I look at on a steep slope.

Quinoa Morocco was the main dish because it could wait a while for us to get home and get around to sitting down for supper. The ingredients marinate each other through the good offices of a tasty vinaigrette, the book asserted. Timing was everything in these instances.

Stan showered, and noticed I'd alphabetized the titles on the reading shelf in the bedroom while bent over drying his legs.

He once, and then twice, said, "It's your house," just saying, then stopped making that observation, as of course it was my house, and why undermine generosity? Life contained random acts of surprising me. I'd come into the kitchen and find dishes loaded in the dishwasher. The little things. He said one night in pitch dark that to solve an unsolved problem, he'd really have to want it. So I had that feel: He wanted me. Well, that made possible the little things. Like tonight his hair was damp. This would be the time to give him a trim. I sat him in front of the vanity mirror. When I said he was handsome, that's what got us to one of our favorite little things.

After cavorting, there was dinner, and after dinner there was chocolate chip marble swirl in the freezer, or a walk and Guinevere's Atypical Flavors. A walk and we could have both.

"Monday I left my name at the Tutorial Center," he said. "Picked up a student who learned her lesson the first semester: she just couldn't afford to get behind in her work. Hence, me, a tutor. Her problem is determinants, and what's that all about, and I'm getting a notebook open on the table with a pen ready, and she hands me a credit card."

"I've rarely had that problem," I said.

"And when you did?"

"This can't be a problem," I said.

"Of course not. She had four bucks and change in a back pocket. Her grandmother sent her two tens and a five for her birthday. She whittled that down when she remembered cash bought things. I whittled what she had left and asked if she'd look me up after twenty birthdays."

"You remember Donald Sterling," I said, "Mrs. King's detective? He stopped by this afternoon."

"We're done with those people."

"We're invited," I said. "Carmel, appreciation night. There was something else. Sterling asked me to talk with Joel Cabot. See where it goes setting up a son's reunion with his mother."

"What a nerve."

"What I said."

"I hope he left unhappy," Stan said. "Kill two birds."

"Mrs. King doesn't want to meet her son," I said, "as things stand. Sterling thinks I could decide what would come of a meeting. A thumb's-up from me could change her mind."

"How would he know?"

"He knows her," I said.

"You said no. Doesn't matter—and just a second. Is Sterling in contact with Cabot?"

"The FBI is," I said. "They also verified in person with Mrs. King that Cabot is her son, alive and well-heeled."

We went in and out of Guinevere's in a hurry. Eight bucks for a dinky cone.

Outside, Stan was scrubbing his temples with his eyes shut, chin on his chest, saying, "Idiot." I've seen him in this crouch. He needed time. I'd wait until he came out of it. Not sure he did, but after a couple false starts, he said, "I think I met Aubrey."

I could ask how he was sure, but past experience told me not to bother. He was on the hunt for that very fact, and besides, sound bounced right off him when his eyes were shut.

A yes and a pause repeated over and over indicated that steps toward the resolution of a question were stacking up, an argument accomplished, no mistakes, no need to back up.

"I met her yesterday for a tutorial," he said. "The whole time I knew this girl was a phony. It was annoying, swiveling around avoiding her knee. I got my back against the wall and stretched my legs out on my side of the booth. I had to leave an arm on the table to write. My hand was fair game. She kept pestering my hand."

"How did she get your name?" I said.

"She didn't. The week before, she was at the next table. When the guy I was with left, she pulled up a seat."

"Remember when you met Blake at the Space Center?" I said. "As I recall, a high-heel leather boot next to your cheek was your first awareness of her."

"Same as this 'Remi,' as Aubrey was calling herself. She was in high-heel leather boots. Another Blake, I thought."

"She wanted a date?" I said.

"She knew about you and me," he said. "I'm sure."

"She assumed the fetish stuff was my hold on you?"

"She invited me for a tutorial at her place. Took it for granted, you and she had a grip on the same magic."

I pointed in two different directions. Let's walk. We took off for the English Department the long way.

"Women don't hustle tutors in the student union," he said.

"Granted. Can't top the Space Center."

"You weren't there," he said. "*Location* doesn't matter. Her whole performance was a creation. Not like the theater. She missed the important point: how people work. She showed me a whip in her bag. And giggled. It was creepy, like demented creepy, like a weird laugh going wild at a non-joke. A matter of some debate that a human made the sound."

"You're frightened," I said. "You're seeing her again?"

"Tomorrow, the laws of matrix multiplication," he said. "She's up to something."

The story of the following events came to me from Sterling. At the time of her scheduled meeting with Stan, Aubrey was in Carmel buying flowers with Joel Cabot. The salesperson recalled they were looking for a flower commemorating a reconnecting. She suggested a dozen red roses, appropriate on any occasion. Cabot decided on white lilies of the valley, and wondered if there was a card that might capture the sentiment he was trying to express. He was meeting with someone for the first time after forty-one years.

The gated entrance to the King estate is accessed from a circular courtyard that lets visitors out on the edge of a fountain. Cabot got out of the passenger side of the car with a box under his arm, and pushed a bell. The guard who emerged from the security hut inside the gate said that he had taken at most a step or two when three shots rang out. The guard saw flashes emerge from the passenger window, but he didn't see clearly the person who fired them. The visitor spun around and flattened backwards against the gate, at which point the guard ducked behind a tree and got out his pistol.

So far the guard had simply put into words what was caught on a surveillance camera. A figure in a black motorcycle outfit got out of the car, threw a book on Cabot, who was by then sitting against the gate. She fired two additional shots into him, got back in the car, and drove off.

There is a museum on a high road that used to be a highway leading north out of Carmel. It was a service station in the 1930s, with two pumps that are preserved today. A glimpse into a hundred years ago, they look like skinny red phone booths with crowns on top. The museum was closed on the day of the shooting. It wasn't until the museum opened for business the following Tuesday that Joel Cabot's car was found in the shed in back.

] *Chapter 30*

WET ALL AFTERNOON in the East Bay above San Jose. Flash flood warnings for higher elevations the next twenty-four hours. Stay off the roads if you don't have to drive. No surprise: Aubrey was a no-show. Stan waited a quarter-hour, vacated the booth and wrote off a coffee but not two cookies. He packaged one in a pocket and stood at a window to the street nibbling the other—a decision of some consequence, as it were. A week earlier, as Aubrey designed her farewell, Stan was nothing more than the second to the last step in a plan, as good as written off. Not only would she not see him again, she wouldn't give him a second thought.

While Stan was looking at the wet walk from the café to the BART station, a woman called his name from the counter.

"You're Stan?"

"I'm Stan."

She handed Stan a package. A manuscript addressed to Elizabeth Cromwell. *A Cry from the Earth.*

"She hoped she could be here in person," the woman said, "but just in case, she said to tell you to look up the Swift Arrow Press."

"The Swift Arrow Press?"

"That's what she said."

I had just got off the phone with Sterling when Stan walked in the door.

"Joel Cabot was shot dead on his mother's doorstep not an hour ago," I said. "Sterling was with two federal agents. They were just wondering if I knew who they should be looking for."

"Let me get dry," he said.

Stan was in sweats, bent forward over the side of the bed, pulling on socks. I lifted his head and ran a comb from back to front and found a groove to make a part.

"You look handsome," I said.

"I added things up wrong," he said, elbows resting on his knees, speaking to the carpet. "Cabot's days were numbered when Petra picked up a copy of Fanon in Paris."

We were in position now to trim his hair. Let's do it. "Keep your head down." I snipped hair along the back of his neck, the ballpark cut at first, cautious snips cleaning up.

"You'll have to explain that," I said.

"Aubrey killed Logan," he said. "Logan got out of prison. It killed him. If he'd maintained his innocence, no parole; no parole, he stays in; he stays in, he suffers; he suffers, he lives. Classic Ingrid. That was the design. At the end, Ingrid alerted Aubrey she should keep an eye on Logan. If he got out, she knew what to do."

"But Cabot? I'm confused. Why would Aubrey kill Cabot? Pretty big jump there."

"They'll find that the gun that killed Logan also killed Cabot— and some of Ingrid's other shootings. I'm sure it's all there in *A Cry from the Earth*, except for the supplement."

"Supplement?"

"They had a publishing company ready for its maiden release. That's the stuff in the package. With everything prepared, Aubrey went to press. The hit on Logan will be there, possibly tacked on at the end, the why he's dead. Call it a supplement. She also had to add on Cabot. We all thought Cabot must have investigated his roots—must have. Now I know he didn't. When the FBI made their call, he was shaken. He was in contact with Aubrey. He told her he was going to see his mother."

"That will be explained?" I said.

"That's the suffering thing. It doesn't ever end. Aubrey didn't have to improvise. She knew the principle. She wasn't after you and me. I had vaguely in mind that she wasn't, but I never thought of Fanon. I thought Aubrey had wormed her way into tutorial stuff with me to stick me in a Logan-type frame-up. I was there to see her today to understand how she would go about setting that up. Cabot would kill you. At the same time, Aubrey would tie me up in some honey-trap with no alibi."

"All the while, we didn't matter," I said.

"Except for one thing," he said. "You and Ingrid. I'll come back to that."

He fell back on the bed. His head hit a pillow, looking at the ceiling.

"Read your Fanon," he said. "It's not up to the oppressor. Mrs. King, in that particular, was sentenced to a life without her son.

"When the translations of Ingrid's and Petra's journals and Dodd's daybook were published, Mrs. King would know everything about her son—in time to know her son was dead."

"Aubrey would kill him," I said.

"His future. All along. Mrs. King would suffer till death. We didn't toss a brick into that when we clued the FBI. We jiggled the schedule. That's all."

"The supplementary blood debt," I said.

"Ingrid got sick. Cabot lived as long as he did because Ingrid knew she could trust Aubrey. Otherwise, she would have turned to William to kill him. Aubrey was a lucky break for Ingrid. William had become a bit of a marshmallow by then. Ingrid saw to it that he pulled some triggers early on, to inoculate him from straying from the fold, cement his status."

"A murderer," I said.

"She left it up to Aubrey to bring the slaughter home. The

oppressor will say the judgment's not fair, it's not proportionate, it's not distributed where it belongs, on the guilty. When Cabot was kidnapped, Ingrid knew the day would come: the boy's gotta go."

"Okay," I said, "so he was kept alive…"

"Like Dodd kept Sarah alive. Aubrey put her own two cents in. Leave him dead at his mother's gate. She could have killed him anywhere."

"Just came to her?" I said.

"Where do people like that come from?"

He gestured at the manuscript. "You may find a note in there from Ingrid. Maybe not. I think you will, though. Aubrey tried to say something to you that day the two of you passed outside Emmon's house.

"I remember. Nonsense."

"A Looney Tune," he said. "Still, she was passing on something that made sense to her."

"Detective Benedict might have made sense of it."

"Ingrid left instructions that you should be at the burial," he said. "You rarely saw her. Doesn't that seem odd?"

"At this moment, no. I knew I was the other voice in her head: *My life is wrong.* Call it a conscience. Just hanging around William in front of me was an embarrassment to her. She knew what I thought of him. Being with him demeaned her around me.

"She avoided your judgment?" he said.

At supper Stan sat across from me in silence. I'd done a good job on his hair. I could goad him to thank me, but I wanted something subtle. I'll work on it.

"Over the years," he said, "you didn't hang around people."

"I was saving myself."

"You were sublimating," he said.

"I was waiting for a man who would use big words on me."

PANAMINT VALLEY was awash in color last spring. The *Chronicle* had a spread three weekends running. So this year we made plans, circled dates on the calendar, told everybody they would be making do without us. But, as it happened, no flowers this year. Still, the time was right for a desert visit. Stan's brother and his wife would drive down from Provo for a family hello in Vegas.

The news of that trip and some photos would make it east before us. We were thinking October, when the leaves were changing, drop by the parents, come to grips with Russian peculiarities. His mother, for example, will call him Konstantin, or Konstantin with a patronymic, Dmitrievich, to emphasize that he is his father's son. It's a mother's endearing prerogative, and a slippery slope. I might just pick up the habit. Another thing, quite a few Nordic peoples migrated to both the British Isles and to the Russias, the three territories that claimed heritage from the Rus. Stan's father will stare because he can't get over my Russian looks. Then there's Russian food, and the subset of family favorites.

Stan is quite confident I'll be fine. I'm increasingly persuaded I'm clocking the future with my eyes wide open—you know, *that* illusion. But how would I know what's blurring the lines of the one true path? Well, I'm on my way.